LAIRD OF LIES

HIS HIGHLAND HEART SERIES BOOK 5

WILLA BLAIR

OLIVERHEBERBOOKS

Cover art by Dar Albert at Wicked Smart Designs

Published by Oliver-Heber Books

0 9 8 7 6 5 4 3 2 1

"This story is action-packed and full of twists and turns that will keep readers on their toes. It is fast-paced and has a sweet romance that will warm your heart. Well written and full of imagination, this story is a must read for historical romance fans!"

— THE ROMANCE REVIEWS

"...a rich, enjoyable read."

— SATIN SHEETS ROMANCE

THE HEALER'S GIFT

"A Highland romance with a truly great hero...the story is compelling..."

— IND'TALE MAGAZINE

"A story of mystery, regret, hope, danger and trust...The characters are endearing, the story is fulfilling, and the set up for the remainder of the series presents an open invitation to dive right in. THE HEALER'S GIFT is a highly recommended read."

— FRESH FICTION

HIGHLAND SEER

"...this is different enough from other Highland romances to stand out from the pack. Ms. Blair's writing style is natural and evocative..."

— ROMANTIC HISTORICAL REVIEWS

"16th-century intrigue, muscled men with claymores and a doomed romance — is it any wonder I was reluctant to leave the rich, riveting world of HIGHLAND SEER?"

— USATODAY HEA

WHEN HIGHLAND LIGHTNING STRIKES

"Ms. Blair is a consummate storyteller...Can't wait for more from this magical author."

— MY BOOK ADDICTION AND MORE

"Ms. Blair has an easy to read talent for bringing a story to life."

— LONG AND SHORT REVIEWS

HIGHLAND TROTH

"Scottish romance at its best!"

— IND'TALE MAGAZINE

"...an exciting, romantic, historical tale full of angst, action and searing hot passion...With plenty of adventure and the twist of an old murder, HIGHLAND TROTH by Willa Blair, kept me hooked from beginning to end. A wonderful Highland romance."

— FRESH FICTION

HIS HIGHLAND HEART SERIES
HIS HIGHLAND ROSE

"Masterfully and brilliantly written Scottish Romance...!"

— MY BOOK ADDICTION & MORE

HIS HIGHLAND HEART

"The plot was honestly a masterpiece. It was well thought out and orchestrated. Right out the gate I was hooked! The hero had immediate book boyfriend appeal."

— LONG AND SHORT REVIEWS

"Willa Blair knows how to make a story come to life and sweep you away on a beautiful journey into the Highlands...This is a Scottish adventure you won't want to miss!"

— BOOKS & BENCHES

HIS HIGHLAND LOVE

"Beautifully written and masterfully executed!"

— MY BOOK ADDICTION AND MORE!

"Fiery passion burns bright in HIS HIGHLAND LOVE! Readers who enjoy Highland romance should definitely try Willa Blair's books."

— BOOKS & BENCHES

"If you love romantic highland stories of warriors and danger, love and honor, you'll find this story intriguing as well as enjoyable."

— THE READING CAFE

HIS HIGHLAND BRIDE

"Ms. Blair has delivered a wonderful and captivating read in this book where the chemistry between this couple was strong; the romance hot..."

— BOOK MAGIC, UNDER A SPELL WITH
EVERY PAGE

"This is a very enjoyable and well-written book to satisfy any historical romance lover, especially one who enjoys forbidden love!"

— IND'TALEMAGAZINE

CONTEMPORARY ROMANCE
WAITING FOR THE LAIRD

"Willa Blair spins a beautiful romance set in the Scottish Highlands full of suspense, history and mystery... I highly suggests you pick it up and enjoy."

— NIGHT OWL ROMANCE

"About 3:00 am I finally had to force myself to stop...yes, it was that good. Give yourself a treat and grab this book..."

— THE READING CAFE

"A contemporary romantic tale with a touch of history—and ghosts...Waiting for the Laird by Willa Blair is a delightful romance and unexpected adventure set in Scotland."

— BOOKS AND BENCHES

WHEN YOU FIND LOVE

"When You Find Love is a beautiful romance filled with combative personalities, a family curse and a love that can't be quenched. Character-driven plot with supernatural undertones make this a must-read. The ending was so fantastic, I didn't want it to end. If you love fantasy romance, you'll be smitten with When You Find Love."

— N.N. LIGHT'S BOOK HEAVEN

SWEETIE PIE

"Willa Blair is known for her Scottish historical paranormal romance. She changes genres with a modern Scottish lass who escapes to the Big Island of Hawaii. SWEETIE PIE is a delicious pupu - Hawaiian word for appetizer. Blair delivers a sweet novella that captures the Aloha spirit of the island."

— K. LOWE

Every book I write is a labor of love born from imagination, nurtured by fellow authors' suggestions and critique, polished by editors and publishers, and brought to completion with the support of friends and family, readers, and reviewers.

My most sincere appreciation goes out to every one of you, and especially to my husband.

Your love and support keep me writing!

AUTHOR'S NOTE

Highland history is full of battles, fascinating characters, love, hope, and tragedy. In my books, I often "set the stage" with historical events, and at times, with actual historical characters. But I also use creative license in populating my stories with fictional characters rather than historical ones, so as not to unfairly portray or impugn important historical actors.

In this case, the lairds of Sutherland and MacKay and their progeny are fictional rather than the historical persons.

The historical events such as Domnhall of the Isles and the Earl of Mar's movements— as far as various sources maintain — are true.

In late spring of 1411, Domnhall (Donal/Donald/MacDonald) of the Isles captured Dingwall, the seat of the Earl of Ross. He then captured and some sources say burned down Inverness on his way to a battle outside Aberdeen with the Earl of Mar over control of the Earldom of Ross and its territory. According to various sources, Domnhall planned to burn Aberdeen to the ground to draw the Earl of Mar into battle. Mar was Albany's (the Duke of Albany and Regent of Scotland) proxy. The battle between Domnhall's forces, made up of Isle men and Highlanders, against Mar's mostly Lowland forces of the Stewart rulers of Scotland finally took place on 24 July 1411 and lasted just one day. It is said that the fighting was so fierce, the ground turned red with blood, hence the name: Red Harlaw.

Overnight, Domnhall withdrew toward Inverness for reasons that remain a mystery. Later, he moved to Dingwall, and held it until Mar recaptured it in the summer of 1412. Over time, Mar succeeded in claiming and holding the disputed territory.

PROLOGUE

SCOTTISH HIGHLANDS, SUMMER, 1400

"*W*ait for me!"

Stellan Sutherland heard his twin's faint call to him, but he kept going, his pace fast, his thoughts faster. He would have to break the awful news he'd just received, but how? He couldn't bear to see the hurt in Anders' eyes, and to be the one to put it there. His own distress was too recent. Too fresh and too painful for any nine-year-old to bear, but especially one who wore his heart for all to see like Anders.

If Anders got close enough, he'd know immediately what was amiss. He'd know the reason for Stellan's anger as clearly as if he'd spoken the reason aloud. Da had informed his heir, his eldest son, of his plans, with no thought to how they would affect both twins.

So he kept moving, stumbling down the swale into the next glen and leaping across the swift-flowing burn, climbing the next hill and the next. Sutherland territory stretched farther than anyone could see, farther than he could go afoot at this pace with no food and only icy water from a burn to drink.

He hadn't planned this infuriated march. He'd simply bolted from the keep after Da had announced his plan to split them up.

To put an end to the canny bond they shared, the bond he feared, but they cherished. The twin bond that let them understand each other without words, to know how the other felt without seeing so much as an expression on the other's face or the set of his shoulders.

The thought of being away from his twin for years stole Stellan's strength and he halted in the heather, panting, bent forward, hands on knees. He heard Anders shout again for him to stop. His twin was still out of sight, below the crest of the last hill, unaware Stellan had stopped and was finally waiting for him.

It was time. They were far enough from Dunrobin to give voice to their anger and grief and not have word of their indulgence in such raw emotions get back to their da.

Anders caught up with him a few minutes later.

Stellan barely got his breath back when the look on his twin's face took it from him again.

"What has he done?"

Anders' demand jerked Stellan upright and he grimaced against the stitch in his side. "Ye dinna ken?"

"Ye are so riled, I canna pick one thing from another. So tell me."

There was no easy way to break the news he'd begun to hope Anders could pluck from him in silence. He must say the words, and the pain in his torso intensified. "Da has decreed we are to be sent to foster."

"Where? What has ye so upset?"

Anders still didn't understand. Stellan sucked down a lungful of air, then with a twist of his lips, told him, "I am to be honored to foster with Domnhall, the Lord of the Isles, for seven years. Da thinks to send ye far away, to the Norse land, surety for the treaty between we northern Scots and the Norse king."

Anders shrugged. "But we will return to Sutherland."

Stellan shook his head. "He thinks to have ye betrothed there. To someday rule the Norseland for Sutherland. Or for Scotland."

Anders' mouth fell open. "Never to return home? That canna be," he objected. "I will go with ye to Domnhall."

At last, his twin understood why Stellan was so upset. He let his gaze drop to the ground. "Da will send us where he wills. We must do as he says and go."

"And ye are willing to let him?" Anders planted his fists on his hips.

Anders' growing anger hit Stellan's chest like a scorching shaft of summer sunlight.

"I dinna believe ye," Anders continued. "Ye always have another plan, a way around our da."

"What would ye have us do?" Stellan demanded, his earlier anguish returning. "Run away together today?" He waved a hand at the hills marching on ahead of them to the west, seemingly forever.

"Nay! We are lairds of Sutherland. The clan needs us, or will… someday." Anders sank to the ground and sat, his gaze confused and dismayed.

Stellan was the stronger of the two, but his heart broke for both of them. "We believed so. Our grandfather decreed it may be so. As we have always done everything else, we would rule together. But grandda is dead. Da's time has come and he will do as he pleases."

Anders drew his dirk. "We will swear a blood oath to survive and reunite to keep Sutherland safe and strong."

Stellan nodded, impressed at Anders' initiative. "Once we inherit, it will be so. And," he added, holding up his hand to stop Anders before he began to sanctify the oath with his blood, "we willna fall for any lass— or Norse princess —unless we can bring her home, so we can fulfill our destiny to be lairds together. As is our right and our grandda's wish."

Anders scored a line in his palm. When it seeped red, he handed the blade to Stellan, who did the same. The cut stung from the sweat on his palm, but watching the line of red well up in his hand, he didn't care. The promise they made this day would set the course of their lives. They clasped hands, mingling the blood they had once shared in the womb.

"So it will be as we have sworn this day," Stellan said. "We may be forced to part for a term of years, but we will return. Someday, we will rule Sutherland together."

"So it will be," Anders repeated, "And when the day comes that Sutherland is ours, we will keep it safe and strong— together."

CHAPTER 1

NORTHERN SCOTLAND, SPRING, 1412

The fire in the great hall's hearth warmed Stellan Sutherland as he waited for his twin, Anders, to shake the sleet from his hair in the keep's doorway and join him by the fire. May was late for this kind of weather, but they were far enough north, one never knew what to expect. "Come on, laggard. It'll melt, but ye willna."

Anders grimaced, gave his plaid a final shake and stepped in. "Sod off. 'Twould run down the back of my neck, as cold as the trail of a witch's finger on my skin."

"And when have ye felt the chill of a witch's finger?"

"Never. And I dinna plan to start now." Anders settled on the bench opposite his twin and signaled a passing serving maid for an ale. "'Twas a long, cold ride from Inverness. If I were eldest, I'd have been sitting here by the fire for the last fortnight, drinking and fondling the lasses while ye froze yer arse riding home through snow and sleet."

Stellan ignored the jibe. He was older than Anders by mere minutes, a fact that meant nothing to them, but carried great weight with their father, the Sutherland laird. He could have told Anders about hunting in the same sleet storm earlier in the afternoon. And he couldn't recall the last time he'd touched a lass, but certainly not in the last fortnight while Anders visited Inverness on business for Sutherland. Instead he asked, "Did ye get what Da sent ye after?"

Anders nodded. "Aye, and more. I'll go tell him once I've thawed my feet."

Stellan itched to know the details, but he knew he would get nothing more from Anders until his twin made his report to their father. Stellan settled back to let Anders enjoy his ale and his warm feet. They would go together to their father's solar.

Anders thanked the lass who brought him a mug of ale. She gave him a grin and a wink, turned to Stellan, curtsied and went on her way. Anders took a long drink, following her with his gaze until she was out of sight, lowered the cup and rolled his eyes.

Stellan gave him an answering grimace. The lasses flocked to Anders' easy charm like gulls to a beached fish. It didn't seem to matter that they were identical twins. No one flocked to Stellan. At best, when the lasses saw them together, their assessing looks and smoldering smiles occasionally spilled over from Anders to include him. Stellan considered himself open and friendly. Some of the time. When it suited his purposes.

Female giggles echoed from the direction of the hallway to the kitchen. Stellan hadn't heard that sound since Anders left for Inverness.

"I see ye haven't lost your charm," he chided.

Anders sighed. "'Tis no' just me, as ye ken fine. 'Tis the two of us, together. Which is how some of them would like to try us."

Stellan snorted. On his own, the lasses were friendly, but when the twins were together, well, the lasses had always been fascinated by the little lairds, as they'd been called when they were bairns. Their fascination had grown along with them.

"Ye are welcome to them," he said. "There's none here I'd have without the lass thinking to be the next lady of the clan. I'd never be rid of them." Anders protected Stellan from ambitious lasses who wanted to be the clan's lady by allowing him, once in a while, to pretend to be his younger twin with a lass who'd caught his eye. During Anders's latest absence, Stellan had toyed with the idea of impersonating his brother with one of the lasses, but decided it wasn't worth the trouble. Most knew Anders had gone, not Stellan.

"Aye, that does tend to make one think twice." Anders tossed off the last of his ale. "Very well, I'm ready. Let's go speak to Da."

They stood and made their way to the laird's solar. The door was closed, a good indication Laird Sutherland was within and working. Anders knocked.

"Come," their father's deep voice penetrated the thick, oaken door.

Stellan gave Anders an open-handed gesture to precede him. It was Anders' turn to report to the laird. Stellan used every opportunity to make their father see Anders as capable and in control as much as Stellan. Their da thought only of Stellan as his heir, ignoring the possibility that if something happened to his eldest, Anders would be the one to take over, and unaware, as far as they knew, of their vow to rule together.

Anders cut Stellan a sour look that spoke volumes, opened the door and went in.

Stellan waited long enough to hear Anders greet their father and garner his attention, then joined them. Anders knew what Stellan was doing, and appreciated it, but Stellan felt his frustration nonetheless as a tightness in his gut. Anders deserved to be valued just the same as his minutes-older brother, but their father adhered to the notion of primogeniture, that only the eldest would rule in his stead.

"So, ye are back." Seated behind his worktable, Laird Sutherland was a large, imposing man with glints of silver in his hair.

"Aye, father, just long enough to melt the sleet."

"And have a drink by the fire, I'll wager."

Anders colored and grinned. "I learned from the best these last five years since we returned from fostering."

Sutherland nodded agreement, since he was well known to do the same, and set aside his quill. "So ye did." He gestured at the seats across from him. "What did ye learn in town?"

"They're making progress rebuilding. There are rumors Domnhall plans another incursion, but 'tis only talk," Anders said as they settled. "No sign of his men in any numbers. Only the normal few ye'd expect to find anywhere in Scotland on business for the Isles. 'Twas a wasted trip."

Sutherland frowned, then lifted one shoulder. "That was nay a wasted trip. Ye have brought good news. The longer Domnhall holds off, the better. No one kens why he walked away from Red Harlaw instead of finishing the fight. 'Tis something to worry us, but for now, we have other problems. If our neighbors would follow Domnhall's example, we might get through the spring without more bloodshed."

Stellan turned to his twin. "No' much chance of that. In the time ye have been gone, MacKay has raided crofts on our border three times."

"So many? What about Gunn?"

"Harald Gunn sent me a missive a few days ago. He met with the MacKay recently and said with spring coming on, they're more interested in planting than stirring up trouble. I hope he kens I have nay reason to believe him."

"Likely," Anders said and nodded.

"'Tis time to see what there is to be seen toward the northwest," Sutherland continued. "Stellan, ye will take some men and ride our borders with Gunn and MacKay."

"I'll go," Anders objected. "Ye need Stellan here."

Surprised, Stellan glanced at his twin, and gave him a slight shake of his head. But he kept his expression neutral as he turned his gaze back to their father. Why the quick offer to go? Anders hadn't been back long enough to get bored with life in the keep. And if their father was ever to see the value in his second son, Anders needed to spend time with him at Dunrobin, doing the things that Stellan usually did with the laird.

"Ye are just returned. In fact, ye are still dripping from the weather ye rode through," Sutherland stated, his tone firm and unyielding. "'Tis time for the heir to visit our outlying crofts."

Had their father finally come around to accepting he needed to prepare both sons to succeed him? "I'll leave in the morning," Stellan said, determined to take advantage of this opening for his brother. He collected Anders with a glance and stood.

After a moment, Anders stood, too, and they left the solar together.

MARIOTA MACKAY REMOVED the hood and jesses and let her hawk Valkyrie fly free. They'd both been cooped up too long indoors, but the skies cleared around midday and she loved the feel of the sun on her face. Valkyrie soared over the glen, making Mariota wish she could see through the raptor's eyes, feel the wind and weightlessness as her favorite hunter did.

She would spread her wings and never look back.

But that was a dream. And her fathers' edicts were real. Not only could she not leave MacKay land, she could not stray out of sight of the keep's imposing walls. She could not ride, or hunt with a bow, or speak her mind, or live her life the way she wished. And his men enforced his every word.

"Lasses do as they're told," her father growled the last time she reminded him she was a better shot with her bow than his men. And Valkyrie could spot and flush prey. To her, it made all the sense in the world. To him, well, she was not a son. And after a boar gored and almost killed him five years ago, he'd never have one of his own.

She was the clan's hope for the future. Or rather, the man she'd eventually be forced to marry would be.

And if something happened to her father or her before that day came? The Lord of the Isles was ready to pounce. Or so her father believed. He'd become obsessed with two things in the last year. Finding a husband for her, and guarding MacKay against their neighbors, clan Gunn and the mighty clan Sutherland, as well as Domnhall of the Isles.

Valkyrie wheeled, catching Mariota's attention in time to see her stoop and dive on some prey. Good. A kill would do much to ease the frustration her winged hunter had felt at being enclosed for the last week. She was trained to bring her kill to Mariota, a necessity if she was to be part of the clan's hunts. If the MacKay ever allowed it.

Mariota watched her take wing and held up her gloved hand, a signal for the bird to return to her. As Valkyrie neared, she dropped a rabbit in front of her mistress, landed on Mariota's fist, flapped her wings to settle her balance, and stilled.

"Good lass!" Mariota told her. "A coney for the pot. Cook will be pleased with ye, even if Da is no'." She replaced the jesses, retrieved the rabbit, and made her way around the glen to the keep's gate.

"Got one, did she?" The guard, her friend Seamus, called down to her.

Mariota held up Valkyrie's kill. "Aye. She always does. I'm headed for the mews, then the kitchen. Can I bring ye anything? Or are ye coming down?"

"Go on about yer business, Mari. I'll visit the kitchen myself soon enough." He gave her a grin and a dismissive wave.

Mariota nodded and after returning Valkyrie to her perch in the mews, entered the kitchen with her prize.

"Been out, have ye?" The cook took the coney and laid it aside. "I should ha' kenned ye would now the weather's cleared. What will yer da say?"

"Nary a word. I stayed in Seamus's view the entire time." One of the clan's senior guards, Seamus was highly accomplished for a man only a few years older than she, but he had always been kind to her.

"As if that lad would tell yer da any different. He fancies ye."

"Dinna ye start. Seamus is a friend and naught more."

"He'd like to be. More, that is. Poor lad. 'Twill never happen."

Mariota's shoulders slumped at the reminder, however oblique, of her duty to the clan to wed a stranger.

"Ach, me and my big mouth." Cook crossed her arms over her ample chest. "Go get cleaned up, then come back. To apologize, I'll make something special for ye."

Mariota nodded and gave her a smile. "Seamus said he'd be in soon. Ye might make enough for two."

"Aye, and I will." Cook shooed her out.

Mariota headed for her chamber, eager to wash the rabbit's blood from her hands and kirtle. In the great hall, she noticed Alber sprawled alone in a chair by the fire, tankard in hand, and grimaced. She looked away and mounted a few stairs, hoping he was far enough in his cups not to see her. But her luck was no better this time than it ever was. He noticed her.

"Have ye killed a MacCleod, then, Mari? From the look of ye, ye did a poor job of it."

Alber's taunt rankled. She pretended she didn't hear him, and continued up the stairs without hesitation.

"Ach, nay, of course no'," he continued, louder. "Yer da willna let ye hunt, so ye canna fight for MacKay, either, can ye? Ye and yer wee bow and arrows. Ye need a real man with ye."

His snicker was the last straw. Mariota stopped halfway up the stairs and peered down at him. Alber was a few years her senior, big and heavily muscled, he could have grown into a good-looking man if it wasn't for the constant sneer on his face. A scar from the battle of Red Harlaw didn't help. It ran from his nose to his jaw on the left side of his face, as if his opponent had tried to blind him and missed. Alber claimed to have killed so many that day, her da thought of him as one of his best fighters. His ruthlessness made him a hero for a few weeks, until people realized he enjoyed the praise, and his tales of his prowess in the battle grew beyond anything the other men fighting there could confirm.

When they were younger, he'd cornered her in the stables and tried to kiss her as he shoved his hand down her chemise. For his trouble, she'd kneed him as Cook had taught her. He'd dropped to the straw, swearing. "Too good for the likes of me, are ye?" He'd spat and curled up, threatening, "Ye'll pay for this."

"No' as much as ye'll pay if I tell Da what ye just did."

Since that day, he hadn't touched her so familiarly again, but never failed to bump into her or brush her shoulder as he passed by in a crowded room. He always had something disparaging to say if he caught her alone, but so far, she'd managed not to let him corner her. She shuddered to think what he'd do, given the chance. Bad enough what he probably said about her out of her hearing. He'd never forgotten that day, or forgiven her. Nor had she forgotten what he tried to do to her. She often regretted not reporting him to her father.

Today, after her brief taste of freedom with Valkyrie, she was in no mood to put up with Alber. "At least I brought food for the pot. What have ye done today, save sit on yer arse and drink? *Real man?* As ye are now, yer next opponent in battle will finish what the last started and cleave yer head from yer shoulders."

He lurched to his feet with a roar.

Mariota sniffed and continued up the stairs. He'd never follow her. If she screamed, her father would exile him, unless he chose to run him through on the spot. She went the rest of the way considering which she would prefer. Alber's curses followed her up the stairs.

STELLAN PULLED off his gloves as he entered the keep and made his way to the laird's solar. The door was open, so he didn't bother to knock. "I'm back," he announced, and moved to the hearth to warm himself by the fire. After a week's hard riding, being back inside Dunrobin felt good. He looked forward to sleeping in his own bed tonight rather than on the cold, hard ground, or in a crofters' cot. Days were getting longer and warmer, but by sunset, the air still carried the bite of winter.

"Ye are late. Was there trouble?" Sutherland laid aside his quill and leaned back in his chair, his gaze following Stellan as he warmed his hands in front of the fire.

"Nay. We saw nay sign of it at the crofts we visited. Ye said ye were told MacKays are hunting Sutherland territory. We saw naught of them, though with everything in the woods starting to sprout leaves, there's nay lack of places for them— or their quarry —to hide." Stellan shrugged. Some of the chill of riding seemed to have eased off, so he settled in a chair across the table from his father. "What are ye working on?" Numbers and notations covered the pages of the open journal on the worktable before him.

"The planting schedule. Barring another hard freeze, we should be able to start plowing and planting the fields soon, especially those closer to the water."

"We dinna need another lean year come harvest time. Or poachers."

"Indeed. Our stores are depleted enough as it is, and this time of year, we have to go farther afield to find game."

"We spotted a huge stag up north and tracked him for a few hours, but lost him in the woods. 'Tis why I'm late returning. I'll take a few men tomorrow and try again."

"Have a care. The hinds will be fawning soon."

"We saw none. They're hunkered down with their fawns, or will be soon. I ken 'tis the wrong time of year to take a female."

Anders sauntered in. "To ye, any time of year is the wrong

time to take a female," he quipped. "Ach, were ye speaking of lasses or deer?"

"In either case, I was no' speaking to ye," Stellan replied, grinned, and gripped his brother's forearm in greeting.

Anders grinned back, taking no insult. Unlike his minutes-older brother, he was free to consort with any lass who showed an interest. Stellan, as heir, had to be much, much more careful.

"So, ye saw nay sign of MacKays, either," Anders went on, clearly aware of the reason for Stellan's grim mood. "Do we ken what they are up to?"

"According to the Gunn, naught," Sutherland said.

"Do ye believe him?" Stellan didn't.

"I believe only what I see or hear with my own senses," Sutherland answered.

"Or the report of yer sons," Anders prompted.

"Or a trusted ally, which Gunn is no'."

"So, nothing has changed," Stellan summarized, then stood. "I'm for some food and my bed."

"I've eaten," Anders told him, "but I'll join ye for an ale."

"Welcome back," their father told Stellan. "Go on, both of ye, and leave me to my work." Sutherland waved them out.

CHAPTER 2

"Let's go riding." Mariota hooked her arm through Seamus's when she found him in the middle of the bailey, and turned him toward the stables. "I want to get out for a while and 'tis a fine morning."

"Yer father does no' want ye to leave the keep."

"Da does no' want me to leave alone. I willna be. Ye will be with me."

Seamus didn't look convinced, so Mariota stuck out her lower lip, doing her best to look pitiable and sad. When Seamus sucked in a breath, she knew she'd won.

"We'll go," he told her, "but we must return before noon."

"Why do ye say that? We always do."

"I'm meeting someone."

"Perfect. If ye'll beg Cook for some food so we can break our fast, I'll fetch Valkyrie."

He stood firm when she tried to turn them back toward the keep. "I dinna ken if this is such a good idea."

He couldn't back out now! She could taste freedom. And her favorite mount, Epona, needed to run. Chafing over her father's restrictions, Mariota hadn't been able to ride her in weeks, and she was used to more freedom. She thought she'd found a champion in Seamus, and feared he was wavering. "I promise we'll be back in time. With Valkyrie along, we can hunt and make the morning worthwhile. She might take another coney for the pot. Da canna complain about that."

Mariota kept her expression neutral as Seamus considered. He feared her father's wrath. Everyone did. But the gate guard would not let her ride out without an escort, and Seamus was the most amenable to her of the MacKay men.

Just as she was becoming tempted to stamp her foot in frustration, he nodded.

"Fetch her, and yer bow. I'll meet ye in the stable."

Elation filled her, but she kept it off her face. "Thank ye." She headed for the mews to collect Valkyrie. She kept her bow there, too, so in minutes she was in the stable, instructing the lad working there to saddle Epona and Seamus's favorite mount.

By the time the horses were ready, Seamus arrived with a packet of food and two skins. He held up one of them. "Wine."

Mariota nodded. He knew her preference for watered wine over ale. They mounted up and Mariota settled Valkyrie on the bow perch pommel the hawk master had carved for her. She led the way from the stable to the gate and called, "Open up."

"Ye are no' to go riding," the guard answered.

"No alone, nay. But Seamus is with me."

"Open up," Seamus added. "We will no' be gone long."

Mariota held her breath. With Seamus by her side, she hadn't expected resistance from the guard. "What did Da threaten all of ye with?" She kept her voice low enough only Seamus would hear her.

"Trust me, ye dinna wish to ken."

"Ouch."

"Pitch yer voice higher and ye'll have the right idea."

Mariota scowled at that. Surely her da wouldn't do anything so barbaric. Her expression smoothed into a smile as the gate inched open. As soon as there was enough of a gap for the horses to slip through, she kicked Epona into motion. In moments, they were free.

They rode hard across the open field outside the gate, but had to slow when they entered the woods. At the first clearing, Mariota stopped and loosed Valkyrie. "Hunt," she told her. The raptor eyed her, then took to her wings and was soon lost to sight above the trees.

"She'll call if she spots something," Mariota reminded Seamus. "Until she does, let's ride."

They continued into the woods. In moments, Valkyrie's piercing call sounded above them. "That way," Seamus said, pointing.

In the next clearing, they found Valkyrie perched on her kill, a young fox kit. "Fox is not good to eat, but the fur will be welcome," Mariota commented as she dismounted.

Seamus pulled his dirk, skinned the carcass, and left the meat for Valkyrie. The fur he rolled and tied behind his saddle. "She didn't take long. Will she keep hunting?"

"Aye." Mari took the water skin from Epona's back as she watched Valkyrie tear strips of meat from the fox's haunch. She looked away long enough to rinse Seamus's hands and knife of blood. "She won't take much from that."

In moments, the bird launched skyward and they remounted.

Seamus picked up his reins. "Which way?"

"Toward the burn, I think," Mariota said. "We can wash up, refill this, and water the horses there, even if Valkyrie doesn't spot any prey."

At the burn, Seamus checked his horse's hooves. "Damn, I thought so. He's thrown a shoe."

"He's lamed?"

"Nay, but I canna ride him back to the keep without risking him. I'll have to walk him back."

At that moment, Valkyrie called. "She's spotted something. I'll go check," Mariota said.

"Dinna go far," Seamus warned. "Ye need to come with me. I canna leave ye here or yer da will have my cods, and I canna get to ye with any speed if trouble finds ye."

"I'll come back as quickly as I can." Mariota rode away, leaving Seamus to deal with his mount. Relishing her freedom to be alone, she forgot her promise to stay close by. She kept going, following Valkyrie's cries until she realized how long she'd been wandering away from Seamus, and called the bird down.

Mariota knew she would be in trouble going so far from the keep. Seamus was well behind her, stuck waiting for her with a lame horse. If he got worried and didn't wait, he'd be hours walking trying to find her. Though she relished the time to herself, away from everyone, out of the keep, and away from her father's odious commands, it wasn't worth the punishment her father would mete out to Seamus if he found out.

This solitude, and feeling almost as free as Valkyrie on the wing was an illusion, and there would be consequences if she didn't get back to Seamus soon. She dismounted and walked across the clearing toward where Valkyrie had landed with her kill, another bird. Mariota would let her feast on it before they headed home. She had earned the treat. But they needed to head back, or Seamus would indeed start searching for her, and he'd never go with her out of the keep again.

An arrow came out of nowhere and buried itself in the ground next to Valkyrie. The hawk dropped her kill and launched herself into the air.

Mariota spun, searching for cover and for where the shot had come from. Before she could pick a direction and move out of danger, Alber showed himself.

"Ye are a long way from home, lass," he taunted her. "And alone. Ye dare to claim I canna fight? I can best any man, but soon, I willna need to."

He laughed, making Mariota's blood turn to ice in her veins. What was he doing out here? He'd followed her. Her taunt had hit closer to the mark than she realized.

"Yer lap dog, Seamus, is far away," he said.

She didn't need the reminder. If she wasn't so focused on Alber, she'd curse herself for ignoring Seamus' warning and wandering so far. What price was she about to pay for her taste of freedom?

"He can do naught to help ye, now can he? And I can do with ye what I will. For as long as I want." He stepped closer, lips pulled back in a malicious grin. "Ye'll have to marry me by the time I'm done with ye. Go on, scream if ye wish. Ye willna be heard."

What? All this was so he could take over the clan? "I dinna need to scream," she ventured, anger welling, though she fought the urge to run. Alber would be on her before she could take three steps. All she could do was hold her ground and keep his attention on her. Fear made her knees weak and her heart pound, but he wouldn't expect her to have the strength to defy him, and she had a secret weapon.

She whistled, calling Valkyrie down to attack, and swept her arm toward Alber.

He laughed and grabbed her hand.

Mariota tugged, fighting to get free, knowing she was too close for what was to come.

Valkyrie's attack was as swift as it was unexpected— at least for him. Before he could pull Mariota against him, the hawk's steep dive ended in a rush of air that blew Mariota's hair back. As Valkyrie's wings flared out around Alber's head, he dropped Mariota's hand. She stumbled back as he tried to protect his throat by grabbing at Valkyrie's claws, but he was too slow. Valkyrie raked his neck and pecked his face, tearing a chunk out of his cheek. Mariota whistled her away before his frantic grabs could harm her.

Valkyrie launched herself skyward.

At least her bird was safe. Mariota wasn't. The look on Alber's torn face promised a painful death if he managed to get his hands on her. He staggered a step, his hands outstretched to throttle her, but he swayed before he reached her. His skin, what of it that wasn't bloodied, had gone a pasty white. Mariota forgot her fear of being grabbed. She might see this man die before her— so much blood coated Alber's face and neck. Instead of rushing Mariota, he pawed at his face, then turned back to his horse, and clung to its saddle, no longer able to taunt or threaten her.

Valkyrie had given her time to escape him. She dared not waste it. Mariota ran to her mount, heart pounding louder in her ears than her footfalls. She glanced back and took her first easy breath since Alber's arrow had narrowly missed her hawk. He still clutched his saddle. She mounted and rode hard the way she'd come, her hawk pacing her in the sky above her.

Still at a gallop, she found Seamus, pulled on the reins and wheeled Epona to a stop.

"Mariota! What's wrong?"

Breathless, she told him what had happened. "He may be coming behind us," she warned, "but Valkyrie did some damage. He's bloodied. I dinna ken how bad."

Frowning, Seamus said, "I'll ride double with ye. My mount can run without a rider on his back. We need to get back to the keep. Ye are nay safe out here."

"Da will never let me out of MacKay's walls again."

"If Alber catches ye, yer da will be the least of yer worries." He mounted up behind her. "Now let's go."

&

THEY REACHED THE KEEP SAFELY, but Mariota knew that wasn't the end of her peril. She still had to tell her father what happened.

"I told ye to stay inside the gates," he raged, pacing his solar after he sent men to look for the injured Alber. "Ye disobeyed me yet again. Must I lock ye in yer chamber?"

"I did as ye asked, Da. I wasna alone until Seamus's horse threw a shoe. And Valkyrie spotted prey, so I went after her. But Alber found me. He threatened me. I had to call Valkyrie down to stop him from… hurting me."

His frown and the way his jaw clenched told her he understood what she hadn't said. Alber would not get out of this unpunished, either.

"If ye had stayed in the keep as ye ought, this wouldna have happened. Seamus will be punished for aiding ye."

"Ye canna do that, Da. Blame me if ye must. I convinced Seamus to ride with me. But no' for what happened to Alber. He did no' have to follow. Or threaten me. He tried to kill Valkyrie, first, but his arrow missed. He got nay more than he deserved."

"And so shall ye. Get ye to yer chamber. I'll deal with ye after the men return."

Mariota realized she'd get nowhere arguing with her father. Meekly, she nodded and did as he ordered.

An hour later, he called her back. His men had found Alber.

As she approached the solar, she heard her father's voice and one of his councilors, as well. James was one of the men her father trusted to advise him, a strong and experienced warrior. Mariota paused outside the door.

"Ye are going to have to do something about him," James was saying.

Mariota knew who he meant.

"I am considering it. He would deserve lashes, but according to my daughter, her hawk may have taken care of that already."

His bark of laughter elicited a chuckle from James, but sickened her. Would her father do something to Valkyrie?

"Perhaps he'll have a scar on the other side of his face to

balance the one he got at Harlaw," James said. "'Twould only be fair."

"He canna go unpunished for this," her father said, "but nay matter what I do, lashes, time in the dungeon or the stocks, it will just make Alber angrier and more determined to do harm. He hasna been himself since Harlaw, but never this bad."

The silence stretched long enough that she knew James must have simply nodded or shrugged.

"Ye might want to name a *tanist*," James said.

The change of subject surprised her. Why had he brought that up?

"If the worst happens, he can take over, and Mariota willna have to be in control," he continued.

Her father gusted out a heavy sigh. "Aye, I've thought of it."

He had? Why hadn't he discussed the idea with her first? She could have been open to the assistance a *tanist* would give her, but now? She could feel her muscles tensing and her heart race with her growing fury. She considered bursting in on the meeting and confronting her father over his betrayal, yet again, of the trust that should exist between a laird and his heir.

Before she could take a step in that direction, sanity returned. He wasn't alone.

The council wanted her to be passed over? Her stomach sank. Whether she wanted to be heir or not, she didn't know how she would bear the embarrassment of having her father's council refute her. She'd always imagined refusing to become laird on her own terms, or abdicating after she found a man who truly loved her. The idea of marrying for love and leaving MacKay in the control of her hand-picked successor was a pleasant fantasy. Hearing the reality of her father and his council preparing to replace her made her long to return to her chamber.

But she'd been summoned, and making her father send for her again would only make matters worse. She cleared her throat to warn them of her presence and took the difficult paces to and through the door.

"Yer men found my attacker?" She was still angry enough to challenge him.

"My men found Alber unconscious, blood still seeping from the wounds on his neck and face. No matter what he said or did, he does no' deserve to die," her father raged once he gave her the news. "Certainly no' in this way! Killed by yer damn hawk? If the lads had no' found him when they did, he could be dead."

"He threatened to ruin me. I had to defend myself."

He stood and leaned over his desk toward her. "Ye, lass, are of an age to cause more such trouble. There are rough men here. More since Domnhall sent troops to fight Mar. I'll put an end to this nonsense. I will see ye married. Soon. Then yer husband can keep ye out of trouble."

"To Alber?" Mariota gasped. This was to be her punishment? Mortified, she glanced aside at James, who was sitting quietly off to one side. He watched her with an expression she could only interpret as disgust. She straightened her shoulders. She used to think he liked her. Now that she knew better, she would not betray her feelings in front of him.

"Nay. And no' to Seamus," her father continued, drawing her attention back to his words. "He may be yer friend and protector, but marriage to him does naught for MacKay. We need an alliance. And I know where to seek one."

Mariota drew a relieved breath. She'd misunderstood his threat and feared he would go along with Alber. She should have known better. Still, she couldn't believe she had to have this conversation in front of one of the council. "Nay, Da, I willna. I dinna wish to marry. No' with Seamus, and certainly no with a stranger."

"Ye ken yer place, daughter. Ye will do yer duty for the clan."

She fought to keep from fisting her hands. Even if her father didn't notice, James would. "Ye are punishing me for Alber's actions."

"Perhaps I am, but for yers as well. Ye must learn what ye do has consequences. In this case, ye nearly cost a man's life."

"I told ye what happened. He brought that on himself. Why are ye protecting him rather than me?" If nothing else, she had to make her father understand how dangerous Alber was to her.

He glanced aside at James, and the two exchanged a frown, then he turned to glare at her. "I will no' argue with ye, daughter. Leave me now, or there will be even more consequences."

He'd confine her to her chamber, or deny her Valkyrie, or something else she couldn't bear. She lifted her chin, turned, and left the solar.

"A lass like that needs a very strong husband," she heard James say before she'd taken three steps past the doorway.

"Aye, she does," her father said. "I'd hoped to find one at Sutherland, but I may have to look elsewhere.

Mariota could easily imagine they would consider a brute like Alber to be just the type of man to tame her.

She would go to her chamber, but not for any longer than necessary. She needed time to gather her things, and to find a way to get out of the keep's walls without being seen. Running away was dangerous, even foolish, she knew, but she also knew her father. He'd do what he'd promised and marry her off, probably to some old laird of an enemy clan, for the sake of one of his damned alliances. She couldn't bear the thought. She'd rather live on her own in a hut in the woods. With Valkyrie to help her hunt, she'd never starve. But first she had to free Valkyrie and get away.

Then she'd deal with the rest of her life.

STELLAN RAISED A HAND, ordering the hunting party to halt just below the next rise. They'd tracked the huge stag for three days, headed north toward MacKay. Stellan knew they were still on Sutherland territory, but they couldn't go much farther. If they didn't get lucky soon, the stag would escape them.

Their horses nickered softly, but no one spoke. Stellan dismounted, crept to the crest and stretched out on the ground to peer over it. The big stag had disappeared over the hill and into the thicker woods just beyond a wee glen that marked the boundary. Into MacKay territory.

His friend Tormund crept up and stretched out beside him. "See him?"

"Nay, and we're at our border with MacKay. If he doesna wander back this way, we willna be able to keep after him."

"Bollocks. We've been chasing that bastard for days. We canna lose him to the MacKays."

"We can and we will. He's crossed the border." Stellan raised a hand to forestall Tormund's objection. "Likely he wanders back and forth at will. If we wait, we'll see him on this side again."

Tormund eyed the sun's position low in the southwestern sky, snorted and pushed up onto his knees. "Unless the MacKays get him first. That's it then. I'm for making camp. Let's let him live another day."

Stellan nodded and got to his feet. As he did, the stag meandered out of the trees and back across the glen's small clearing well ahead of them, nibbling at green shoots as he went. "He does no' bloody care that he's run us all over the countryside. Look at him."

Tormund crossed his arms over his massive chest. "He kens we're here."

"Aye. And if we go at him, he'll duck back into those trees in MacKay territory."

A hawk circled over the stag and emitted a piercing cry.

The stag's head came up and he froze.

"He's too big for the likes of ye," Tormund muttered, clearly addressing the raptor.

Before Stellan could answer, the stag bolted—straight for them.

"What the hell?" Tormund raised his bow, but Stellan put a hand on his arm.

"Wait till he's well on our side. Wait." Stellan's gaze swept the area between their hilltop and the stag, looking for the stone marker he knew was in the glen. He spotted it as the stag crossed into Sutherland and began to run uphill. "Now!"

Tormund loosed his arrow and struck the stag in the throat.

It went down, stumbling, onto its foreleg knees, and rested there, wheezing, as blood began to soak its shoulder.

Stellan nocked an arrow and loosed it, finishing the beast. "I didna want to see him suffer," he said, waving at the others to bring the horses up.

Tormund nodded and they started down the hill. An arrow whizzed by and buried itself in the ground behind them. They ducked and scrambled for the cover of a tree trunk.

"Sodding Sutherland thieves!" The angry call came from MacKay land. Another arrow followed it.

"Stay back," Stellan warned his men, turned and faced toward the buck. "We've stolen nothing."

"The buck was on MacKay land. 'Tis ours!"

"We've chased that buck over half of Sutherland. It crossed into MacKay and back out again before we killed it. Ye have nay claim."

The rumble of deep male voices came to them, none clear, until one rose above the others to object, "That blasted bird spooked it and it ran. We'd have it but for the hawk."

"Ye did no' ken the buck was even there until the hawk screamed a warning," another said.

The voices dropped, but continued wrangling. Stellan sat back against the tree trunk and looked across to where Tormund was doing the same. They traded a look and shrugged.

"Think we can retrieve it?" Tormund's grin gave away the sarcasm in his question.

"Go right ahead," Stellan told him. "It ye want yer arse shot full of arrows trying to pull it up here."

"Guess we'll have to wait until they give up and leave."

"Aye. If they do. MacKays are no' kenned for being reasonable."

The arguing continued in the MacKay camp with occasional forays to yell insults at the Sutherlands. With dark encroaching, the MacKays lit a campfire that glowed through the trees on their side.

Tormund groaned when the glow of the fire became visible. "Damn MacKays. That's our buck."

"They'll be watching it from under the cover of those trees. Let's make a show of withdrawing."

Tormund grinned and nodded. "Anders is going to be sorry he missed this."

Stellan stayed down but ordered his men back over the hilltop. He didn't bother to lower his voice, wanting the MacKays to hear him.

On the other side of the hilltop, out of earshot of the rival clansmen, he told his men, "Let them drink themselves pished. Once they do, we'll haul the buck over the hill and be gone before the sun comes up. Tormund and Gregor, ye've got first watch. Wake me when they get quiet."

Two hours later, Stellan took four men to pick up the buck and bring it back over the hill. It was a Sutherland victory his da would appreciate. The only life lost was the buck's.

CHAPTER 3

Finding a way to escape MacKay was taking Mariota longer than she'd hoped it would. She couldn't free Valkyrie, claim a horse, and get all three out of the keep, herself included, without garnering too much notice. Her father had laid down the law with the guards. Under no circumstances was she to leave the keep. Not alone and not with anyone else, especially Seamus, who had been relegated to the nighttime watch, though perhaps to soften the blow, he'd been named chief of the watch. She was sorry for the trouble she'd caused him, but her da could have done worse.

Alber had been under the care of the healer. Despite all the blood Mariota had seen and her da's claim that he'd been found near death, his injuries were not as serious as she'd imagined. In Valkyrie's favor, he'd never look the same again, not that Mariota thought he'd been an attractive man to start with. Her hawk's claw marks would scar his neck. The chunks the raptor had torn out of his face would heal, but would leave unsightly pits on the side opposite the Harlaw scar. Bruises, though those would fade, further detracted from his appearance. So she'd been told. She hadn't been foolish enough to get anywhere near his chamber.

He was under no such compunction. Mariota found him waiting outside her chamber after the evening meal the day after he was brought back to the keep.

"What are ye doing here?" She shouted at him, hoping someone would hear and come to her aid.

"I've come to finish the business between us. Yer damned bird did this to me," he said and lifted a hand to his face, open wounds seeping still.

Hadn't the healer bandaged them? Or had he torn the covers off to try to frighten her with his grotesque appearance.

"She protected me."

"She's no' here now." He moved more quickly than she thought him capable of, grabbed her arm and forced her against the wall, his other hand splayed over her face, fingers gripping the sides of her head in a punishing show of strength she feared would crack her skull. "Ye are mine and ye owe me. I'll make ye hurt as yer damn bird hurt me, then I'll have ye."

Mariota tried to scream, but he flattened his palm against her nose and mouth, denying her breath. She was on her own. But she'd beaten him before, once by herself and once with Valkyrie's help. She'd do it again.

She tried to twist away, but it was a ruse and he fell for it, stepping wide to contain her as she writhed. With no mercy, she kneed him between the legs, surprised he fell for the same maneuver again.

His howl echoed down the hallway. She suspected it could be heard in the great hall. In moments, running footsteps proved her right.

"I owe ye naught and will never wed with ye," she spat. "I dinna ken what is wrong with ye. But ye got what ye deserved."

Two men reached her first, followed by two more and several women.

"He attacked me again," she said. "I stopped him."

The women took in Alber lying on the floor, hands between

his legs cupping himself, tears mixing with the blood seeping from his face from his fall and laughed. "Ye got him good, lass."

"Get him away from me, please. Lock him in his chamber and tell my da."

"We'll take care of him," one of the men said, his frown at Alber promising something other than care. He nodded to the others and they dragged Alber down the hall toward the stairs. In moments, she heard the hard thump, thump, thump that told her they dragged him *down* them, too.

So, she wasn't the only one having trouble with him.

"Did he hurt ye?" One of the older women asked in a sympathetic tone, reaching out to touch her arm.

"He tried," Mariota told her and the others who remained. "I didna let him."

"Ye are a braw lass," one of the others said. "I canna imagine fighting off a man that size."

"Thank ye." Her pulse pounding in her ears, she added, "I'd like to go rest now, but later, I'll be happy to show ye what Cook taught me. Or ye can ask her." She wrapped her arms around her waist to keep them from seeing her tremble.

With understanding nods, they left her in her chamber. She locked the door and gave in to a fit of shakes, angry tears stinging the corners of her eyes. She was out of time. Once Alber recovered, no matter what her father might say or do, he'd come after her again.

A knock on her door startled her. Not Alber, please! Nay, he wouldn't knock. "Who is it?"

"Yer da sent me to guard yer door, lass. Ye'll be safe." She recognized the voice of one of the men who'd carried off Alber. So, she was confined to her chamber after all.

Left with no alternative, she waited until midnight, made a rope out of bedsheets and with her few belongings wrapped in a spare plaid tied on her back, climbed out of her window and down to the bailey. The night was quiet and the guards' attention was outside the walls, not inside, so she was able to sneak to the mews and free Valkyrie. Outside, she tossed her skyward, knowing the hawk would keep pace with her. If Mariota was caught, the hawk would return to the mews by morning. The stable tempted her, but she knew she'd never get out with her horse. Keeping to the shadows, she hurried to the postern gate, and once through it, made her way on foot to the village, staying under the trees and out of sight of the guards on the keep's walls. She knew the value of a horse to each villager, and she hated to do it, but she was desperate. She saddled and stole one she knew, vowing to return it as soon as she could. After leading it quietly away from the village and the MacKay keep before mounting it, she rode into the night.

❦

STELLAN and his men continued to hunt, making their way slowly back toward the keep with the buck tied over the back of one of the horses. They'd stopped only once to field dress the buck when he was certain they were far enough into Sutherland territory the MacKays wouldn't dare follow. Hoisting it up by its hind legs and a rope slung over a tree branch, they cut its throat and drained its blood, gutted it and left the entrails for the local predators. Then they'd moved away and found a spot near a burn to get some sleep before continuing their journey home.

Stellan woke to a guard's hand on his shoulder, early sunlight in his eyes, and the sound of a horse moving nearby rustling in the undergrowth beyond their camp, headed their way. With no fire to warn of their presence, he expected the rider would be on them in moments. He stood and toed two more men awake. "Someone's coming," he told them quietly.

They nodded, got up, and soundlessly reached for weapons.

Stellan bit back an oath when a lass on a stocky draft horse stumbled on their camp. She looked half asleep and barely aware enough of her surroundings to avoid getting knocked off by tree branches as she rode. Her mount looked more suited to pulling a plow than carrying a rider. This lass was no threat to anyone but herself. Why was she out here alone?

"Lass," he said softly as he grasped the horse's bridle to keep her from jerking awake and galloping away. They were covered in the stag's blood and would frighten her when she noticed it.

Then she shifted and dark eyes glinted, peering out from the edge of her cloak. Against her chest, a hawk in jesses gripped her sleeve.

Suddenly, the lass became much more interesting. What was she doing with the raptor?

"What? Ach!" Her eyes widened as she took in her situation. "Who are ye? Let me go."

"I'll let ye go when ye are awake enough to ride safely. I'm Stellan. Who are ye?"

She studied him, her eyes widening as she took in his and his men's bloody clothes. No amount of dunking in a shallow burn would remove all of it, though they'd tried.

"Did ye kill the men following me?"

"Men are following ye? Who?"

"MacKays." She looked around as if looking for a way out.

Tormund came up and gave her a nod before turning to Stellan. "Likely 'tis why that lot were so close to our border last night, aye? Searching for her and found our buck."

"We havena killed anyone but a buck, lass, and ye are safe with us. Now, who are ye?"

"Mariota. I'm… lost, I think. Can ye help me?"

Stellan couldn't believe what he was hearing. "What are ye doing lost in the woods alone?" No lass in her right mind would venture out with nothing but a hawk for company. Or protection?

"I wasna safe where I came from."

Not safe at MacKay? What had happened there to send her

out into the night? "'Tis lucky ye found us. We're headed home to Sutherland," he said and nodded toward the buck's body tied over one of the horses. "Come with us and we'll see ye taken care of. But first, let's get ye down. We're about to break our fast. Ye must be hungry."

"I am," she told him and tried to dismount, but the weight of her hawk made her movements awkward and dangerous.

If she fell, she could be hurt, and so could her raptor, so Stellan reached for her waist. She nodded and clung to her hawk while he lifted her down, her arms wrapped around it to keep it still. He held her waist, her slender form burning his hands until she seemed steady on her feet. Once she was off her horse, he realized she was tall enough that the top of her head reached his jaw. Her chestnut hair blazed with golden high-lights in the sunrise, her coloring much like her hawk's. A sensation Stellan had long suppressed filled his chest with heat that radiated throughout his body. He hadn't felt attraction like this in months, certainly not for a lass he'd just met. But her large eyes, the color of woodland moss, held him in thrall as she looked up at him, studying him much as he did her. He forced himself to release her. She was a lass who needed his help. Scratched and limping as they made their way into the camp, she couldn't continue her escape on her own. But where was she going? For a moment, he considered whether she'd stolen the hawk, but her clothes were too rich for a serving lass on the run, and the hawk tolerated her touch. This lass was someone of substance.

He helped her to a seat on a log near the fire someone had stirred back to life. "We have trail rations," he told her. "Oatcakes and dried meat and the like."

"I'm grateful for anything ye can share," she told him. "I had to leave too urgently to gather many supplies."

"Is that why ye are limping?"

"Nay, I twisted my ankle a wee getting down to a burn for

some water during the night. 'Tisna bad." She demonstrated by turning her booted foot one way, then the other.

He noted the quality of the leather and workmanship. Not something a serving lass would own. "Where were ye thinking to go, lass?"

She accepted the food one of his men brought to them, shrugged and took a bite of oatcake. "I thought to reach Inverness. Or Sterling, perhaps."

Inverness was rebuilding after Domnhall burned down much of it on his way to Aberdeen and the battle at Harlaw last summer. It was not a fit place for a lass alone. But Sterling? To the royal court? He contented himself with asking her, "Alone?" He couldn't get past the idea that she was mad— or that desperate. There were a lot of mountains between here and her goal. And a lot of dangers. But he held his tongue, wanting to hear what she would reveal— and how she expected to survive.

"With Valkyrie, I would never starve. And I'm hard to kill," she added softly, as though to herself.

"One well-timed arrow and ye would truly be on yer own," Stellan observed. Even he and Anders took precautions when they traveled for the clan. Including men and weapons. As many as they could reasonably carry. He'd seen no sign of any with Mariota. But perhaps she sought to hide any she carried because, once again, she was surrounded by men— strangers this time — and was afraid they might try to do her harm like the MacKay soldier

"I nearly was. That is how the fight started with the guard. He shot at Valkyrie. Thank the saints he missed."

"Yet he and his men are after ye?" Why did he get the sense that she was holding back something important?

"I wounded him. He sought retribution and I had to hurt him again. I wasna safe at home any longer."

This lass harmed a MacKay guard, twice? Perhaps she was mad. "I'm sorry for that. Could ye no' appeal to the MacKay?"

"I tried." She huffed out a breath. "He didna believe I could best one of his favored warriors."

Stellan leaned back to study her. "I mightna either, save that ye are here." Travel-worn and weary, she was still lovely. Something about her made him want to put his hands on her again. He clenched his jaw and laid them on his lap instead.

She made a moue of her mouth. "I had nay choice but to leave," she said and bit into a chunk of dried meat, then went about chewing it, effectively halting her side of the conversation.

Stellan knew she'd never make Inverness or Sterling with nothing for protection or supplies but her hawk. She'd be safe at Dunrobin, and could live there in comfort until such time as she revealed more about herself, until someone sent for her from MacKay, or until they could send her onward with an escort. Stellan knew he was taking a dangerous step— MacKay could say he stole the lass —but her plaintive tale gained his sympathy and his cooperation.

"Ye will come with us to Dunrobin," he told her. "Ye will be safe there and welcome for as long as ye wish to stay."

"I dinna expect that—"

"'Twould be best if ye didna appear to be a lass as we travel," he told her, cutting short her objection. She should be as familiar with Highland hospitality as he, and know that she could count on Sutherland aid.

She turned those moss-green eyes on him, one eyebrow arched in... what? Query? Or disbelief? It didn't matter. He wanted to lose himself in her gaze.

"Aye?"

Her question broke his concentration on the color of her eyes. Moss green, yes, but with flecks of brown like fallen bits of bark on a mossy rock.

"What should I appear to be?"

He realized she was teasing when the corner of her mouth crooked up.

"A sprite would do, I suppose," he said, going along with her jest. "Though I think ye are too tall to be convincing. Perhaps a tree, then?"

She snorted. "With a hawk perched on a limb, aye?" She held her hawk out to one side, her arm extended.

"That looks tiring. Suppose we simply lend ye some clothes and ye can look like a lad. Tuck yer hair up in a bonnet and from a distance, nary a man will be the wiser."

She nodded her agreement.

"How did ye come by having Valkyrie with ye?"

"The usual way. I found an egg in a nest up a tree. I used to be quite good at climbing when I was a lass." Her expression grew solemn, even sad.

Stellan assumed it was because proper young lasses were not allowed to indulge in activities like climbing trees.

"I raised her from the egg," she told him between bites of food, and with little encouragement from him, told him how the MacKay hawk master had taught her to train Valkyrie, and how they had bonded.

Stellan enjoyed how when she spoke about something she clearly loved, she became more animated.

"She is one of the best hunters among MacKay's mews."

He started to ask her who she really was, when Tormund brought a set of clothes for her to change into. She took the spare clothes with polite thanks, and walked behind some undergrowth to change.

Her limp seemed less pronounced already, giving Stellan hope that she'd soon lose it altogether.

When she returned, he handed her a man's bonnet to hide her hair. They might be unlucky enough to happen upon MacKay men foolish enough to be heading south, looking for her on Sutherland land.

She twisted her hair into a loose braid, tucked the thick strand into the bonnet and pulled it onto her head.

Stellan hid his disappointment. He could think of several fantasies involving that hair, but it was hidden now, out of sight and touch. "I think ye will do," he told her, though she'd had to roll up her sleeves to reveal her hands. And the leggings were similarly shortened to keep her from tripping over them. From a distance, she'd look like a lad in an older, larger brother's clothes. Up close, she was all lass, and Stellan was having a hard time pulling his gaze away from her form that the clothes revealed. God help him if she turned around.

Tormund joined them and nodded. "Ye could be a ghillie, helping with the hunt. 'Tis good, Stellan."

Mariota smiled at Tormund's comment. "'Tis? Good. Are these yer clothes? My thanks."

"One of the other lad's," Stellan said, unreasonably jealous of the smile she'd turned on Tormund. "He'll get them back when we get ye settled at Dunrobin."

"Thank him for me, nonetheless," she said.

Stellan's estimation of her rose higher. "Do ye need more time to rest? Ye were half asleep when ye arrived."

"Nay, I am restored. Thanks to ye. Let's keep moving and get more miles between me and MacKay."

It still bothered him that the MacKay had not protected a mere lass against one of his fighting men, which meant there had to be more to Mariota's story than she had revealed. Though by her clothes and the hawk she carried, she seemed to be no mere lass. But he admired her spirit and liked her manners. And then there was the heat that filled his belly— and lower —every time she met his gaze. He wanted to know more, to spend more time with her, and the best way to do both of those things was to take her home to Dunrobin.

If MacKay men were truly pursuing her, he'd just as soon get her behind Dunrobin's walls and out of danger. That applied to him and his men as well. He wasn't eager to have to protect her during a fight with an unknown number of MacKays. So Stellan kept them moving, glad the trip back to Dunrobin's large tower house went much faster than the trip out. They weren't meandering around the countryside on the trail of the huge buck, but rode straight through to the Sutherland keep and arrived just after midday.

❧

WHEN THEY REACHED Dunrobin's bailey, Stellan helped Mariota dismount, as he had when she'd stumbled across the Sutherland camp, with Valkyrie secure against her chest. Now, as then, the span of his large hands on her waist made her insides melt. She'd never seen a more handsome man, not one who appealed to her the way he did. His thick, dark hair had a touch of curl at the ends, enough to give it a wild, unkempt look, especially after he ran a hand through it. His shoulders were broad, his arms and chest well-muscled, his legs long and as well-muscled as the rest of him. Looking at him made her think of the tales she'd heard from her married friends. What would it be like to kiss him? And more? Who was he at Sutherland? The head huntsman? If so, he'd be important enough to be considered a candidate to betroth with her. She might like that very much indeed.

She realized all the while she'd been admiring him, his hands still spanned her waist. His thumbs had begun to stroke the sides of her abdomen, sending tingles spiraling into her chest while he studied her. She put her free hand over one of his, reluctant to stop his simple caress, but a few seconds more and people would start to notice. The bailey was bustling and she noticed no few gazes on them as people passed. Were they what caught the interest, or simply the way she was dressed? "Thank ye, Stellan. I'm quite steady now."

He dropped his hands to his sides, then lifted one to run through his hair, mussing it further. "Sorry, lass." He looked Mariota over once again. Making certain she could stand on her

39

own? Then he glanced up and waved a hand. "Ah, Nan," he called out.

A lovely young woman approached, and Mariota's heart dropped into her belly. His wife? Mistress?

"Stellan," she said, her voice throaty and soft as she said his name. "Who do ye have here?"

"Mariota MacKay, my cousin, Nan. If ye would, Nan, please find the steward and help him get Mariota settled in a guest chamber. With a bath," he added, glancing at her. After she nodded, he continued, "and a tray from Cook sent up to her. I ken we're late for the midday meal."

"'Tis lovely to meet ye," Mariota ventured, not certain she or Nan could pull their attention from her cousin.

But Nan surprised her, turning to fully face her and smiling warmly. "And I ye, as well. Let's get ye comfortable. We'll have time to get acquainted after ye have had a chance to rest."

Mariota liked that idea. But she turned to Stellan before Nan led her away. "Thank ye. Ye and yer men have been more than kind. To whom do I return these clothes?"

"Nan will get them back to me. I'll take care of them." He was staring at her chest. Nay, not at her. "Ach, Valkyrie!" Mariota was so distracted, she'd nearly walked off with her hawk.

"I ken ye are weary, lass. If she'll accept me handling her, I'll take her to the hawk master in the mews and have him settle her there," Stellan promised. "She'll be well cared for."

"I'd like to meet him. If I may take a moment, I need my things, too."

"Of course."

He helped her retrieve her pack. She took it from him, dropped it, and bent to search within it. In a moment, she found what she sought, slipped the hood over the hawk's head and secured it. "I've got her."

"Ye're certain ye dinna want me to take her?"

"She's my responsibility," Mariota told him. She might be

tired, but so was everyone else. "I willna leave Valkyrie's care to a stranger. Once I meet him, once I see her safe, I can rest."

Stellan nodded, understanding plain in his approving smile. "Come with me, then. Nan? Can ye join us?"

"Of course." She bent to retrieve Mariota's pack, but Stellan took it from her and led them to the mews.

"We house our own hunting hawks and falcons here," Stellan told her when they reached it. "I'll see if Ian is within."

"I'm here," a middle-aged man said, exiting the door to the mews. "One of the lads told me ye might have a guest for me."

"I do," Mariota told him and introduced herself.

He raised an eyebrow but didn't comment on a lass in a lad's clothing.

"Ian Sutherland," Stellan told her. "Sutherland's hawk master these past fifteen years, aye?" At Ian's nod, he continued. "Since my brother Anders and I were lads. While she's here," he told Ian, "Mariota needs a safe place for Valkyrie."

Mariota pulled aside her cloak and displayed her raptor.

"Hooded. Wise lass. She's calm with ye."

Mariota smiled at the praise. It was certainly something she was unused to. "Thank ye."

"Let's get her settled, aye?" Ian opened the door and gestured them inside.

Mariota stepped into the structure, dim save for shafts of light slanting through tightly spaced bars on a large window. Perches at different heights were occupied by hooded birds, but several stood empty. Ian led her to one away from the occupied perches. "'Twill do, I think."

"It will do nicely," Mariota agreed and shifted Valkyrie to the perch. She removed the hood long enough for her raptor to have a look around, and to see and sense the hawk master, then she replaced the hood.

"I'll see her fed and watered while ye rest, lass," Ian told her. "*Dinna fash* for yer bird."

"Thank ye." Relieved, she turned to Stellan. "Valkyrie is in good hands, as ye said she would be."

"Let's get ye settled, too," Stellan told her. "Thank ye, Ian," he added before gesturing for Mariota and Nan to precede him out of the mews.

Nan took her hand, a gesture she found reassuring. It struck Mariota that everyone here seemed calm, even happy. She saw none of the tension or conflict that seemed a normal part of life at MacKay. Surely there had to be some here. She'd give Stellan time to show her the real Sutherland.

"Nan will take care of ye," Stellan said after they'd gone a few paces. "I need to see to the horses and help with the buck before I come in."

Mariota nodded, grateful for the attention he'd already given her. "Thank ye, Stellan," she told him. "For everything."

She and Nan headed across the bailey toward the keep's door just as another man came out— one who looked exactly like Stellan.

Mariota stopped dead, twisted around to make sure Stellan had not somehow gotten around her and into the keep and back out again. Nay, he was still with the horses and his men. Fighting to keep her mouth from falling open, she hissed, "Dear God, there are two of them?"

Nan laughed and called out. "Anders, come meet Mariota. Mariota, this is Stellan's twin."

"What a lovely lass ye have brought me," Anders said, stopping to take her hand and bow over it. "Mariota?" He looked her up and down and grinned.

"MacKay," she managed to say without stammering.

"Stellan just returned from the hunt with her," Nan told him. "Lass, I ken ye have a story to tell, but perhaps it should wait until after ye have a chance to rest."

And have time to absorb the fact that there were two devastatingly handsome Sutherland men for her to feast her eyes on. "Aye," she managed to say. "Thank ye."

"I look forward to seeing more of ye," Anders said with a grin. Mariota glanced back as Nan led her away. Anders stood watching them walk away. So did Stellan, visible beyond his brother's shoulder. She whipped her head forward and took a breath.

"One of them is good looking enough, but two? More than a lass can take, aye?" Nan teased.

"Much more," Mariota agreed and put a hand over her heart.

CHAPTER 4

$\mathcal{B}$y the time Stellan and his men delivered the butchered buck to the kitchen, he was again covered in blood, and still had to explain Mariota to the laird. But first, he needed to clean up. He enlisted Cook's help. Rather than have the lasses carry hot water up to his chamber, he used the tub in the screened-off nook off the kitchen, stripped and slid in with a satisfied groan. Cook had left soap and towels. He was content to stay until the water cooled, but the laird awaited. So did Mariota.

Anders shouting his name woke him from the doze brought on by warm comfort and exhaustion. Moss green eyes and the feel of Mariota's slim waist under his hands tormented him. He was glad of the growing chill of the water.

"Ah, there ye are. So Cook is stewing ye for our supper?"

"No' likely," Stellan answered, stood and let the water run down his torso before grabbing the top bath sheet from the stack and wrapping it around his waist. "What's so urgent ye have to come find me here?" He stepped out of the tub and frowned at his twin.

"I ken ye picked up a stray. And this will interest ye. 'Tis good,

I think. I felt yer surprise and attraction to her long before ye got back."

"Did ye? That hasna happened in, well, I dinna recall the last time."

"At least six months. I've seen her, by the way. Lovely. Nan introduced us. Now the bad news. Da wants us. Now."

Stellan grimaced. "Now, of course." He grabbed the next bath sheet and rubbed his hair as dry as he could. "I have to dress."

"Best hurry, then. I'll go stall him," Anders said and left before Stellan could ask him to bring down some clothes.

Stellan headed for his chamber wrapped in another bath sheet after checking to make sure it was dry and not riddled with translucent wet spots. He knew the gamut that awaited him in the great hall. He crossed quickly, making a point to ignore the admiring glances the kitchen wenches and other clan womenfolk sent his way. Why hadn't he sent for clean clothes before he got in the damned tub? None of the lasses at Sutherland interested him, but he and Anders had always interested them. He'd known since his beard came in not to give them more to feed their fantasies.

In his chamber, he wasted no time getting dressed in clean clothes, and hurried back downstairs toward the laird's solar, glad to see the lasses paid him less attention now that he was clothed. Less, but not none. One or two smiled at him with invitation in their eyes as they fingered the edges of their chemises. He looked away and kept moving. They must think he was his twin.

Anyone who didn't know them well had trouble telling them apart, a fact they'd taken advantage of many times before they'd spent the years between ages nine and sixteen fostered away. As lads, they'd get a treat from the cook, return as the other brother and get another. When they returned from fostering, they went right back to switching identities to fool their tutors so that Anders took Stellan's French classes and Stellan took Anders' history classes, saving them both from courses that made them cringe. Those days of impersonating each other were behind them, save for those rare instances when a lass caught Stellan's eye.

As Mariota had.

When Stellan entered the solar, Anders and their father were standing at the worktable, studying a map.

"Ye needed to see us?" Stellan moved toward them.

Sutherland straightened and crossed his arms. "Are ye surprised? What the hell were ye thinking?"

His father's vehemence took Stellan by surprise. "That the lass was lost, exhausted, and needed help. She's a MacKay."

"I'm well aware. Mariota."

"Aye, 'tis her name." A shiver ran down Stellan's back. What did his da know?

"I received a missive from the MacKay. The second on the subject actually, two days ago."

"What subject?"

Anders moved around the table to stand with his twin.

Sutherland gestured them to chairs. "His heir, his daughter Mariota, is of marriageable age."

Stellan exchanged a shocked glance with Anders. Stellan felt the bottom drop out of his gullet. She was the MacKay *heir*? No wonder he'd felt she was withholding some of her story. The twins exchanged frowns. What an impossible situation he'd put them in. He groaned, not just because of who she was, but because of his attraction to her. A lass he could never have, as tied to her clan as he was to his. This was trouble, indeed.

"Did she leave because she was to be wed?" It made better sense than the story she told about being attacked, and her father, the laird, not protecting her. Or did it? She'd taken a huge risk in running away. Only a lass driven to desperation would do such a thing.

"Last fall, when ye both were away," their father continued,

"MacKay proposed an alliance. I posed it to Cameron. Ye ken he looked in another direction for a wife."

"Mary Elizabeth Rose, the Rose laird, aye."

"MacKay never actually designated which of ye lads he would like to see wed to his daughter. Now, it appears something has happened to give her marriage some urgency. He writes that he wants a Sutherland son to come to MacKay to meet her. And for the betrothal."

"He's jesting. Or ye are." Anders frowned. "When did ye say ye received his missive?"

"Two days past."

"Which means he sent a ghillie four days ago or more. She hasna been gone from home that long. She found us in our territory last night, so her da sent the missive before she ran off. Or escaped, by her telling. And she's fallen right into our hands." Stellan filled them in on what he knew of Mariota's story. "She was exhausted by the time she found us. She wouldna have made it much farther, and I dinna like to think what might have happened if she'd run into anyone other than us."

Anders frowned. "He doesna care whom she weds? Any Sutherland male?"

"Any son of mine," Sutherland corrected. "Save the heir, of course."

Anders gulped.

Stellan would have laughed but the situation was too serious.

"How many men would have to go with us to ensure he didn't kill us out of hand once we crossed into MacKay territory?" Anders asked, finding his voice.

"None. He guarantees safe passage."

"He doesna ken we have her," Stellan said, trying to figure out how many ways this situation could go wrong.

"Nay, and by now, he's probably quite concerned about our response since he canna produce her."

"But we can," Anders said.

"Why Sutherland and no' one of his other allies. Gunn or Sinclair or MacLeod?" Stellan frowned. "He must be nervous about Domnhall."

"I would be if I were he," Sutherland said. He shrugged, then studied both twins and seemed to come to a decision. "I will notify him that she's made her way here. Since he will doubt she has remained untouched, I must agree to the betrothal. If his response is still favorable, she must return home until the wedding."

To Anders, of course. Stellan shook his head. "Da, ye canna. She claims to have fled because she feared a clansman." She hadn't said what sort of assault she'd endured. Was her father trying to marry her off because she was ruined and he wanted to make sure she was wed before a bairn arrived? His frown deepened. He hadn't gotten the sense from her of that sort of violation. She'd fought her attacker. Wounded him, she'd said. If he'd tried to do more, Stellan doubted he'd succeeded.

"If she's betrothed to a Sutherland, do ye think her da will allow her to be harmed?"

"We canna be certain…" Stellan protested, still bent on protecting her.

"Anders, ye will go— with an escort. Stellan," he added, holding up a hand as both he and Anders opened their mouths to object, "Ye seem to have gotten attached to the MacKay heir. Forget her. I will have other plans for ye."

Sutherland had clearly made up his mind to propose Anders as her betrothed. He was out of other sons who could marry outside the clan. Stellan frowned. There was no other option, given her status— and his own. But as foolish as it felt, he had to try.

"Da—"

"I'll hear nay more about this for today. I have a letter to write. Both of ye, out." He gestured at the door.

꧁

MARIOTA ROSE from her bath and wrapped herself in the plush robe Nan had found for her, secure in her conviction that she'd been right to leave MacKay, and that luck, or the Celtic gods, or some forest spirit had been with her to guide her right to the Sutherland hunting party. The encounter could have gone very badly for her, she knew, if she'd run into a wild predator, or worse, one that walked on two legs. But the danger she left behind was worth the risk. And now, she was safe and well cared for by genial people, including two of the handsomest lads she'd ever had the pleasure to meet.

But for how long? She started pacing, afraid that the Sutherland would waste no time letting her father know where she was. She should have refused to give her clan name when she stumbled on the Sutherland hunting party. The sudden clench in her belly told her she hadn't run far enough. To Inverness or Sterling, perhaps would have been better. She could still go. There she could disappear, and make a life for herself. And Valkyrie? Nay, that would not work. Perhaps she could convince the Sutherland to keep her presence a secret from MacKay and allow her to stay. If worse came to worst, she could leave her hawk behind and rest easy knowing she would be well cared for.

But if her father came for her, what could she do to protect herself? On a sigh, she stilled, reached for the shift and kirtle Nan had also provided, and dressed. She knew better. Her da would not risk a clan war on her word that she'd been threatened and attacked. He hadn't believed her up to now. Chances were, he was happy she was gone.

Hindsight told her she should have made more of a protest to him. She risked his ire, but she was his heir. He would have to listen to her eventually— preferably not standing over her broken and bloody body. Any of the rest of the clan who observed Alber's behavior could support her claims, explain how she came by the bruises or worse that he inflicted on her. Yet he hadn't believed Seamus. Nor the men who'd dragged Alber down the stairs. She'd never forget the sound of the thumps as he dropped from step to step. Witnesses had done her no good. Why hadn't she shown her bruises to her da? Why hadn't she asked the healer to support her? Her da respected the healer most among all the women of the clan. Mariota clenched her fists. Being the dutiful, submissive daughter had done her no good at all.

Her father also refused to accept and understand her rebellions. Things he would approve of in a son he punished her for. He blamed her instead of the man attacking her. It wasn't fair. If she'd been born a lad, her life would have been so much better. Painful memories threatened to come to the surface, bubbling up from where she'd thought them buried long ago. She quickly put those thoughts aside.

Still, there were advantages to being a lass. Advantages that in hindsight she saw she had used little or not well. Advantages she would be smarter about in the future.

Hindsight had nothing to do with how she felt about the man who'd taken care of her when she stumbled into the Sutherland camp and continued to look out for her. Stellan Sutherland. She could scarce recall the names of the other men in his hunting party. Only him. How ironic that she would encounter one of a pair of twins. She liked both of them. Each had much to recommend him.

Perhaps she'd find some answers if she spent more time with them. Or met more of the Sutherlands— lads and lasses. Stellan might not be the only man in the clan who could make her heart beat faster. Perhaps he was just the one who'd shown her kindness and her traitorous heart mistook that for something entirely different.

Or perhaps not.

❧

STELLAN KNEW he probably shouldn't, but he had to know whether Mariota was comfortably settled in a chamber of her own as befitted a visiting heir to another clan. And to alleviate his concern for her. "Come with me," he told Anders as they crossed the hall toward the steward. "So there's no question of her having been alone with me."

"Aye, two of us in her chamber will appear *so* much better to the wagging tongues in the keep," Anders chided. "Are ye certain ye want to do this?"

"She's my responsibility." As far as Stellan was concerned, that ended the matter. Anders' shrug indicated he understood. The steward told them where he had placed her, and Stellan led the way upstairs.

He started to knock on the door, but Anders grabbed his forearm before he could make contact. "What if she's asleep? Ye said she was exhausted."

Stellan studied the door, torn between his urge to see for himself that she was well, and his twin's caution that she might be getting the rest she so clearly needed.

Rather than give up, Stellan knocked softly. If she was asleep, she wouldn't hear it, but if she was awake—

The door opened and Mariota stood before him. His breath seized in his chest for the moment it took him to rake his gaze over her from head to toe. She had bathed and dressed in clean clothes. Hers? Or borrowed from a Sutherland lass? Nan? No matter. Someone had braided her hair. Her mossy eyes, wide with surprise at her unexpected guests, or so he presumed, stopped him from speaking long enough for Anders to step forward.

"We came to see how ye fare," his twin said after a sidelong glance his way. "It seems yer beauty has struck my brother dumb. In case ye canna tell us apart, I'm Anders. He's Stellan."

"The one who brought me here," she said and stepped back, gesturing for them to enter.

"I dinna think we sh—" Anders began to demure when Stellan stepped forward.

"Ye look well," Stellan told her as he took one of the two chairs by her hearth and gestured her to the other. Anders could stand. Struck dumb, his left cod.

She was even more lovely than she had been when she happened upon them. No surprise there. She'd traveled far and had been at the end of her tether. Her determination and bravery in escaping an untenable situation continued to impress him, though he knew venturing out alone in the middle of the night or full daylight— even with her hawk —was a damnably foolish thing for a lass to do.

"Thank ye, I am. The healer visited and pronounced me well enough," she told him. "I require naught but rest to heal."

And protection from the man who chased her from her home, Stellan surmised, but kept the thought behind his teeth. He would not open that wound. If Mariota wanted to talk about it, she would bring it up.

"Yer healer is a formidable woman," she said.

Anders laughed.

"It comes from riding herd on Sutherland men," Stellan replied, "especially those who tend to need her services quite often. My brother and I included."

"Ye have been wounded in battle?" Her hand lifted to her throat.

Stellan liked her show of concern for him. For them, to be sure, but her gaze remained on him.

"Mostly in training, and in the fights two growing brothers indulge in. There's been nay permanent harm to either of us."

She released a breath and nodded. "I'm glad to ken that. If ye dinna mind, I'd like to visit Valkyrie and see how she's settling in."

"I understand," Stellan told her.

"I ken where it is, but I'd feel better if ye would come with me."

She stood, so Stellan rose, too, and gestured to the door Anders had left open. Wise thinking. If anyone passed by, they could see that nothing untoward was taking place.

"I have something to take care of," Anders said as they left her chamber. "So, I'll leave ye to it," he added as she closed the door. "I hope ye will find yer stay here to be all that ye need." He glanced aside at his twin.

Stellan gave him a frown, reading more into his words than Mariota was likely to. Apparently she needed a husband. A Sutherland son for a husband, but not *the* heir.

He escorted her out of the keep and across the bailey.

Mariota beamed when she saw Valkyrie, sitting calmly, well away from Sutherland birds, jesses securing her to her perch, hood in place but loosened so she could toss it off if she wished.

Stellan was struck by the realization that this was the first fully open smile she'd displayed. It entranced him and made him wish she'd turn it on him. But it faded as he watched to something… less… polite, but not openly glad.

"I appreciate that yer hawk master kept Valkyrie apart from the others. She needs time to settle in to her space. But 'tis clean, warm and dry." She removed the hood and stroked the raptor's head with a careful fingertip.

Though Valkyrie wasn't hooded, and the remains of food she had been given told him the hawk master had done well by her, Stellan knew Mariota was wise to be cautious. Valkyrie might appear calm but in a strange place, being cared for by people she didn't know, she could strike out unexpectedly.

"I'm well pleased," Mariota said as she stroked the raptor. She turned to Stellan. "I canna tell ye how grateful I am to have encountered ye and yer men, and that ye chose to take care of me. To bring me here. I only hope I willna cause strife between our clans."

"If it happens, 'twillna begin with Sutherland," Stellan assured her. Her gaze remained on him, then dropped to her boots. What had made her suddenly shy? He sensed heat between them— his own, certainly, but hers, as well? He could be misinterpreting her gratitude for something entirely different.

"Ye must still be knackered, lass. Now that ye ken Valkyrie is well taken care of, let me return ye to yer chamber. Ye may wish to rest there until dinner."

Her gaze lifted to his and she blushed. "Very well. Thank ye."

Stellan escorted her back into the keep. On the way, he couldn't help replay what he'd learned in the laird's solar from his father. As he introduced her to people they met on the way, he stood aside while they exchanged greetings, thinking he could understand Mariota withholding that she was the MacKay heir. She didn't know him or his men and could have feared being kidnapped, her return contingent on money or some other boon she couldn't count on from a father who had done a poor job of protecting her. As they mounted the stairs to the level where she had a chamber, he wondered if he should confront her about it? Or would he learn more if he waited for her to tell him? And how she chose to tell him?

At her door, they paused and she turned to him. He might be indulging in wishful thinking to presume that she was as attracted to him as he was to her. Her gaze remained on him as if she waited for... what? For him to kiss her? To ask to join her in her chamber? Or simply to say something polite and leave her to her rest? Even before he knew she was the MacKay heir, he should have known not to get his hopes up. Her presence here could cause trouble between their clans. After he found out, he knew there was no hope, but somehow, the attraction, or the idea of it, and the idea of holding Mariota again, kept running through his mind. And his blood. He lifted her hand, then dropped it.

"Rest well, lass," he told her and, furious with himself, left her at her chamber door.

CHAPTER 5

At dinner, Stellan led Mariota to the high table as her station as the MacKay heir demanded. She seemed nervous when Stellan seated her where his father, after greeting her warmly, indicated, on his brother's far side. But her gaze, when she turned it from Anders to Stellan, seemed to hold an air of awareness that heated his blood. He was glad their father was talking to Nan on his other side and not aware of the byplay.

It struck him that she didn't know they knew who she was. Did she understand who he was? Or wonder which twin was the Sutherland heir? Their resemblance to their father, and their presence at the high table, made it clear they were his sons.

"Tell me about yerselves," Mariota said to Anders, but her gaze dropped before she added, "How is it being one of twins?"

So, she wasn't sure who she was dealing with.

While Anders strove to answer her, Stellan had the opportunity to just look at her. To study her profile, as she faced forward, looking out over the hall at the people of his clan. He wondered what she was thinking, but the light from the hearth fire and torches along the walls of the great hall lit her face and danced in her hair, distracting him. She listened to his twin with interest, nodding, thoughtful, occasionally laughing at his quips, and Stellan found himself getting more entranced with every smile she turned on his brother. Some of them spilled past Anders to him.

When she looked past Anders and asked him how they bore fostering apart, he found himself tongue-tied before her yet again. His brother's throat-clearing broke Stellan out of the prison of his rapture. He shrugged and thought for a moment. "It was an adjustment neither of us expected to have to make. It pained us both," he added with a glance at his twin, who nodded. He didn't like thinking about those years, but his words earned him a sympathetic frown, and Mariota put a hand on Anders' arm. In such close proximity to his twin, Stellan felt her palm burning through the sleeve of his own *leine*.

"I'm so sorry," she told him, turned to Anders and added, "for both of ye."

"'Twas good for us, as it turned out," Anders told her, knowing Stellan needed a moment.

"What?" Her surprised expression amused Stellan.

"It gave us a chance to grow as individuals," Stellan told her, his voice gravelly with the need for her coursing through him. "To hone interests and skills each of us had that might have been subsumed in being together and doing the same things all the time. We didn't enjoy the separation, but we learned from it."

He forbore to mention how much Anders had learned from the lasses everywhere he went. He didn't want to plant ideas in Mariota's head, or in Anders', for that matter, where she was concerned.

She hadn't been told that the laird decreed Anders would take her home and likely betroth with her. That would tell her Anders wasn't the heir. Stellan liked that idea less and less the more time he spent with her. As dinner progressed, they traded a lot of glances that to him felt more heated each time it happened. But she also shared a trencher with Anders, a sight more intimate than Stellan liked.

Still, Stellan sensed nothing seductive in her interactions with Anders or in his twin's reactions to her. He liked that, but it also worried him. She was the heir to another clan, and he to his, though his father didn't know the twins had sworn an oath to rule together. Unless their clan went to war to subsume MacKay territory, he and Mariota could never marry. The Sutherland had to propose Anders for her. And Stellan knew two more things. His father would never initiate such a clan war over Stellan's attraction to her, and if MacKay brought a war, there was no guarantee that Sutherland would win.

After dinner, Mariota pleaded exhaustion. "'Twas a full day. I beg leave to find my bed," she said. Though the image of her in the bed in her chamber caused Stellan's pulse to speed, he knew he dared not escort her. Stellan met Anders' gaze and silently urged him to offer his escort. The twins needed their da to see them following his wishes. Stellan needed that most of all if he was to be able to spend any time with her.

"My lady?" Anders stood and offered his arm. She accepted with a disappointed glance Stellan's way, and Anders escorted her from the great hall.

Stellan turned back to his father to ensure he knew which twin remained, but he stood.

"I've work to do. We'll speak tomorrow. Nan, would ye like an escort to yer chamber?"

She sent Stellan a speculative look, then shook her head. "Thank ye, nay. I'm going to visit with my friends over there." She nodded across the hall.

Sutherland grunted his agreement and took his leave.

Now that his father was gone, Nan gave Stellan one more chance at her company. "Care to join us?"

"Thank ye, nay," he told her, preferring to wait for his twin.

She shrugged and left him alone at the high table.

He stood, too. But instead of leaving the hall, he took one of their accustomed seats by the great hall's hearth and waited for Anders to join him. When he did, Stellan tipped his mug. "Slàinte, brother. What do ye think of our lass?"

Anders choked on the mouthful of ale he'd just taken in and sprayed it toward the fire, which leapt when the alcohol hit it. "Yer lass, ye mean," he said when he could breathe. "I could feel the heat pouring off ye."

There were times when the bond between them was damned inconvenient. "Da wants ye to return her to MacKay. What do ye think he means, save that he's expecting ye will wed her—perhaps even while ye are there?"

"He may think so, but ye found her. Ye seem to like her. And I've been around enough lasses to divine that she likes ye. Though, enough? That remains to be seen. Ye should be the one to travel with her, to meet her da, even to marry the lass—though I dinna ken how. No' me."

"There's one problem with that," Stellan said, staring into the fire.

Anders flinched. "Aye, she's her father's heir. Her husband must rule MacKay with her. And ye are da's heir, so he expects ye will rule here after him. I'm the expendable one."

"Nay to me. Nay to the vow we made."

Anders nodded, then grinned. "Do we switch? Ye go as me, and I stay as ye?"

"And when we are discovered?" Stellan couldn't imagine the outcry that would result.

Anders shook his head. "If ye decide against the match, ye can leave her there, and come home. As long as ye manage to control yerself and dinna ruin the lass so ye are forced to marry her."

"Aren't ye forgetting Da said they probably think that has already happened? Our fathers can decide to betroth ye to her. To me as ye. To one of us!" Stellan tossed off the rest of his ale, tempted to hurl the cup into the fire for the satisfaction of watching it shatter. They'd known a day would come when the Sutherland would try to settle wives on them. Mariota had unwittingly made that day today. "God's bones, even if I burn for her, she's a lass I can never have. Because of the trouble it would cause with MacKay, Da willna accept her for me. And we swore when we thought ye would be sent to the Norse land forever that we would marry only a lass we could bring home. No' a Norse princess who would keep ye there. And no' the MacKay heir."

"We were nine," Anders replied, his tone dry, his gaze on the low flames in the hearth.

"We were wiser than our years." Stellan clenched the fist holding the cup. "I ken ye dinna want her, but I might."

Anders cut his gaze to his twin and raised his cup in salute. "Then ye will find a way. Ye had best plan to go with her so ye can find out if she's worth the trouble the two of ye will cause."

❧

THE NEXT MORNING, Mariota made her way downstairs to break her fast. She found a place to sit off to the side where she could look over the entire great hall and watch the comings and goings of the people in it. A lad here and there caught her eye, handsome or tall or muscular, but not having met them and knowing nothing about them, she felt no stirring of interest like she felt for Stellan. Some men merely passed through, others sat and ate with friends or family. Children and dogs moved between tables, playing, begging food and attention, all so normal she might have thought she was still at MacKay.

Except for the twins. They entered the hall together. She couldn't miss seeing them. They drew her eye, no matter how fleeting the glimpse she got of them. Nor could she look away as they scanned the crowd, many of whom seemed focused on the pair, as well. Anders, she presumed from his grin, saw her first and elbowed his brother. Stellan met her gaze and nodded. They both moved toward her. On cue, her heartbeat picked up its pace and her palms began to grow damp. Anders smiled at her but she couldn't stop looking at his solemn-faced twin.

"Good morrow," Anders greeted her with a grin.

Anders' grin was about the only way Mariota could tell them apart. She summoned a smile to answer him, then turned it on Stellan. "Do ye wish to join me?"

"Aye," Anders answered, speaking for them both.

Stellan caught the attention of a serving lass and ordered their meal, then sat next to Anders.

Opposite her. Where she could not escape looking at him. Not that she wanted to avoid seeing him. But would anyone notice her gaze locked on him? Would he?

"I hope ye had a restful night," Stellan said while they waited for their breakfast, his gaze on her as unrelenting as hers on him. Something passed between them, an imagined whisper of his breath on her face that made her toes curl in the slippers Nan lent her. His eyes, the color of old amber or pine bark held her captive.

She sucked in a breath. "I did. Thank ye." She took a moment to get her wild thoughts under control. Anders' eyes were the same color, but she felt nothing from them. She prayed he was the Sutherland heir, not Stellan. Only Stellan seemed to be able to make warm tingles swirl through her without actually touching her. "I've been enjoying watching yer people while I broke my fast. There's little difference here from mornings at MacKay."

"I imagine many of the same things must be taken care of each day," he said as he accepted a trencher and cup of cider from a lass who lingered to smile at him and Anders, then turned her attention to Anders when only he smiled back.

Mariota wanted to laugh at her blatant interest in Stellan's twin, but that wouldn't be polite. Instead, she took advantage of Stellan's willingness to talk. "I am sorry ye have to fend them off," she remarked with a nod at the retreating lass's back, oddly pleased that Anders had sent her on her way. Why, she couldn't say. It wasn't as though she was interested in him. She noted that Nan intercepted the lass and spoke a few words to her before she moved on. Warning her to behave? "Or does yer cousin Nan do that service for ye?"

Anders glanced around and caught Nan's smirk. He gave her a frown in return and turned his back.

"Aye, well, she thinks she must dissuade any lass who shows an interest," Anders groused. "She doesna always succeed," he added with a smirk much like his cousin's.

"I would enjoy making more friends here," Mariota said, after exchanging a grin with Nan. She shifted her gaze back to Stellan. "Several, in fact. I'm somewhat isolated at MacKay."

He shrugged off the lack. "There are plenty of lasses here for ye to meet. Ye ken Nan."

Anders quipped, "And ye have me," he added with a glance aside at Stellan. "Who else could ye possibly need?"

Stellan.

Stellan's lack of reaction to his twin's jibe disappointed her. Had she been reading too much into his care for her? Was he just being the responsible brother?

Anders rambled on about several of the lasses she should meet, and pointed out one of those already in the great hall. As if drawn by his comments, that lass finished her meal and walked by their table.

"Brìghde, come meet our visitor," Anders directed before she could move past. "Brìghde is a friend of mine," he told Mariota, "and now she can be yers, too."

Only a friend? Or was she more than that to him? She found it hard to believe a man as attractive to the lasses as Anders could be satisfied with mere friendship. Then again, he'd offered just that to her.

Brìghde greeted her politely. "I'm pleased to meet our visitor," she said with a smile. "I heard but little about how ye came to be with us. I'm eager for the rest of yer story."

Mariota wasn't certain how much of her problems she wanted bandied about the Sutherland clan, but if Brìghde was friends with Anders, and not one of the lasses trying to hang onto him, she would be a good friend to have. "I'm pleased to meet ye, too. I've met only the twins, Nan, and yer steward and healer," she said.

Brìghde laughed and glanced at Anders. "I can help with that. Join me. I'm off to visit the cobbler to retrieve a pair of boots he repaired. On the way, I'll introduce ye around. We lasses must stick together, aye?"

Mariota, reluctant to leave the twins, felt suddenly shy. Anders seemed content to interact with the lasses, but Stellan's gaze was on the door to the laird's solar. While his lack of attention on her was disappointing, it convinced her that at least one of the twins had more important work to do than entertain her. "Thank ye. That would please me greatly."

And might give her a chance to see how this clan differed from MacKay. She might learn things that would be useful when she became laird. Not just Sutherland strengths and weaknesses that her da would look for as a matter of course, noting vulnerabilities that she might need to use against them in the future, but also things she could use to help her people. How tasks were distributed among the people of Sutherland, how they managed their food stores, crops, livestock, what they did for income for the clan, and so forth. She rested her chin on a fist, realizing she both wanted to run away and to learn how to do leadership right — which she didn't think her father did. There was always so much discontent at home, but she didn't understand what caused it or why it was so widespread. Perhaps it wasn't just that Alber was there, but that men like Alber thrived under her father's leadership.

And why did everyone she'd seen so far at Sutherland seem

the opposite— content, even happy. Even the lasses vying for the twins' attention and failing to receive it didn't seem to mind. Was it a game? They knew they'd never wed with either of them, but the fun was in the flirting and the attempts? She'd seen a few couples behave that way at home, but nothing like the scale the twins inspired.

She straightened. To accomplish all of that, she would need more time than her da would likely allow, but she could make a start right now.

Brìghde proved to be pleasant company. They went first to the cobbler to retrieve her boots and she made a point of introducing Mariota and praising the cobbler's work, making the older man redden above his bushy beard, but he smiled at the compliments she heaped on him. From there, they ventured around the bailey to the various crafters and tradesmen.

The latest tapestry on the weaver's loom drew Mariota's admiration, and she studied it with delight, a hint of a smile on her lips. Rather than the usual battle scene, it depicted Dunrobin's large, square tower and outer walls surrounded on each side by one of the four seasons. Spring and the shore of the Dornoch firth to the east, summer to the south, autumn to the west and winter to the north. It was far from finished, lacking about a third of the finished size and the handwork that would make it truly unique and beautiful, but the weaver's artistic design was clearly well underway. "I hope I may come back to see this work when ye finish it," she told the smiling weaver. "'Twill be lovely wherever 'tis hung."

"'Tis meant for the new Lady's bedchamber," she said proudly. "'Twill be finished long before 'tis needed, of course," she added with a glance at Brìghde. "But I've already received other requests for similar, smaller works for the healer and others in the clan."

"I'd love for ye to one day make something similar for me at MacKay," Mariota told her, truly impressed with the design and artistry the weaver had already demonstrated. "Perhaps one day, ye would visit so ye can see the keep and the area around it."

The weaver dropped her gaze. "I'd be honored, milady."

After they left her, Mariota couldn't resist asking, "How long ago did Stellan and Anders lose their mother?"

Brìghde shook her head. "'Tis a sad tale. She died birthing a lass who also didna survive. Their da was so heartbroken at the loss of his love and wee daughter that he has never remarried, nor intends to. By the clan's new lady, the weaver of course, means Stellan's wife, once he becomes laird."

Nay! Mariota's belly hollowed. Stellan was the heir, not Anders. The twin she'd hoped to attract was forever out of her reach, as tied to his clan as she was to hers.

She took a breath, forcing herself to set aside her dismay. If there was a way, she would find it. "Why would the laird nay make an alliance through his own marriage?"

"I believe he sees himself as the clan's past and Stellan as its future." She shrugged. "But I dinna ken, and though Anders is my friend, he doesna speak of it to me— or anyone."

❧

LATER, the twins found Brìghde and Mariota in the mews, admiring Valkyrie. Stellan overheard enough to impress him yet again as Mariota told Brìghde about climbing trees as a lass and raising her hawk from the egg she found high in a nest, and about learning to shoot a bow.

"Could ye teach me to shoot?" Brìghde asked. "If I could handle a bow and arrow, I could help defend the keep."

"I'd be happy to," Mariota told her. "Nan, too, if she wishes it."

Anders snickered at that. "Can ye imagine those two on the walls?"

"Brìghde, aye," Stellan told him.

"I'd fear for our men if Nan were armed," Anders continued.

"She'd as likely shoot herself or the man next to her as over the wall."

Stellan's mental image of the scenario Anders painted, though it was highly exaggerated, made him laugh.

"Who's there?" Brìghde's voice preceded her out the door of the mews. "Ye two. What do ye think so amusing?"

"Naught," Anders replied, still chuckling.

"We were having a serious conversation, and heard yer laughter. Ye were listening."

"'Twas naught," Stellan told her, having recovered his composure.

"What brings ye both?"

Brìghde's query made Anders grin and Stellan frown.

"We heard voices and stopped to find out who was in there," Stellan answered, pointing at the open door.

"Stellan wanted to escape our da and the planting schedule," Anders declared, earning a glare from his twin. "I had a purer motive," he continued, "to make certain ye hadna shared all of Sutherland's secrets while ye have been about."

"Only those concerning the two of ye," Brìghde jested.

Stellan couldn't miss how Mariota paled. Something had upset her, but what? He fought to wipe his frown from his brow. Anders calm demeanor told him Brìghde knew nothing of any secrets he and his twin kept. Certainly not the most important one. He was certain Anders would not have mentioned their childhood vow to any lass. Or anyone else. Nor had he. Had their grandda done so before he passed on? Stellan had no reason to believe so, since even their father seemed unaware of their and their grandda's wishes. Or perhaps their da just rejected them in favor of his own expectations for his sons. Though they had survived— even thrived —when he fostered them separately, they never lost their determination to honor their vow to rule together.

Mariota seemed to have regained some color. Stellan thought

she might need more air. "Anders, perhaps we should take Mariota riding. Valkyrie must need some time in the open sky."

"A brilliant idea, brother. Mariota? Would that please ye— and Valkyrie?"

"Aye! Of course, it would."

Her enthusiasm was unmistakable. Perhaps he had imagined her pale countenance, or it was a trick of the light in the mews.

"Brìghde, would ye join us?"

Stellan watched with interest as Brìghde fought for a polite reply. He was certain riding was one of her least favorite activities. And Anders knew it.

"I fear… I have other… things… to take care of," she said, forming the words as though speaking them would choke her.

"Another time, then," Anders said, letting her off the hook. "Perhaps we could escort ye toward the keep while Mariota readies Valkyrie for her outing? 'Tis on the way to the stable."

That brought a smile back to her face. "I would be grateful, of course."

With a smile for Mariota and a smirk to his brother, Anders offered his arm, and all three left Mariota to ready her hawk.

"What do ye think of our guest?" Stellan asked after they were far enough from the mews to be out of earshot. He saw Mariota as courageous but impulsive. He was curious how another lass, with a woman's particular understanding, might perceive her.

"She's lovely, a bit quiet, but appreciative of the hospitality she has received here," Brìghde told him. "She seems quite… comfortable… with ye two."

Anders nodded. "She's met Nan, too, but we've spent the most time with her."

"I appreciate ye taking an interest in her," Stellan said. How much had Mariota told her about the danger she'd been in at home? He didn't want to make an issue of it with Brìghde if Mariota hadn't shared any more of her personal life than the clan already knew.

"I am always happy to be of service to ye both," Brìghde answered.

Stellan noted her choice of words, Anders' grin in response, and wondered just what sort of service she'd offered his twin— or was hinting at to him. Were they more than friends? Would she be hurt by their father's intention to betroth Mariota to him? He dared not ask her, but Anders would answer him. Later.

CHAPTER 6

Stellan and Anders rode out of Dunrobin flanking Mariota, with six guards following them. They headed first along the firth to let her enjoy the views and the breeze off the water. "This is beautiful," she told them. "Do ye ken how to sail?"

"Of course," Stellan told her. "The fastest way to almost anywhere is by water."

"No' to MacKay," she said. "Or is it, from here? I've never considered that."

"'Twould depend on the weather and the seas rounding the north between Caithness and the Orkney islands," Anders said. "'Tis farther, but if the seas are calm and the winds favorable, 'twill be faster."

"Than a fast horse? I dinna think so," Stellan objected.

Anders shrugged. "Perhaps one day, we'll have to test it. Will ye sail or ride?"

"I'll decide when the time comes," Stellan prevaricated, taking note of Mariota's interest in their byplay. Her gaze danced from one brother to another, depending on who was speaking, though occasionally it remained with him, as if she wished to see how he reacted to Anders' provocation. She didn't swoon over them together as most Sutherland lasses did. He found that refreshing. He didn't have to be on his guard around her. Not in the same way, at least. She seemed straightforward and direct in her questions and comments, without the innuendo he was used to.

"Surely someone has done both by now," she interjected. "Or several people, on different occasions."

"Perhaps. I'll ask our guards if they ken," Anders said and turned his horse to drop back to their followers.

Stellan knew what he was up to, giving him and Mariota time to be as alone as they could, without either twin ever being entirely alone with her. Most of the clan would think nothing of the twins entertaining the visiting MacKay heir, but neither of them could afford to be accused of ruining her, or doing anything else that would further their father's plans for the betrothal, not until they were ready. Nor could she.

"How is Valkyrie over water?" His question was not meant simply to engage her in conversation. He was curious, never having heard of a hawk hunting in the sea.

"Let's find out, shall we?" Mariota removed Valkyrie's hood and jesses and after a moment to let her get her bearings, flung her into the air. Valkyrie climbed and soared overhead, circling above her mistress, partly over water and partly over land.

"She seems unruffled," Stellan observed as the hawk's flight drifted on the breeze more inland toward the meadowland at the foot of Dunrobin's cliff and structures, then along the tree line of the forest to the north.

"She's hunting, and happy to be a-wing," Mariota said. "I envy her freedom when she flies. But I canna envy her when she is confined to a perch."

"Do ye see yerself the same way? Confined as the heir?"

She opened her mouth, then closed it, surprise written in her narrowed gaze. She took a breath. "How could I no'? Dinna ye, as well?"

So she hadn't been aware they knew who she was! Stellan didn't know whether to be surprised or amused. Did she think they gifted every lass with this much of the heir's time and attention, or seated her at the head table? Would knowing she was found out make a difference to her? Judging by the way she pursed her lips, it must. Stellan started to apologize, but instead took a breath, thinking about her question. It was something they had in common. Something to bridge the gap between them and perhaps bring them closer together. He wanted that, didn't he? He needed to learn more about her. Every time he was near her, he wanted his hands on her waist. He wanted to kiss her and find out if she tasted as sweet as she seemed to be, or if the attraction between them would burst into flames and consume them both. But her question poured cold water on all his desires. They were destined to be lairds of neighboring, sometimes rival clans. Always apart. Not betrothed. Never wed. How fast could one ride or sail from Dunrobin to MacKay, indeed?

He looked away from her, hiding how his jaw clenched. Of course he did feel confined as heir. He imagined any eldest son— or daughter in the right circumstances —did. While many, even most, sons and daughters' futures were prescribed by the circumstances of their birth, some had at least a small measure of freedom to change their fate. To join a fighting force, become a priest or a nun, a scholar. But an heir would always be the heir, always expected to take on that role, that responsibility, with no escape. He, at least, had the comfort of Anders' presence and the oath they'd sworn to each other.

What could he say to Mariota that would comfort her? They had heard some of her story and he sympathized with the lass for making her escape, temporary though it might be. He didn't understand why her father allowed her attacker to remain alive, but in any case, she remained the MacKay heir, and someday soon, her father would demand her return, either in a letter or at the point of his sword outside Dunrobin's walls.

Yet how could she return if her attacker still remained free at MacKay? And how could her father demand it of her?

"I do feel confined," he finally said, lacking an answer to the questions plaguing him. "But I see it as my responsibility, and a challenge to affect the future of the clan that few are given."

"I would like to give it back," she muttered softly.

Stellan wondered if he was meant to hear those words.

"I think I would happily become hawk mistress rather than laird," she said a little louder. "I could do what I love and given the choice, would not be forced to wed anyone I did not like— or anyone at all."

"Ye dinna wish to wed?"

"I dinna ken. Surely I dinna wish to wed some of the men my da is likely to want alliances with. I must be able to refuse them." She looked away from the sea. "Has yer da written to mine yet that I am here?"

Her question seemed casual, but her hands clenched on her reins told Stellan the answer to that question meant more to her than she was willing to divulge.

"Aye, he has." Stellan sympathized with her, but he also saw her reluctance to wed as a mark against her. She knew she had no choice. Despite how she intrigued him, even if they could solve the problem of their positions in their clans, he didn't want an unwilling bride. Perhaps she *should* wed his more easygoing twin. He could make her happier than Stellan, and with Anders as her husband at MacKay, rather than just rule Sutherland together, he and Anders could control much of the north of Scotland.

Later, after supper, while he and Anders settled by the fire as was their custom, Stellan broached the idea.

Anders choked on his ale and coughed. "Did ye spend too much time in the sun today, riding along the firth with Mariota? Ye seem to have lost yer mind— right along with our da!" Anders shook his head. "Da already risks having our neighbors Sinclair and Gunn up in arms over an alliance between our clans."

Stellan shrugged. "Against Domnhall? I doubt he cares what the clans to our north think."

"And have ye forgotten which of us is attracted to her? 'Tisna me. Besides, I've had too many willing lasses to want an unwilling one, especially to wife."

Stellan took another drink, then drummed the fingers of one hand on the arm of his chair. "Dinna refuse the idea out of hand. It solves our problems." When Anders snorted, he added, "Da will sign the betrothal agreement with ye in mind. 'Tis up to ye to make her willing. Seduce her. In bed— nay, not until after the wedding, but with yer charm, the strength of an alliance with Sutherland, and how close we brothers are. Having Sutherland at her back at all times."

"And wedding the brother she can have fun with, rather than the dour "older" brother who is in the same position she's in, aye?" Anders shook his head again. "'Twill never work. She's as attracted to ye as ye are to her. Forget it."

Hope bloomed in Stellan's chest, warm, yet strangely sharp and painful. Anders had sensed that she was interested in him? His twin was much better than he at picking up on such things, having spent much more time with the lasses. Until Anders' comment, Stellan had remained unsure if Mariota felt the same as he did. Now that he knew, he wanted to smile, to laugh, to go to her. But it could never be that simple. Now that he knew, what good could come of it?

THREE DAYS LATER, Mariota was crossing the bailey when the guards up on the wall called for their laird. Not knowing what to expect, she returned to the door to the keep and waited to see what would happen. She'd enjoyed her time at Sutherland so far, and had learned a great deal. Perhaps she'd learn something else useful in whatever was about to transpire with Stellan's father.

She appreciated the care she was being shown by everyone, but especially by the twins. And even more so by Stellan. Yet how could she let herself fall for him, knowing what their futures held?

Brìghde saw her and came to join her. They leaned on the sun-warmed stone by the door and watched the guards scurry across the wall walk, gesturing to each other and down toward the glen outside Dunrobin's walls.

"Who do ye think it is?" Brìghde nodded toward the keep's heavy gates. "Tisna someone they're eager to allow entry, no' until the laird gives his aye."

The door at their side opened and the Sutherland laird came out, followed by stern-faced Stellan. The pair proceeded across the bailey without hesitation.

"We will soon hear what has caused the commotion," Mariota said confidently. The Sutherland laird was decisive and not at all soft-spoken, not in her experience anyway, so they would know soon enough who was at the gates.

The laird and his heir mounted the steps to the wall walk and had a few words with the guard captain, then turned to regard the ground below them. Mariota was about to say they'd never find out at this rate when Stellan caught her gaze and beckoned.

Her belly clenched. His summons could mean only one thing. Her father had answered the Sutherland's letter. He had arrived to take her home.

Brìghde patted her shoulder and pushed her across the bailey.

Stellan met her at the bottom of the steps and escorted her up them to the wall walk. She gasped when she looked over the nearest gap in the rampart. Below, her father rode with fifty men. One, positioned just behind him, made her stomach turn and her skin break out in a cold sweat. "Ach, nay, he didna," she muttered, shocked that he had brought her attacker. Shocked, too, that Alber still lived after what he tried to do to her the last time. And that witnesses, even after the fact, within the clan could confirm her story. Was her father telling her he didn't believe her? Given Alber's position in the horde, had her father promoted the man bent on ruining her? Destroying her father's plans for an alliance with another clan? Could he possibly be so blind? She wanted to appeal to the twins for help, but not until she was sure what her father intended.

"Ye didna expect him to come for ye?" Stellan took her arm and moved her toward his father.

"Nay, 'tisna that. 'Tis who he brought with him. Alber. The man who has attacked me three times." She finished the sentence as they reached his father.

The Sutherland frowned at her words. "He brought that man with him?"

"Aye, Laird Sutherland. He's there, in the front row behind my da."

Stellan nodded. "I see him. I recognize him by the scars ye say Valkyrie gave him."

It had only been a sennight since she fled MacKay, so Alber's wounds had not had time to heal completely and were still cruel red lines on his face and neck. She hoped his cods looked no better. She'd done her best— twice —to crush them.

"Well," Sutherland said, studying her face as if it held the answers he might need before talking with her father, "what do ye think yer da hopes to accomplish by this show of strength?"

Mariota bit back a laugh. "If need be, to compel my release. To force me home, of course. And perhaps of most import, to bring a Sutherland husband back to MacKay with me."

"I dinna see the point of bringing yer attacker here," Stellan remarked. "As a threat? Or is he going to exact punishment where ye and all of Sutherland can see?"

"I canna say." Mariota shrugged and added, "But I worry what it means." She had hoped if her father came for her, it would be to show her that he valued her, even applauded her initiative to protect herself and its outcome, and would deal respectfully with her— and with Sutherland —on the matter of the betrothal.

Sutherland nodded. "We'll take care of ye, lass." He stepped to the wall. "MacKay, what brings ye here?"

"Ye ken fine why I'm here. And I came with enough men to prize her from ye, if I must."

"Including the man who attacked her, forcing her to run from MacKay for her own safety?"

"Ye believe a lass about a man's intentions?"

Mariota's heart sank. For a moment, she'd been fool enough to allow herself to hope that some vestige of care for her had brought her father to Sutherland's gates. So much for that. Or for seeing Alber punished.

"I believe yer daughter. She is heir to an important clan, a lass who has shown herself to be sensible, accomplished, and quite determined to protect herself. I believe her over a man only brave enough to assault lasses, and who canna fight off a hawk."

Laughter rumbled across the lines of MacKay warriors, all save for Alber. Even from atop the wall, Mariota could see his face go red and his eyes narrow with fury. She feared the Sutherland laird had just made himself a target.

"Bring out my daughter," MacKay demanded.

"I have a better idea. Clearly ye received my response to yer letter. Come in and discuss this. I grant ye safe passage inside my walls. Ye alone and none of yer men. And most certainly not that one," Sutherland added pointing at Alber.

Alber stood up in his stirrups with a shout.

MacKay's head whipped around. "Sit down and *wheesht* or I'll send ye back with more damage than the hawk did to ye."

Mariota's mouth fell open. Finally! Her father had disciplined Alber where others could see it happen. She grasped the stone wall in front of her, anxious over how Alber would react.

Alber's jaw flexed, but he resumed his seat and calmed his mount, disturbed by his outburst.

"Yer men can camp in the glen," Sutherland continued as if Alber had not had the temerity to interrupt a negotiation between two lairds.

"I will bring ten inside with me."

"Six and nay that one," Sutherland repeated.

MacKay tried to stare him down.

"Choose yer six, and send the rest to set up camp across the glen. I willna tolerate them below my walls."

Only then did Mariota realize the army her father rode with would be enough to lay siege to Dunrobin. She hoped he was not foolish enough to try it. Clearly, Sutherland knew it, too, and was prepared to withstand it.

After a beat, MacKay turned and called out six names. Mariota was shocked to hear Seamus's among them. She had been so focused on her father and Alber that she hadn't noticed him among the troop.

Once the bulk of MacKay's men moved away, Sutherland ordered the gates opened. "Best ye go greet yer da, lass," he told Mariota. "Stellan, stay with her. I'll nay have one of his men grab her and hie back out of our gates."

Stellan nodded and went down the steps in front of Mariota.

She wondered how long her father's patience would last. She might not be inside Sutherland's walls for long— his presence here demonstrated that he would not simply allow his heir to run off. Despite his lack of confidence in her, there was an alliance on the line, after all.

She was grateful for Stellan's care, and that his da was not foolish enough to trust hers. After what she'd just seen and heard from her da, her hands shook and she could barely draw breath. The only good news so far was that Seamus rode with him, and was coming inside Sutherland. She could find out from Seamus what had happened at MacKay since she left, and what her father was thinking, bringing Alber with the group of warriors intended to guard her on their return home.

≈

STELLAN COULDN'T BELIEVE Mariota's attacker was here with the MacKay. His outrage at the insult burned white-hot in his blood. He knew Sutherland would normally say the other laird could bring any of his men he desired, but Sutherland already denied the attacker entry, thank the saints.

Anders met them as they reached the bailey and stood shoulder to shoulder with his twin, blocking Mariota behind them from MacKay's reach. "I kenned aught was amiss."

Once again, Stellan had reason to be grateful for their uncanny connection. He gave Anders a quick update.

Anders understood the situation immediately. "The lass would be in danger inside our own walls if Alber had been allowed in. What would her father do if the man harmed her here? Blame us?"

"I wish yer da hadna taunted him," Mariota told them. "He's dangerous."

Sutherland joined them as the gates swung open. Before the MacKay could enter, he told his sons "Ye two will alternate guarding her, backed up at all times by Sutherland men. Ye willna let that man she fears get close to her. MacKay sent him away, but I dinna doubt he will try to cause trouble, and we are responsible for her safety while she resides with us."

"The MacKay will want her under his control, his guards," Anders argued in a low voice. "If that contingent includes Alber at any time, it will be the fox guarding the hen. And that can only go badly."

Stellan agreed. "And on the way home? Too many things can go wrong."

Sutherland nodded. "I ken it. But how do we prevent it?"

Mariota's gasp alerted them to trouble. Behind the MacKay, among the six, Alber rode in, on his face a malicious grin and evil gleam in his eyes.

The Sutherland held up a hand and his men stepped in front of them, swords at hand, halting the procession of MacKays through the gate.

"I did not give that man leave to enter my keep, MacKay. What do ye think ye are doing?"

"Asserting my right to have the guards around me that I most trust."

Stellan found himself shocked. The MacKay named his daughter's attacker a guard he trusted most, and dared call him back once the Sutherlands left the wall walk. Did the MacKay think they wouldn't notice? A glance aside showed him that Mariota had paled. Stellan wanted to get her out of the bailey, away from this confrontation, but he dared not do so without his father's order. So far, she was behind a wall of Sutherlands, but at the first sound of swords being drawn, her safety would be at risk.

Sutherland regarded MacKay with disdain. "Before we even begin to speak, ye disregard my orders? In my own keep?"

"I bring the men I choose. The men I trust. Alber is one of MacKay's heroes of Red Harlaw."

Stellan and Anders traded a look. Was that how the man had gotten his laird under his thumb?

MacKay demanded to see his daughter. Mariota stepped out from behind the twins, but didn't greet her father. Instead, she made a guttural sound of disgust. The fury in her eyes relieved Stellan. He had feared she might show alarm at her father's declaration— and demonstrated lack of support for her —but clearly she was made of sterner stuff.

"Turn him around," Sutherland demanded, "or this conversation is over and ye will leave Sutherland territory."

"Nay without my heir."

"Yer heir stays here, if that is her choice, until 'tis well established that she can return to MacKay without further incident."

The MacKay's gaze cut to his daughter.

Beside Stellan, Mariota straightened tighter than a bowstring.

"I choose to remain where I am safe and valued," she announced. "If ye vow that is MacKay, I will go with ye, but not with Alber in the troop. Send him back, or I will remain here."

"Then there will be clan war."

"I will leave Sutherland, if I must, to prevent it. But I willna return to MacKay."

"Daughter—"

Mariota shook her head. "Dinna threaten my hosts, who have been naught but kind to me, better than the treatment I receive at home. I will go where ye will never find me, and yer precious notion of using me for an alliance— with any clan —will die. Is that what ye want, da?"

MacKay glared at her, and at Sutherland before turning around to shout, "Alber, join the men across the glen."

Alber shot a hate-filled glare at Mariota, jerked his mount around and rode out of the gate.

The MacKay watched him go before turning back to Sutherland.

"Satisfied?"

Sutherland looked to Mariota.

She lifted her chin, then nodded.

Stellan suspected this was the first time she had been able to force her father to do anything for her.

Too bad it took the combined might of Clan Sutherland to make him capitulate. And what would come of it? A proud man, a clan laird, forced to back down in favor of a lass, and in front of one of the most powerful clans in the Highlands? Stellan didn't see anything but trouble to come.

CHAPTER 7

"Let's take this to my solar," Sutherland told the MacKay, who nodded. "Stellan, Anders, ye, too, and two of yer men, Laird MacKay. Mariota?"

"I beg leave to join ye in a few minutes, Laird Sutherland," she asked politely.

"Of course, lass."

Stellan had no doubt she intended to survey the MacKay camp from her window before coming back downstairs. It might be visible between merlons in the outer wall.

"These men will escort ye," Stellan told her, indicating two of his men who remained nearby.

Mariota thanked him and headed inside with her escort.

Sutherland gave Stellan a look he understood. He lagged behind long enough to alert the guards on the wall walk to keep Alber under close watch. They must make sure he continued across the glen to join the MacKay camp— and didn't try to return.

That done, Stellan followed his da and the others inside the keep. The remaining three of MacKay's companions settled in the great hall and began drinking Sutherland ale. So much for protecting their laird in a potentially hostile situation. Stellan shook his head and left them under his men's watchful eyes.

In the solar, things were already going badly. The two lairds were on their feet, only the desk between them keeping them apart, all but snarling at each other while they waited for Mariota, reminding Stellan that MacKay had led an army that included Sutherland men against Domnhall at Dingwall only a year earlier and lost. The two guards who'd accompanied MacKay into the solar stood behind the chair he'd obviously vacated to get closer to Sutherland as they argued.

Stellan joined his twin near the door, glanced at Anders, then frowned at the two lairds.

Anders leaned close enough to speak into Stellan's ear. "Da wants to know why MacKay doesna protect his heir and why he let things get so bad that Mariota felt like she needed to escape his care."

Stellan winced. The MacKay would be furious enough with his daughter without their da twisting the knife.

"Ye ask about things that are none of yer business," MacKay insisted. "My heir is a foolish lass who invites attention from unsuitable men. 'Tis all ye need to ken. And why I must take her home before she causes the same sort of trouble here."

That did not ring true to Stellan. He glanced aside. Anders was wearing a frown that made him look more like Stellan than himself. Anders didn't believe the MacKay, either.

Mariota had never struck Stellan as foolish, though the way she left MacKay came close. She'd taken a calculated risk in escaping MacKay the way she did. She was fortunate to have a hawk that could feed her and watch over her, and to protect her by surprising anyone rash enough to attack her. Valkyrie had already done so at least once— they'd just seen the proof on her attacker's face and neck. Mariota claimed to be good with a bow. He suspected she was also capable with a blade, as well. He wondered who had trained her and put that thought away to ask her later. Impulsive, aye. Determined to protect herself, aye, from at least one unsuitable man. Her situation at MacKay and her father's inaction had left her with no choices to save herself except to kill her attacker and face the consequences, or to leave MacKay and build her own future. Both were dangerous. He admired her bravery in choosing to leave. So why was her father intent on painting her as a fragile, empty-headed lass? In Stellan's experience, she was anything but that.

"Yer daughter has nay been a source of discord here," Sutherland told the MacKay in answer to his outrageous statement. "So my question still stands. Why no' listen to her, investigate her claims, and take action? Ye say 'tis none of my business, and ye are right, but now that I've met the lass, 'tis what I would have done."

"Ye think to instruct me in how to train my daughter?"

"Nay. Ye seem to have trained her well enough to be able to take care of herself across the Highlands. Is that it? Do ye want her to be the one to punish her attacker for ye? Do ye think that will make her stronger? A better leader? 'Tis my opinion that is the laird's job."

"Now ye instruct me on how to be laird?" MacKay's face was red, and veins bulged at his temples.

Stellan began to worry that his father was pushing too hard, and that MacKay would stomp out of Dunrobin, forcibly removing Mariota with him as he went. They could not allow that. The danger to her was too great.

MARIOTA HAD BEEN PLEASED to see Seamus in the Sutherland great hall, though his back had been to her and he probably had been unaware of her walking behind him. He was still seated by the hearth with three other MacKays when she descended the stairs from her chamber. Of the three, only he was not drinking.

His gaze was on the short hallway to the laird's solar, as though he wanted to be in there, not out here.

She diverted long enough to go to him. "Seamus, we must talk."

He stood and nodded while he moved away from the other three men. "We must, but for now, ye are best served by joining yer father. I canna guess what he and the Sutherland might be discussing before ye arrive. Ye dinna want them making decisions for ye without a chance to influence them."

"Nay, I dinna want that. But I couldna walk by without a word with ye."

He gave her a tight smile. "I'm glad ye did. Now go defend yerself from the lairds."

She laughed, more to reassure him than because anything about her situation was amusing. Still, speaking to her friend had made her feel ready to face whatever might happen in the next few minutes. She would talk to Seamus later— privately would be best, if she could manage it.

She passed Brìghde and Nan, both seated near the laird's solar and gave them a brief smile. Nan grinned back, but Brìghde clenched a fist over her heart. Mariota understood and appreciated their support.

She entered the Sutherland's solar and noted the tension in the room was already thick. "Da," she said, but had no chance to say anything more.

Her father rounded on her, fury in his eyes, his face red and his fists clenched. "What were ye thinking? Sneaking out. Running so far away. To Sutherland! Those men could have killed ye or worse."

So, after all the times she'd tried to make him see sense, they were going to have this out in front of the Sutherland laird. Her father had to be outraged, not to control himself while they were in company. "Really, Da? What is worse than Alber beating and choking me? Oh, and the rest he has threatened to do?" She stood her ground when he took a step toward her, then mirrored his move and took a step toward him. If he only respected strength, she'd show him strength. "How could ye bring him here? Do ye think I'll be safe on the way home with him nearby? In the dark in the woods?"

Her words seem to give MacKay pause, but not for long.

"My men, any of them I want, go wherever I send them. Or bring them. Ye claim one of my best warriors has tried three times to hurt or kill ye. How are ye still alive?"

Mariota snorted a laugh. "Because he lied about Red Harlaw, Da. He's a drunk best at currying yer favor, and ye believed him, as ye have believed every tale he ever spun for ye. If yer other men didna fear to tell ye the truth, ye'd ken before now." MacKay's fists clenching and unclenching with her every word signaled to her to give it a rest, at least for a few minutes. His face had turned bright red, and he looked close to doing something he would forever regret.

The Sutherland, thankfully, read the same signal. "I will have calm in my own solar, MacKay. I ken she's yer daughter, but I willna have her harmed in my keep— by ye or anyone else."

MacKay twisted to face him. "Who said she would be harmed?"

Sutherland continued as if the MacKay had not spoken. "I willna tolerate the presence of the man she accuses of threatening her to the point of running from her home. What was yer purpose in bringing him to collect her?"

MacKay continued to take offense. "'Tis my business and nay yers."

"Very well, but he will remain outside my gates. Do not think to bring him in, no' even for meals. If ye didna bring sufficient supplies, my men will take food out to yers."

"Or we will leave— all of us," her father added while glaring at her, "right now."

Sutherland shifted his gaze to her, then back to her father. "Is that truly yer purpose here? Ye have proposed an alliance— twice —with me through a marriage between our clans. Do ye no' wish to discuss that?"

Sutherland's ability to keep his tone level and reasonable in the face of her father's irritation impressed her. She hoped when her time came to lead— if it ever did —she would be able to control her emotional reactions to conflict such as this.

MacKay frowned, then reared back and shook his head. "I—nay. I have changed my mind, Ye are too close. I dinna want my lands annexed by another clan. All too easily done with a Sutherland married to the MacKay laird, and in the discord sown by the Domnhall and Albany."

"Ye accuse me of plotting to steal MacKay? Ye are the one who proposed the alliance. Twice now, by my count. What value did ye think I would see in it?"

She heard irritation creep into Sutherland's voice. She had no doubt her father heard it, too.

"Exactly as ye imagine, a stronger front against Domnhall and the Regent's man Mar."

"Who fight over Ross, no' our land. With Gunn and Sinclair to our north, and Norsemen beyond that? They'll nay interfere with us in our lifetime." Sutherland snorted.

"Ye are no' daft enough to believe that."

Mariota could see that Stellan wanted to intervene. He pursed his lips when Mariota met his gaze, trying with her expression to ask for his help. Clearly, he was considering what to do to stop this before the two lairds ruined relations between their clans for generations to come. She thought Anders wanted to intervene, as well, but they had better sense than to interfere in a dispute between clan lairds. She couldn't think what they could do to diffuse the situation.

Stellan mouthed to her, *faint*. He nodded and directed his gaze to the floor.

Mariota frowned. She understood, but she didn't want to.

True, she could distract the lairds and it might even give her father a chance to prove he truly cared about her— or not. But she was stronger than that. She'd just stood up to him in front of the Sutherland and his heir. She was her clan's best archer and a hawk mistress. She didn't want to give up any ground she'd gained with him by appearing weak, so she gave her head a subtle shake.

Stellan's frown deepened. He studied the lairds for another moment then turned his gaze back to her, shrugged, and again mouthed, *faint,* with a more forceful nod toward the floor.

The lairds had continued to harangue each other while she and Stellan traded glances. Their voices had grown louder, their shouts more insistent. Rather than having their fathers come to blows, or worse, she sighed and dropped into a heap on the cold, stone floor.

❧

STELLAN FOUGHT the urge to rush to her side. The only reason Mariota had done this was to distract their fathers. That wouldn't be much of a diversion if he rushed into the fray. And his father was not so distracted that he would not note which son had gone to her aid. He couldn't betray his interest in her, not here. Not now.

"Ach, fer... why?" MacKay groused and pointed at her. "Pick her up and put her in a chair," he told his men.

Sutherland looked askance at his sons, but all Stellan could do was shrug or he'd give away Mariota's ruse to her da. Sutherland clearly knew it was a feint to break up the escalating tension in the chamber. Anders shook his head and started forward to help, but Stellan grabbed his arm and held him back. Let the MacKay men deal with her, or the Sutherlands would be seen as interfering. Still, despite the fact that this ruse was his suggestion, Stellan was appalled for Mariota's sake. The men handled her like a sack of grain while her father looked on, his expression annoyed, lips twisted and jaw tight. Stellan saw not one bit of fatherly concern in MacKay's expression or his posture. Or was he annoyed by how the men handled her? His gaze tracked their movements, but in doing so, he watched his daughter, too.

"Does she need the healer?" Sutherland asked, trying to elicit something other than annoyance from her father.

MacKay shook his head. "Nay. She'll come around soon."

Stellan didn't know how she managed not to react, but Mariota defied her father by remaining limp. Slumped in the chair where the MacKay men had dropped her, she kept her breathing slow and her muscles loose. Stellan wanted to applaud her performance, but the only thing both he and Anders could do to help her was to reinforce it by acting concerned. "I'll carry her to the healer," he offered, "or her chamber."

"I'll help ye," Anders spoke up.

But one of them had to stay in the solar with the lairds. Both twins knew someone had to remain to observe, and possibly to help their father keep the MacKay from doing something ulti-mately harmful to his daughter or her future. Anders' offer finally succeeded in galvanizing the MacKay to action.

"One of my men can take her, if one of yer lot will show them the way." He frowned. "She should have come 'round by now."

To Stellan, the MacKay still sounded more irritated than concerned, but to be fair, his frown could indicate either. Still, Mariota's situation at home was becoming more and more clear, the more he learned from her and observed her father. Behind his back, out of MacKay's sight, Stellan clenched his fists, angry and heartbroken for her.

"Anders, show them the way," his father directed.

With a glance at Stellan, Anders complied. One of the MacKay guards lifted Mariota out of the chair and followed him.

Stellan kept his gaze on Mariota as the MacKay guard carried her out the door. He hoped the man didn't drop her. The way he kept shifting his hold, Stellan feared for her. But he couldn't follow. The lairds were also watching her departure.

Then they turned back to each other. "I hope yer daughter will be well," Sutherland said. "'Twas never my intention that she suffer harm in our care."

"She hasna," MacKay told him in a much more level tone than he'd managed during the last minutes of their exchanges. His color had improved, as well, with only a slight stain of the former red that had suffused it.

"Would ye like to go with her?"

"Nay. Yer healer will see to her. My men will advise me if I am needed."

"Very well. I ken how a father can worry over his bairns. I worried over my lads while they were fostered away, and found that I missed them, but I was confident the experience would be good for them."

Stellan knew his father was trying to appeal to MacKay's paternal side, but it still warmed him to hear that their father had cared about them. And missed them. While his decision had seemed harsh at the time, he and Anders had told Mariota the truth when they said they had learned from the experience. They'd had many opportunities since then to understand how very wise their father could be.

Stellan hoped that held true today.

MacKay crossed his arms over his chest and Stellan feared he would choose to renew their arguments rather than following his father's lead.

"At least ye had sons to follow after ye. Mine—"

He stopped and appeared to be gathering himself. Was he going to bemoan having a daughter for an heir yet again?

"I spoke out of anger," he finally said.

Stellan glanced toward his father, but the Sutherland's attention was fixed on the MacKay laird. Stellan wondered if his father was as surprised by the admission as he was.

"I am still willing to consider a betrothal with yer younger twin," MacKay continued, "but I believe the best thing I can do for Mariota after her adventure with ye is to take her home. For both of us to have time to deal with problems there before entering into such an agreement."

"If that is what ye wish. There are, of course, details to be worked out, but I will remain open to the idea," Sutherland told him, then escorted him to the door of the solar and bid him good day.

Stellan leaned against the wall at his back to hold himself up. Mariota had not only put a stop to the argument between their fathers with her feigned weakness, she bought time for herself and, it appeared, a more sympathetic attitude from her father. He didn't want her to leave, but perhaps it was the best for her.

CHAPTER 8

Mariota stayed limp and unresponsive as her father's guard followed Anders out of the solar. It took all the control she had not to break his nose when his hand slid around her back and she felt his fingers begin to fondle the side of her breast. She knew better than to count on her da to do anything about it, so she would have to. She knew which guard carried her by his grunts and groans as he shifted her in his arms, acting as if she weighed as much as a horse, all, she supposed, to distract from what he was doing. She heard male voices and chairs shifting. They were passing through the great hall. Surely someone would notice where his hand was and stop him. Anders, whom she was certain would have flattened the man had he seen, was in the lead and looking away from the man following him.

Suddenly Seamus' voice rang out. "Mari! What happened?" She dared not open her eyes, but felt heard the guard's hold on her shift as Seamus' footsteps approached.

Through slitted eyelids, she saw Anders turn and put a hand on his shoulder to hold him off.

"She fainted. We're taking her to the healer."

"Fainted? Mari's never fainted in her life."

She wanted to kick him. To hiss at him to be silent, but she was stuck playing the weak female. At least with Seamus' approach, her tormentor had moved his hand to a more appropriate location down her ribs. She'd take care of that one later. She'd beaten Alber, she could take this oaf easily.

Seamus stayed by her side as they continued on to the herbal. "What made her faint? How long has she been out?" He kept peppering Anders with questions. It was nice to hear Seamus' voice and know someone cared about her well-being. But Anders didn't have time to answer him.

Suddenly they stopped and her tormentor dropped her onto a cot. At last! If she'd had some warning, she would have done him some damage as she fell, but she didn't get the chance.

"Ye men, out," the healer snapped.

Mariota heard them move away and opened her eyes.

The healer motioned for her to stay put and quiet until she was certain they'd gone out of earshot. Then she spoke, "Well, lass, what is this about?"

"Sorry to intrude," Mariota told her in a low voice in case someone ventured nearby, "but my da and the Sutherland were at each other's throats. Stellan thought it would distract them if I fainted."

"Ach, lass. 'Tis sorry I am that ye felt ye had to do that."

"I hated doing it, but between Stellan, Anders and I, none of us could see another way to keep them from coming to blows— or worse."

"Are ye well, then? Ye werena harmed when ye fell?" The healer kept her voice low, though her concern was evident in her warm tone. "Or he dropped ye here?"

"Nay, I'm well, save for the guard's wandering hands. I would have preferred Anders carry me, but he couldna, no' in front of my da." Mariota was sorry not to have a chance to speak to Anders or Seamus before they left the herbal. She appreciated having the twins and Seamus as allies. She also appreciated the chance to get away from her father after he proved yet again how little he cared for her. She knew Anders and Stellan would be on alert, for her sake, to anything the two lairds said or did that would affect her. But she didn't know what they could do to help. Ultimately, her father could pull her out and force her back home, with Alber nearby. The thought sickened her. Still, Seamus would be nearby, too. That was some consolation.

"Anders is a good lad, despite being fond of the lasses."

"They've both been naught but kind to me," Mariota said, defending Stellan as well as his brother.

"I would expect naught less," the healer remarked. She glanced toward the door and said, "I'll be back in a moment."

She left and Mariota heard her voice in the hallway. "I'm going to keep the lass for a while. Ye may leave. She's perfectly safe with me."

Anders and Seamus thanking her were the only responses Mariota heard. Like as not, her guard had already joined his fellows in the great hall rather than return to the solar. That would give Seamus a chance to replace him there.

"They're gone from here," the healer assured her. "I'm sorry ye are nay treated better by yer folk."

"Nothing like Sutherland. If only I could receive the same kindness at home," she said.

"I heard that the MacKay came to fetch ye home. But I never kenned why ye left in the first place."

She was grateful Stellan and Anders kept her story about Alber's attacks to themselves. It was hers to tell, and she found a willing and sympathetic listener in the healer. "'Tis nay as though none are good to me, but they canna stand up to the laird, and Da hasna punished Alber so far as I ken. But one of the head guards, Seamus, is a friend and I may find out more from him, as soon as I can talk to him alone.

"Wait, yer attacker is here? Yer da brought him to help escort ye back to MacKay?" The healer shook her head, disbelief written in every crease on her forehead.

"Aye." Mariota couldn't think of anything to say that would make it sound better. Or justify it.

"He'd best nay cross my path. I'll make his life miserable while he remains at Sutherland if he so much as looks at ye crosswise. Were things always this bad at MacKay? Ye seem like such a strong, smart lass, yer father must have loved and cared for ye when ye were young. What changed to turn him mean?"

Mariota tensed. She knew why, and didn't want to share that story. Things had been bad enough after the accident. But perhaps things had gotten worse after Alber arrived. She had been about nine, which would have made him eleven. Old enough to cause trouble, yet she didn't have any strong recollection of spending time with him. He must have kept to himself, or stayed out of trouble until he was older. He hadn't fostered away. Her father had kept him close, but perhaps once he was old enough to spend most of his time training with the other men, her father's interest in him had waned.

So, what about her changed with him? She couldn't answer that, either, save her encounter with him the first time she bested him. Had she hurt his feelings so badly that he still carried the resentment to this day? It didn't seem possible, unless there was more she didn't know. Had her da seen him as a surrogate son? Promised him things that were never bestowed? She just didn't know, and because of where they were now, it mattered. "Who can say why any lad becomes the man he is?" She was prevaricating, and she could see the healer knew it, but the woman shrugged and let her comment pass.

Mariota's guilt surged anew. By her rejection all those years ago, she might be more responsible for Alber's actions than she'd ever considered. The thought made her belly sink. She couldn't see any way to fix this, now that Alber seemed determined to exact his revenge.

STELLAN CAUGHT ANDERS' eye when he reentered the solar. Anders nodded. That simple gesture told him Mariota was with the healer and would remain there until the healer agreed to let her leave. Even her father would not be able to remove her from the Sutherland healer's care if she insisted on keeping the lass. Mariota was safe for the moment. The healer was a powerful ally to have within Sutherland, and this was the second time she had defended Mariota, even though Stellan was certain she knew Mariota had faked the faint and there was nothing new wrong with her since she'd arrived. Perfect. That would keep the lass out of her father's clutches, at least for now. Some of the tension Stellan had been holding onto drained out of his shoulders and belly.

Now to deal with whatever the two lairds came up with.

But before Anders could cross the solar and join him, the two lairds stood and the MacKay and his remaining man walked out.

Sutherland tilted his head toward the door. Anders nodded to someone out in the hall and closed it behind the MacKay and his man. He and Stellan moved to the seats opposite their father's desk.

"Fill Anders in while I consider something," Sutherland directed.

Stellan nodded. "Ye didna miss much after ye left. MacKay willna say any more about why he brought Alber, but 'tis clear he accepts the man's lies about his prowess at Harlaw."

"So why dinna his other men tell him the truth?"

"Perhaps they did. 'Tis an important question, but one we canna answer."

"Perhaps he has something on the old laird, something he doesna want made public," Anders said, his gaze distant while he thought.

Stellan disagreed. "MacKay could simply banish him or even

kill him for what he's done. Why put up with threats to himself or attacks on Mariota? What makes Alber untouchable at MacKay?"

"Domnhall? Or one of their other supposed allies, Gunn or Sinclair? Did he foster with one of them?"

"We dinna ken enough to be certain about any of them."

Anders frowned.

"Her da doesna treat her as his heir," Stellan continued. "Could he intend to name someone else to succeed him?"

"Certainly not Alber!" Anders objected.

"Nay, but if MacKay is all about power and keeping what MacKay has to itself, he might decide to replace her. If he doesn't trust anyone enough to use her to make an alliance, he can just marry her to a MacKay warrior or one of his advisors."

"If he did that, the least he could do would be to let her choose her husband."

"I dinna think that's likely, in any case, but ye dinna hear what he said about his proposal to us after ye left. He claimed to be speaking from anger. He wants to take her home, to let things settle down. I dinna ken whether he has truly decided he doesn't want a neighboring clan involved after all. He could honestly fear MacKay would cease to exist as a separate clan and territory unless he looks farther afield."

Anders clenched a fist. "So she's left with rough men like Alber, or old scheming men, ye mean? Those would be her choices? We canna let that happen to her."

"We canna stop it," Stellan said, and that made his blood run cold. There had to be a way to protect Mariota that wouldn't worsen relations between their clans. Not that he thought they were very good at the moment.

Their father had turned to stare at the low flames in the hearth. Now he turned back to them. "I considered offering Mariota a place here. It would be a monumental step to offer permanent sanctuary to another clan's heir. One certain to cause problems. I'm concerned for her at MacKay, but I see more behind her father's bluster than, perhaps, he wants anyone to see. He's worried."

"For her?"

"Perhaps. In part. It does make me wonder if he would be relieved to have her remain here. Then there's Domnhall to worry us all. He's a fickle ally at best, as MacKay kens fine. MacKay was right to be concerned about the current conflict spilling north at some point. And this man, Alber. There's something between them. Something of long-standing, or his laird would have dealt with him by now."

"He should have dealt with him anyway," Stellan said. "Ye would have."

"Aye, I would, but I am no' the MacKay and I dinna ken what burdens he carries. Well, some of them, aye. The obvious one being a daughter of marriageable age and his heir. I have to wonder if any of this would have happened if Cameron had not met Mary Rose, but had wed with Mariota MacKay. Where would we be now?"

Stellan and Anders traded a glance. To Stellan, such speculation was not useful. They had to deal with the here and now. Their younger brother was besotted with his bride. Stellan knew neither he nor Anders would wish a different lass for him. And certainly not Mariota. Not when she meant so much to him— nay, he must not think about his growing feelings for her. He knew there was no future for them, not as long as they were both destined to follow their fathers.

AFTER WHAT THE healer deemed was a suitable amount of time, Mariota left the herbal. She would have happily stayed there, but knew she could not, and that a confrontation with her father was inevitable, and imminent. Unless the twins were willing to hide her somewhere within Sutherland's walls, she would not be able to avoid him.

As soon as she entered the great hall, she spotted Seamus with the other MacKays by the hearth. So he had not joined her father in the Sutherland's solar? She headed for Seamus. He stood in response to her eye contact and the tilt of her head, then she headed for the back hallway Brìghde had shown her during their tour. It led to the kitchen past the buttery, so no one would think twice about Seamus wandering in that direction. She waited for him down the hallway, close to the buttery's door. Minutes later, he joined her.

"I walked outside for a moment to get eyes off me, and came back in with a group of Sutherlands before following ye. What happened to ye? What's amiss?"

"Naught save trying to keep Da from doing something stupid. I hate playing the weak lass, but it was the most expedient way to distract the lairds from their disagreements. Why are ye out here and not in the solar with them?"

"They finished their discussion before I could get there. Yer da rode out to the camp across the glen. I saw no sign of him while I was outside, though I think he'll be back soon. What can I do for ye, lass?"

"I need to ken what has happened at MacKay since I left," she said. "Did Alber get punished at all? Why was he in Da's personal guard? Why is he here?"

"Ye dinna ask much," Seamus said, crossed his arms over his muscled chest and leaned back against the stone wall on his side of the hallway.

"I ask because my life may depend on it." The words came more easily than she thought they should to describe something so frightening.

That sobered him. "Because Alber is here."

"Of course. Did Da punish him after he attacked me outside my chamber? People saw the aftermath. They, ah, helped him from the hallway outside my chamber and down the stairs. I dinna ken what happened after that."

"Other than a stern lecture, I dinna think anything did."

"Then what hold does he have on my da?" Frustration tightened her jaw.

"'Tis more than his claim of mastery at Red Harlaw," Seamus said thoughtfully. "But I dinna ken what keeps him at MacKay, or keeps him alive. 'Twould seem to me anyone else doing what he has done would be banished, lashed, or dead by now."

"There havena been any witnesses to his attacks on me till after 'twas done," Mariota said. "Save for the damage to him and some bruises on me, he could claim naught ever happened."

"If I had seen him attack ye, I would have killed him then."

If that had happened, perhaps all this would be over and she would have been able to move forward with her life at MacKay. "Thank ye, but I dinna want to be that vulnerable to him again. Ask around, discretely if ye can, about him. Where he's from, anything ye can find out about him. I doubt we can trust what we already *think* we ken about him."

"'Twill get back to him," Seamus cautioned.

"Nay if ye are careful about who ye ask."

"Some of the older men might remember. But they're back at MacKay."

"Then ye must wait 'till ye return, but I need to ken why my da is protecting him over me."

"Ask him."

Mariota bit back a laugh that wanted to become a shriek of frustration. "Ye think I havena?"

"Of course ye have. Have ye considered it may be dangerous for him to tell ye?"

"More dangerous than what Alber has already done to me and still wants to do? More dangerous than me, my father's heir, being ignorant of some secret he keeps?"

"Ye have a point."

"James," Mariota blurted out the name as a memory surfaced. "Da's friend and member of his council. I think he kens something. Mayhap everything." The day she'd overheard him talking to her father and had to tolerate his presence while her father threatened her came back to her in a rush. Nothing he'd said made her suspect him, just his attitude. The way he and her father exchanged glances. Aye, he knew something.

"I'll ask when we get back to MacKay."

Mariota nodded, relieved that she had set something in motion. There might not be any answers to be had, but she knew Seamus would try. He was careful, and he was well-liked. If anyone could find out anything, he would. "I think we've been here long enough," she told him. She tried to door to the buttery. To her relief, it opened.

"Carry out a cask of something to explain why ye have been in here for so long. I'll make my way through the kitchen and come back to the great hall from there."

Seamus nodded and entered the buttery. Mariota left him to explore and took a side passage toward the kitchen. It felt good to have Seamus at her back. He was her best friend at MacKay. She didn't want to get him into any more trouble, but somehow, she had to understand why Alber could do what he did without repercussions. She swore to corner her da again, too. The more she stood up to him, the more respect she hoped to gain. Could she gain enough of his respect for him to share whatever truth he hid, before Alber succeeded in whatever he was determined to do?

In the kitchen, no one seemed to notice her entry, so she grabbed a hand pie from a serving tray and went across the great hall. As she reached the stairs up to her chamber, her father entered from the bailey. She paused, then sank into a seat at the nearest table, hoping he would not notice her among the others scattered around the hall. But his gaze cut right to her, and he beckoned her.

At least he didn't shout her name across the chamber. He had some small semblance of decorum left to him.

With a sigh, she rose and crossed to him. "Da."

"Pack whatever ye brought, and ready yer hawk. We leave at first light."

A chill ran down her spine. "With Alber among the guards? Nay, I willna."

"Ye will do as ye are told, Daughter. Dinna argue with me in another clan's hall. I willna stand for it."

So he was still cross from his argument with the Sutherland laird. "And I willna stand for what Alber has threatened to do to Valkyrie, and to me."

"Ye will have my men around ye at all times."

Why did he think that would reassure her? "I have that at home and yet he's gotten to me thrice."

"I will assign him duty to keep him far from ye."

"Where? Here? The Sutherlands willna welcome him."

"Leave that to me."

She felt her temper rising as her belly clenched. She fought to remain calm. "And on the way home? There will be times I must have privacy, yet he will follow me. He has done so already."

"Mariota, I will keep him away from ye. That is all ye need to ken. Now go to yer chamber and ready yerself."

Could she trust her father with her safety? He hadn't done a very good job of it so far. But what alternative did she have? The sound of a bench scraping on the flagstone floor distracted her as someone stood up from a table. Despite her determination to confront her father, he was correct. The Sutherland great hall was not the place to do it.

"I will comply," she said, relenting for the sake of peace, or at least decorum, "but I have a demand as well. Seamus will travel with me. And three other MacKay men I choose. And several Sutherlands will come as observers to ensure I remain safe."

"Nay. Ye go too far."

"'Tis my life, my future, I bargain for. Why can ye no' see that?"

"They are in my hands. I am yer laird as well as yer da."

Mariota shook her head, resigned to angering him but determined to keep her voice down. "I meant what I said about remaining here. Or I will travel elsewhere and ye will never see me again."

"Dinna threaten me, lass," he warned her, though he matched the volume of her voice. "Better than ye have tried and failed."

"I dinna wish to fight ye, Da. I'm fighting for myself." Did she see a glint of respect appear in his eyes? It was gone too quickly for her to be certain, but it gave her hope.

He heaved out a sigh and ran a hand through his graying hair. "How many Sutherlands?"

"That will be up to them. I will request an escort."

"Nay. I will."

Mariota nodded. She'd won this round. It was time to stop. "Very well. I will go ready myself and my hawk."

After the evening meal, Stellan joined his father in his solar. "Ye asked to see me, Da?" None of the MacKays had attended the meal, and Mariota had sent word that she would remain in her chamber. He expected his father knew what was going on. Given the confrontation earlier in the day, and despite how it had ended, he didn't expect the news to be anything good. On the other hand, MacKay might simply have taken his men and gone across the glen to have the meal where the rest of his men were camped.

Sutherland gestured him to a seat. "MacKay informed me that he and his men are leaving with Mariota in the morning. At her request, he has asked for Sutherlands to accompany them. Since she has agreed to go, I see no way to prevent him. Have ye seen any further sign of her attacker? If he's going to try to cause trouble for us between the clans, tonight is his last chance."

Stellan's heart dropped into his belly. He wasn't ready for her to leave, nor was he ready to accept the idea that he go as his twin, and Anders remain here as the heir. But his father had asked a question. At least it was one he could answer. "Naught,

Da. Our men are keeping him in their sights. So far, they report that he has remained in the camp across the glen."

"Good. Good." Sutherland nodded. "Double the guard on her chamber and in her hall. I dinna want any surprises during the night."

"Why would he try something now? He'll have a better chance of getting to her on the way to MacKay."

"Aye, but let's no' make it easy for him."

Increasing the guard suited Stellan. Could he stand watch outside her door, too? Or better, inside it? He pushed the thought aside. "I'll take care of that now."

"And send yer brother to me," Sutherland added.

Stellan knew why their father wanted Anders. He would be among the Sutherland guards to accompany Mariota back to MacKay. The thought tightened Stellan's gut. There were many reasons why Anders was the right choice to make the trip. Even the right choice to wed with Mariota. And one major reason why not. Stellan's blood heated around her, and his brother's did not.

Though many marriages were made by families among total strangers, it didn't feel right to treat Mariota that way. She was no shy lass dependent on a husband to care for and protect her. She was a skillful hunter and wicked with a bow according to what she'd said. Having seen how well she'd trained Valkyrie, he could believe her capable of anything she set her mind to.

She was supposed to become the next MacKay laird. She deserved to have a man at her side who truly cared about her and supported her. He had to admit that Anders would be good to her — and for her.

But Stellan couldn't accept that.

He found his twin by the hearth and gave him the summons. "I'll want to talk to ye once ye are done with Da," Stellan said.

Anders nodded, his expression grim, mouth tight and brows creased. "As will I," he replied and headed for the solar.

Stellan posted guards on Mariota's chamber as his father had directed, then returned to the great hall to await the news his brother brought. He could feel a sense of submission from Anders, but it was tinged with something else. Defiance. Definitely.

When Anders returned, he wasted no time mincing words. "This is yer last chance to rethink the switch," he said. "I ken ye are nay fond of deception, and this will be an important one, but if one of us goes, despite saying her da changed his mind about an alliance with us, he could still force a wedding at MacKay, thinking he has Sutherland's approval."

"He does have it, at least for the betrothal, with some details to be worked out," Stellan said after a moment's thought. His belly churned with the idea of the risk they contemplated, but he couldn't let circumstances dictate that Anders would have this woman. It might be different if he wanted her, but he did not.

Stellan had to go to prove to himself that he wanted only her, that she was worth the trouble they would cause both their clans. Anders, remaining behind as Stellan, deceiving their father on such an important and fraught issue, would take the brunt of it here. Still, there were obstacles. "If I go as ye, 'twill make nay difference. Save that I would have to admit the deception, and all hell would break loose. I could be forced to stand as yer proxy to wed her."

"I could feign illness," Anders suggested, "then ye could go as yerself."

"Ye would have to involve the healer. She could betray ye if she deemed it important to do so. And do ye think da would send me? I dinna."

Anders glanced toward the solar, then shook his head. "He's sending Sutherlands to protect her on the journey, at least. She's more vulnerable while they travel than she is at home. And have ye considered that there may be some at MacKay who dinna think a lass should be laird? Alber may no' be her only threat. I think we need to find out."

"Her da would say 'tis none of our business." Stellan wanted to agree with Anders rather than argue with him, but they had to think this through, and they'd always been good at debating both sides of the issue. "She's made no mention of anything else. Or of her da seeking to replace her as heir."

Or had she, in an indirect way, with her musings about what her life could be if she were free of that responsibility? If the MacKay did name someone else, it would solve Stellan's problem with Mariota's heritage. She could be with him at Sutherland without causing a clan war. Perhaps.

"It could be why she's no' been trained. He is thinking of replacing her," Anders said, as if hearing his thoughts.

"It may have crossed his mind," Stellan agreed. "But has he done aught about it? Or will he? At any rate, 'tis no' her immediate danger."

"Aye. Alber will be riding with her. I dinna see any alternative to me— or ye —going with her. MacKay might be willing to sacrifice Sutherland guards, but he'll think twice before harming the Sutherland's son."

Stellan shook his head. "I'm nay certain of that. Still, the Sutherland heir could be a convenient target. Or hostage. 'Tis less likely he'd see the second son the same way."

"Then it must be Anders on the trip. 'Tis been years since we switched identities."

"And never for anything so important," Stellan said in agreement, feeling the weight of inevitability settling on his shoulders. He shifted them, not liking the sensation, but seeing no other way.

"I can be ye easily," Anders continued. "Can ye be me? Friendly, fun-loving, with an eye for the lasses?"

Stellan copied Anders' grin. "'Twill take everything in me, but I must."

MARIOTA LOOKED TO HER LEFT, hoping to find Anders among the Sutherlands riding near her, but she didn't see him. Where could he have gone? She looked over her right shoulder and behind her. Ah, there he was, talking to Seamus. Relief let her exhale, but curiosity kept her twisting about to glance their way. What were they talking about? Possible dangers? Or her? Thankfully, her da rode at the head of their troop, out of earshot of whatever they or any of the Sutherland guards might discuss. She'd already gotten Seamus into trouble with her da. She didn't want to do that to him again.

Seamus glanced up, met her gaze and gave her a quick grin which caught Anders' attention. When he looked her way, he added his own cheeky grin. That was so like him. Mariota rolled her eyes, grinned back at them, and turned her gaze forward again. With those two to look at, the view was definitely better behind her. But her horse, the one she'd borrowed the night she escaped from her chamber and needed to return to its rightful owner, was starting to shift underneath her, reacting to her twisting in the saddle. And the MacKay guards on either side had noticed her mount's behavior. She didn't need to be seen staring at either Anders or Seamus. Ahead, her view encompassed the glen they traversed, the woods and hills beyond it, and several MacKay guards with her da and Alber among them.

At the moment, Valkyrie flew lazy circles above them, which caused Mariota's belly to clench with anxiety any time she lost sight of Alber. Her da seemed to keep him close, but she didn't trust his surveillance to be absolute. Still, he appeared to try to adhere to the bargain she'd struck with him. So was he trying to keep Alber under control? Or keeping him close because he remained a favorite? The question burned at her, but as long as he remained tethered to her da, he could not use his bow to shoot Valkyrie out of the sky.

But if her da let him scout ahead, she'd call Valkyrie down and keep her close. Alber could be canny when he chose to be, and she couldn't hear what he said to her da, what ideas he put into his head. Alber had yet to succeed in doing her or Valkyrie permanent harm. Still, she didn't want her father to finally have to believe her complaints while standing over her or Valkyrie's bloody, cold body.

At midday, they stopped by a stream to rest the horses. She shared a simple meal with Seamus, Anders and the other four Sutherlands her father had agreed to allow to accompany them. Valkyrie had provided her own meal— a young coney she dispatched with abrupt skill, dropped it near Mariota, then settled her feathers and ignored the men surrounding her mistress.

"She's trusting," Anders remarked while he picked at his food, his gaze on the hawk.

"I'm here, she kens Seamus, and I think she expects if I am comfortable with ye, she has nay reason for concern."

"I hope she's right," Anders said and resumed eating his own meal. Had the sight of Valkyrie tearing into the coney diminished his appetite?

Mariota thought he'd seemed more subdued this morning than was his usual demeanor, more like Stellan, but she'd never been on a long ride with him, so she couldn't judge. The other men with him seemed content with their own thoughts, though she was aware they had placed themselves around and across from her so they could see in all directions. No one would be able to sneak up on her. She appreciated their vigilance, especially as understated as it was. They kept their weapons to hand, but on the ground or tucked into belt or boot, as much a part of them as their fingers and toes.

She held in a chuckle at the image that filled her mind of the Sutherlands and Seamus sitting around her barefooted, wiggling their fingers and toes to scare off anyone who came too close. She took another bite of cheese to hide her mouth behind her hand. They took their duty seriously. She should, too.

Her da approached and announced, "We ride in ten minutes. Take care of yer needs before then."

Before Mariota could even nod in acknowledgement, he turned and walked away.

"No' in a friendly mood, aye?" One of the Sutherlands whose name she hadn't yet learned said and followed her father with his gaze. "Or is he always so terse?"

She should defend her da, but she had to agree with the man's assessment.

Seamus saved her from having to form a reply.

"He is when he's off MacKay land." He shrugged. "We've a long way to go before his mood will improve."

Seamus glanced at her.

Mariota understood what that gesture meant. They were a long way off MacKay land because of her. She didn't see censure in his glance, but it was too brief for her to interpret it. Still, it raised the specter of guilt within her. If she hadn't run, all these MacKays and the handful of Sutherlands would not be here, camped out in the woods, tense and subdued as her father sent disapproving glares at everyone.

She shook herself. Alber was to blame, not her. Any other lad would have taken her rejection years ago for what it was and moved on, but he took it as a challenge and came at her again and again, each time escalating the violence and threats, with some daft idea of using her to become laird. And she was letting her da force her home to confront more of the same.

Why had she agreed to this?

One look at Anders' sympathetic gaze on her answered her own question. It seemed he understood where her mind had gone and wanted to help. Everyone at Sutherland had wanted to help, but there was only so much they could do without causing even more trouble, for her and for them. And nothing her friends there could do once she left Dunrobin.

For a long moment, she wished she'd left Valkyrie in the care of the Sutherland hawk master and run for Sterling.

Still, that was the coward's way out, and she refused to be a coward. If she had to be the MacKay heir and someday its laird, she could not indulge her worst imaginings. She had to take charge of her fate, her da, Alber, and anything or anyone else who stood in her way. And with friends like Seamus and, possibly, a husband like Anders at her side, she would do it.

Anders must have seen the resolve in her eyes, or perhaps her clenched jaw gave away her thoughts. He nodded and gave her a brief smile, looking more like Stellan than Anders' usual affable self. Somehow, he seemed to know she was thinking serious thoughts. Nothing to laugh over. She nodded back and stood to make her way out of the midday camp to a convenient clump of bushes.

Seamus and Anders stood, too.

She started to tell them to stay where they were, but realized she couldn't see Alber anywhere. Her breath caught in her throat and she looked up searching. When she spotted Valkyrie doing lazy turns above her, she took a breath, kicking herself for not being aware when Valkyrie had finished her meal and taken flight.

Mariota nodded and let her friends take up positions behind her, at a discrete distance, backs turned, while she took care of herself. They escorted her to the burn to wash up, then back to her horse where she replaced the leather glove that protected her hand from Valkyrie's talons and called her hawk down from the sky. She'd feel better keeping Valkyrie close by until they stopped for the night.

That evening, the group built several small fires for the men to huddle around. Mariota refused her father's demand that she sleep near him after she judged Alber too close, and her father's snores disruptive enough to keep everyone near him awake and fuming. Instead, she bedded down at another fire, gratified when

Seamus, Anders and the other Sutherlands as well as several MacKays formed a defensive ring around her.

Alber would not get near her.

She hooded Valkyrie and tied her jesses to a thistle between her and where Anders stretched out. The plant was low enough to see beyond but rooted deep enough to keep Valkyrie close by, but not so strong that the hawk could not pull free if threatened. Mariota debated leaving her without the hood, but decided she'd pass the night more quietly with it on. Normally she'd tie her to her perch on her horse, but there, she'd be outside the Sutherland circle of protection and in danger from Alber.

The night passed uneventfully until near dawn. Something spooked the horses into shifting and snorting where they were tied. The noise woke Mariota and much of the camp. Several of the men got up to check on them. Her father sent men to get reports from the perimeter guards.

"Likely a wildcat," the nearest said when he came back into the camp. "The guards didna see anyone."

Mariota caught Seamus' eye. "Where's Alber?"

He got up and walked casually around the camp, but returned in moments. "In his plaid on the far side of the second fire," he told her. "'Twasna him to spook the horses."

Later that morning, they crossed a narrow glen and once they reached the woods on the other side, she realized Alber was not at the front of their group with her father. Where had he gone? She'd kept Valkyrie with her so far this morning, but knew Alber could circle back and pace alongside her but out of sight behind trees. Waiting for his chance. To shoot arrows at Valkyrie from the trees? Or her?

"Anders, Seamus," she said softly. Once she had their attention, she nodded toward the front. "Alber is missing. Do ye see him behind us?"

Both men shook their heads.

"He may be alongside us, out of sight," she told them.

"Damn the man," Seamus muttered and pulled his reins to turn his horse.

"Wait," Anders called. Seamus turned back.

"If we move away from Mariota, she'll be a clear target. If he's out there, that's what he's hoping for. So we stay by her." He signaled to the two closest Sutherlands. "Elias, Erik, form up with us. Elias, in front of Mariota, Erik, directly behind her."

Seamus called for MacKay guards to close in as well.

Mariota appreciated the wall they formed around her, but she didn't want them to get hurt. Her father had promised to keep Alber under control. "Da," she called out, attracting his attention. He frowned at the close guard around her and rode back.

"What are ye men doing?"

She didn't give any of them time to answer. "Where's Alber, Da?"

MacKay frowned and looked around. He pointed at two of this men among the guard around her. "Find him."

"Nay," Anders objected. "We stay with Mariota. Send some of yer other men to find him."

"My men do as I command," MacKay responded, going red in the face.

"Not this time," Mariota told him. "He's after me. He's in these woods, somewhere close. These men stay with me."

"Damn it, lass," MacKay started, but Mariota stared him down. She was pleased to see that her father also didn't trust Alber, perhaps even that he wasn't choosing Alber over her.

But that would mean there was another reason for always keeping him near. She couldn't think of a reason that didn't make her father's actions seem suspect— that he knew all along what Alber had been doing, and had allowed it. Or worse, that Alber had some hold over him that stayed her father's hand. She didn't like the alternatives.

"Fine. Ye two, back there, search along our back trail," he ordered, pointing at his men following Mariota's group. "And ye two, go left, two more, go right. Five of ye scout ahead. Find the bastard."

As the men began dividing up and moving out as their laird directed, Alber rode out of the nearby trees. "What's amiss?"

"Where have ye been?" MacKay snarled.

"What? Can a man no' take a piss without causing— whatever this is?"

"With me," MacKay demanded turned his horse and kicked it forward.

Alber let his gaze slide over the men around Mariota, then settle on her like a veil of slime. He gave her a nasty grin, eyes slitted but teeth exposed, kicked his horse and followed her father to the front.

"I'm going to have to kill that man," Seamus said.

"After I do," Anders told him.

"Nay, lads. After I finish with him," Mariota told them, giving in to the shudder his gaze had raised from her chest to her fingertips. "He's going to make a mistake he canna recover from. I'll see that he doesna."

&

THEY ARRIVED at the MacKay keep later that day. Mariota dismounted and, escorted by Seamus and Anders, took Valkyrie to the mews and the care of the hawk master. He would keep her safe.

Out in the bailey, Mariota paused and looked around. This was the only home she'd ever known. It was familiar. She had a few friends here, though. Her closest childhood girlfriends had married into other clans and were gone. Was she glad to be back? She wasn't ready to answer that question. Too many issues remained unresolved.

She remembered her manners and turned to Seamus. "Will ye please find the steward and see where the Sutherlands can sleep?"

She and the MacKay guards with her father were home, but the Sutherlands were not.

Anders shook his head. "We'll be in the corridor outside yer chamber."

Seamus's eyes widened. "The MacKay will never allow that."

"If he objects, we'll bed down in the great hall. All Mariota will have to do is scream and we'll be moments away."

How long would it take Alber to assault her and claim she was now his, or get his hands around her throat and kill her? "I'll lock my door," she promised as they reached the door to the keep. Her father met them inside.

"Daughter, get ye to yer chamber. I only want to see ye out of it at meals, and if anything happens, I'll have meals brought to ye."

"And Alber? Is he also confined?" She narrowed her eyes at him.

He met her challenge with a frown. "'Tis naught of yer concern."

"'Tis every bit my concern," she replied, aghast. He still refused to understand. "Who more than me has he threatened?"

"He's been warned to keep his distance or suffer the consequences, and with yer personal Sutherland guard," he said and glanced aside at Anders, "he kens better than to try anything."

"Ah, so ye do acknowledge that he is a danger to me."

MacKay's brow drew down. "I willna discuss this," he growled. "Go to yer chamber."

Mariota pressed her lips together, fuming. How much did Alber care about consequences? In her experience, he did not care at all. And with good reason. He'd never faced any that she herself had not delivered.

She'd best stay close to Anders and his men, the MacKay men who disposed of Alber after his last attack, Seamus, and groups of women. She could not let Alber get her alone again. Ever. She didn't want to have to try to escape her chamber the same way she did the last time. The guards would have learned to look for anything hanging out of her window. She had no choice but to obey— for now.

Inside the great hall, her father took Anders to his solar, probably to give him the limits of what he and his men could do here. Two waited nearby to attend her, and the others, she assumed, remained outside taking care of the Sutherland horses and the one she had used when she escaped. She was debating going straight to her chamber or taking pity on the men and staying where she was for some food when her friend Genevra rushed to her.

"Where have ye been? I've been so worried. Ye disappeared, and yer da lit out of here with a lot of the men, and now ye are back again. Did that Alber steal ye away? Are ye well? Did he harm ye?"

Mariota hugged her friend to silence her. "I've been to Sutherland. Da fetched me back, and though he brought Alber with him among all those men, he promised to keep him away from me. I decided to give him another chance. Da, nay Alber."

"Ye must tell me all about it!"

"Come upstairs with me. Da wants me to stay in my chamber."

"Nay! Ye willna, will ye?"

"For a while, until he settles down. No' for long."

She led Genevra to her chamber, certain that her chatty friend had not noticed the strange men following them up the stairs. Once she and Genevra entered her chamber, she closed and locked the door behind them. The Sutherlands would have to take turns getting some food, she supposed. As soon as Anders got away from her father, he'd figure out where his men were. Seamus would see them taken care of.

Genevra took a seat by the hearth, then pointed out that no one had lit a fire in it. "'Tis cold in here. We should send for someone to take care of this."

"I'll ask the steward to have it lighted while I'm at supper,"

Mariota said. The chamber was cool, but Genevra was one of those lasses who never seemed to get warm enough.

"Very well. Tell me what happened to ye."

Mariota told her what happened the last time Alber accosted her, and why she left, but not how.

"Were ye well treated at Dunrobin?"

"Aye, very well. So well, in fact, that there are five Sutherlands among my guards now." She didn't dare mention her interest in Stellan, or that his twin was one of the men who came to MacKay with her, or the news would be all over the clan in moments. Genevra would see Anders soon enough. The thought nearly made Mariota laugh out loud. She could imagine the comments her friend would make about him and the other Sutherland men. Handsome and strong would only be her first attempt to describe them. Mariota would add kind, courteous, and careful, but that would be only the start of a long list of positive attributes she would use. And that was before she got to describing Stellan. Nay, those attributes, she'd keep to herself.

Genevra shivered and Mariota wrapped one of her shawls around her friend's shoulders. She couldn't imagine her friend riding for days and camping overnight in the woods with more than fifty men around her, trying to stay warm by a small campfire. She didn't know which would get her friend first, the cold or the mortification of sleeping near so many men. Or even one of them. Mariota knew which one she would have preferred, but sadly he had not made the trip with her. Stellan remained behind at Sutherland with his da, in the heir's rightful place. That thought made her frown. Where was her rightful place at MacKay?

CHAPTER 10

*A*fter the evening meal, Stellan joined the MacKay in his solar. As Anders, he could not turn down an opportunity to share a cup with his host. That was easy. Flirting with the clan's lasses, as Anders would certainly have been doing, was not something he was comfortable with, and not only because it didn't suit his personality. It also felt like betraying whatever was between him and Mariota. He couldn't put a name to it, but he could tell the heat between them also affected her when they were close, more so when they shared a look, no matter how brief the glance. Even now.

Did she feel she was betraying him with his twin? She must be confused, and it was his fault. Why hadn't he realized when he and Anders were concocting this mad scheme that Mariota would be caught in the middle, thinking she was now attracted to Anders. Would she fall for the man she thought was his brother and forget about him? Or would she figure out something wasn't quite right?

Should he tell her? Could he trust her not to betray him—even accidentally?

And given that, as Anders, he was here to represent Sutherland and to… possibly… be accepted as the betrothed husband to the MacKay's daughter and heir, Stellan could only sip the ale and do his best not to down it in one gulp.

"Yer da gave me a letter before we left Dunrobin. I've read it. It mostly concerns the proposed betrothal agreement," MacKay suddenly said.

Stellan choked back a swallow, fighting to keep the ale from shooting out his nose. He should have seen this coming. Stay sharp, he admonished himself.

"And?" He asked when he could get air past the burn in his throat and nose.

"Did yer brother ruin my lass?"

Stellan thanked whatever saints watched over him that he hadn't taken another mouthful of ale.

"What? Why would ye even think that? Mariota herself said she'd been treated kindly and with respect."

"A lass alone, coming upon a hunting party in the woods? I count her lucky no' to be dead."

So did Stellan. "She was never in any danger from us— from Sutherlands," Stellan said and mentally kicked himself for the slip. MacKay knew he, not Anders, had been the one to bring her back to Dunrobin.

"'Tis why yer brother isna here in yer place, aye? Because he already—"

"Nay!" Stellan had heard enough of this line of inquiry. "Yer daughter is unharmed, at least by any Sutherland. If ye are so intent on insisting she has been ruined, perhaps ye should force a confession out of Alber. He beat her, he tried to smother her the last time he got his hands on her. Perhaps he did more, and she hasna wanted to admit to it."

"He hasna confessed to such as that. If he had, he'd be dead."

Maybe it was the ale, but Stellan hated the way this man treated his daughter, and found himself unable to hold back.

"Would he? Ye seem to have done little to protect her or punish him up to now."

MacKay rose, and Stellan saw his life about to end, right here, right now. If he could not disarm the older man, he'd be sunk. He dared not kill him. Either way, Sutherland would be furious when he discovered which twin had come here, and MacKay might have the decency to be appalled at discovering he'd killed the Sutherland heir. But maybe not.

Instead of pulling a blade, MacKay walked toward the hearth, his back to Stellan.

"I've done what I must. What I promised long ago." He paused, then added more quietly, "Perhaps that debt is long since paid."

"What do ye mean?" Stellan couldn't wait to hear the man justify his daughter's treatment.

"None of yer affair." He stared into the flames for a moment longer, then turned back to Stellan. "Yer da left open the idea of the betrothal. He offered ye, but didna make it binding, and made it clear Mariota's situation here disturbed him. If her husband couldna protect her here, if he couldna take a significant role along with her, or if it was discovered she'd been ruined by her attacker, he'd withdraw his consent."

So Da had tossed the decision back to MacKay. And given Anders a way out if he didn't think the potential alliance would benefit Sutherland. That surprised Stellan, but pleased him, too, and demonstrated yet again how canny his father could be. Stellan waited, knowing the longer he remained silent, the more likely MacKay would feel the need to say more.

His patience was rewarded when MacKay turned away from the hearth and resumed his seat.

"Ye ken Domnhall holds Dingwall and has yet to return to Islay."

Stellan nodded.

"What do ye think that means?"

"He thinks his control of Ross is firm. He didna continue the fight at Harlaw because he made his point, and rather than lose more men— on both sides —he quit the field. That's my guess."

"I'll be glad to see him gone back to the isles. Friend or foe, he's a dangerous man."

"Ye supported him. Why would ye *fash*?"

"Why would I no'? I've also fought against him."

"Ye ken— my brother fostered with him years ago." Stellan hesitated. He'd nearly said that he rather than his brother had fostered with Domnhall.

"I didna. What has he told ye about his time there?"

Stellan shrugged. What could he say that would not sound like first-hand knowledge? "Ye ken Domnhall controls many islands and coastal areas. Stellan spent most of his time at Finlaggan and didna travel with the laird. He has the same tales of training with weapons that any fostered son would share. If our da thought he'd spend most of his time learning to rule from Domnhall, he was disappointed in his expectation."

MacKay huffed. "A shame, that, I suppose."

"I would be surprised to hear ye say that, save that ye seek an alliance with Sutherland."

MacKay nodded. "I did. I might yet again. Go to yer rest, lad. I've much to consider. Leave me to it."

Stellan breathed a sigh of relief and stood. He might not have to deal with the consequences of a betrothal as Anders after all. "Good night to ye, then."

MacKay nodded again, his gaze locked in the distance, already distracted by whatever thoughts plagued him. Stellan left him to it.

He missed Anders. At home, after an interview with their father, they would sit by the fire in the great hall and talk. He hadn't even been able to bring Tormund among the men with him. He was Stellan's friend. Anders would not have chosen him as a companion for something like this. Mariota was confined to her chamber, and though her father's order had seemed punitive at first, Stellan was beginning to suspect it was truly meant to protect her. He didn't see Seamus, but was gratified to see the rest of the Sutherlands bedded down near the stairs, along with a few MacKays he recognized. Stellan nodded to them, passed through them and climbed the stairs, headed to his chamber.

A door swung open as he approached and Mariota leaned out.

MARIOTA HAD BEEN WAITING for Anders to come upstairs to his chamber, listening and watching from her door. She chafed at her confinement, even though they'd arrived home only hours before. She'd opened the door just enough to see out toward the stairs, but slight enough that she could slam it shut and lock it if Alber appeared.

She opened it fully when she saw Anders and stepped out into the hallway. She said his name softly. "I'm happy to see ye."

"And I ye, lass. But ye shouldna be out of yer chamber. What will yer da say?"

"I willna tell him. Will ye?"

"Nay, of course, nay. Can I get something for ye? What do ye need?"

Her face heated. She needed him. Or did she? Was she simply lonely? Or did she miss his twin and hope Anders could stand in for him? "Just someone to talk to," she admitted. "I dinna like being closed in."

"Like yer hawk," Anders said.

She tilted her head as a memory swamped her. She'd said much the same to Stellan days ago when they went riding along the firth. Maybe he'd mentioned her comment to Anders. Aye, that had to be the reason she felt this frisson of awareness spiraling through her chest.

"Aye, like Valkyrie." She glanced aside at her open door, then leaned back against the hallway wall behind her and crossed her arms. "This isna the best place for a conversation. Would ye come in?" She knew how he would answer before he opened his mouth, but she'd felt she had to try.

"Nay, lass, no' unless ye want to skip the betrothal and be wed in the morning."

The idea held a certain appeal, and if Anders' elder brother stood before her, she'd be tempted to grab his hand and pull him into her chamber, but nay, not this brother. Not yet. She would not be forced to wed someone when she was interested in another. She wanted Stellan, not Anders, despite the problems that would cause. Should she settle for Anders, knowing Stellan was out of reach? Not if she could help it. Not yet. She hoped not ever.

But something about Anders seemed different. Perhaps she was too tired to judge but he seemed more Stellan-like, more reserved, and the thrum of her blood in her ears told her something had changed. This, though, was not the time to try to understand what. "Ye are right. I'm sorry for suggesting it. Ye must be as tired as I. Dinna let me keep ye from yer rest."

"Good night then, Mariota," he told her.

On impulse, she reached up and cupped his cheek with one hand. Heat flared in his eyes and found an answer in her body—an answer she didn't expect. The limpid fullness low in her belly spread throughout her blood, stealing her will to move. Who was this? "Ye...?"

He shook his head and stepped back. "Ye are tired, lass. Ye need to rest. Good night."

He walked away.

She let him. She had to. She was too shocked to move. Was this Anders? Or Stellan? If this was Anders, how had she not felt the heat that just flared between them before now? The heat she thought she only felt with Stellan? The twins looked so much alike, could she be attracted to both of them?

She wrapped her arms around her middle. Nay, they were not

alike, not really. Anders was more free, more jovial. Stellan was more quiet, solemn, duty-bound and... Stellan fired her blood and made her toes curl in her slippers. Could this be Stellan in truth, and not Anders as he claimed? Mariota collapsed against the wall. Now what should she do?

❦

AFTER A RESTLESS NIGHT, on the way to break her fast, Mariota saw Seamus and decided she needed to talk to him. With the friendship that seemed to be growing between him and Anders, perhaps Anders had let something slip that would help her decide which Sutherland son she was dealing with.

Even if her suspicions were unfounded, Seamus would know more about MacKay, including things she wasn't privy to. She wanted his counsel. But when he saw her, he avoided her. Was he still angry with her that he remained on the night shift because of her? She told herself if he'd been on guard all night after traveling all day, and was just coming in to eat and rest, he would not be fit company for any lass. She took her seat and watched to see where he went. The other side of the great hall, of course. He really did not want to talk to her. She'd see about that— later. She knew him well enough to know she'd get no cooperation from him now. Tired or angry, he'd be in no mood to answer her questions.

Instead, she focused on her meal, then went outside. Her da would not approve, but the morning had dawned clear and warm. She did not want to miss a day like this shut away in her chamber. Neither, she decided, would Valkyrie. Two of the Sutherlands exited the keep behind her. Ah, her guards had found her. She stopped them and prevailed upon them to escort her to the mews, then outside the gate to let Valkyrie fly.

"Are ye certain ye should?" one asked.

"I am. But to appease my da, I need a guard to go with me,"

125

she said, doing her best to look pitiable. "Even just to fly Valkyrie in the glen outside the gates, I canna go alone." Even though she'd been tempted to try.

The two men regarded each other and the one who hadn't spoken shrugged. "Very well. Let me advise Anders and we'll go with ye."

"I'll go to the mews and fetch my hawk," she said.

The first Sutherland nodded. "I'll stay with ye," he said. "Anders warned us the danger to ye lives inside the keep as well as out."

"Thank ye both," Mariota added before she turned for the mews, her escort on her heels.

The second man appeared a few minutes later with Anders.

"Lass, ye try yer da's patience," he told her.

"Nay half so much as he has tried mine," she retorted as Valkyrie hopped onto her leather-gloved fist and accepted the hood. "'Tisna good to keep hunting hawks too long in the mews."

"She only arrived home yesterday."

"I dinna care. We need to fly free." Had she really said "we"? Aye, she had.

Anders choked at that, then sighed. "Come along then. We'll nay ride. Just walk outside the gates and loose her. My men will come with us."

Mariota knew when to accept a bargain. "Very well." She'd be well guarded, close to the keep's gates, and chances were good Alber still slept. She would be safe from him for hours yet. She crossed the bailey with her entourage, curious to see if, even with Anders' men behind them, she could get close enough to him to discover whether the heat she'd felt last night had been real and would flare again. There were too many people moving about in the bailey, but they were intent on their own tasks. Outside the gates, the guards' attention would be on the area around them every moment, including on her and Anders. It was now or never. Anders had caught up and walked on her side opposite

Valkyrie. She flexed her wrists, a move certain to cause Valkyrie to spread her wings and shift her feet. That let Mariota feign a stumble into Anders' shoulder.

He did as she'd hoped and reached out to steady her. One arm went around her waist and pulled her closer to him, the other reached between Valkyrie and her face, as if concerned that her hawk would somehow injure her.

The heat built faster than an oil-fed fire between them. His scent filled her nose and made her mouth water. Secure in his embrace, she wanted to lay her head on his shoulder and stay there, but as soon as his men caught up, he released her.

"Steady, there, lass," he admonished, but the heat in his gaze was unmistakable.

"Thank ye for catching me," she said, loud enough for their followers to hear. "I dinna ken what tripped me," she added, twisting around to look at the ground behind them, then shrugged. "Well, let's go," she said to the Sutherlands behind them, turned and resumed walking toward the gates.

"Where do ye think ye are going?"

Mariota groaned. Seamus had come outside, and she knew that tone of voice. She'd been wise to keep her distance in the great hall. But she had no hope of avoiding him now. Had he seen Anders' arm around her? She forced a smile that she didn't feel, turned and lifted the fist where Valkyrie perched. "Just outside the gate to let Valkyrie fly," she said sweetly. "Would ye like to join us?"

Beside her, Anders snorted softly.

"Damn it, Mari. Aye, I will. Yer da has already sentenced me to night watch. What else can he do to me?"

"Banishment?" Anders muttered.

So, Anders wasn't eager to have Seamus along with them, either. Was he jealous? They'd seemed to forge a bond on the way back to MacKay.

Mariota ignored the tension between the two men and

continued out the open gate. The Sutherlands spread out around her. Anders moved to the other side of the gate as if he needed space from her, and took up his post there.

Seamus stayed at her side.

"Why are ye so determined to challenge yer da?" He kept his voice low, but she could hear the anger in it.

"If he only respects strength, I must be strong and challenge him," she told him as she removed Valkyrie's hood, loosed the jesses, and tossed the hawk skyward. She turned to face Seamus.

"So was leaving in the middle of the night yer idea of strong and determined?"

"At the time, aye, it was. I saw no alternative if I was going to stay alive."

"Alber would never— "

"He spread his hand over my face to keep me from breathing — until I did my best to smash his cods. What did ye expect me to do when Da didna bother to see if I still lived?"

"Climbing out yer window was a childish, dangerous stunt, Mari. How do ye think anyone will accept ye as laird if ye use judgement that poor?"

His words hurt, but angered her, as well. "Poor? I couldna count on the MacKay to protect his own heir. So I took my protection into my own hands. I'd say it worked out well." She gestured toward the Sutherland men arrayed at a distance around them, but didn't let her gaze linger on Anders. "Would ye nay agree?"

"Ye were lucky, lass."

"Aye, I was. I ken that."

He huffed out a breath. "Ye have friends and supporters here among MacKays. Ye didna need to bring Sutherlands back and rub yer da's face in their presence. And ours."

Seamus could always make her think twice. But not about this. "I'm sorry ye are hurt by their presence, but ye are wrong. I needed exactly that to break through Da's indifference. And it seems to be working."

"For yer sake, Mari, I hope so."

She turned away from him. Valkyrie stooped on a hapless coney but Mariota didn't signal for her hawk to bring the kill to her. She'd let her have this one, and the next would go to Cook. Just like she'd let her da keep her confined— within limits —but in the end, she would be laird and if her da hadn't done it, she would eliminate the threat Alber posed, one way or the other. Eventually. She watched as Valkyrie tore into the coney, doing as instinct drove her to do.

Mariota glanced toward Anders, recalling the instinctive heat that flared between them— and between her and his brother. Did she really want the responsibility she was destined to inherit? At times like this, wrestling with her da for control of her own life, she wasn't sure if she wanted to be in charge of the clan, or just herself. If she wanted either Sutherland twin, or just Stellan. With Anders by her side, she could bear the future laid out for her. But if what she felt with him was truly only an echo of what she felt with Stellan, she would have to give up her destined future.

Even before she met the Sutherlands, she'd had doubts. There were times when the idea of abdicating attracted her, as she'd once told Stellan. Now, that idea was gaining prominence.

Had her notion of running to Inverness or Sterling been more hopeful or utterly foolish? Inverness was close, but perhaps too close. Easily within her father's reach. And they'd heard Domnhall had done a great deal of damage there last summer before moving on toward Aberdeen. Besides, where would she live in that town with a hawk? Sterling would have been a better choice if the court was there. Surely they had a mews and hunting birds. She would be farther from home and less easily retrieved if she could find a patron at court to protect her.

She decided she was being foolish. A lass alone? She'd already risked too much when she left MacKay the first time, though fortune had smiled on her when she met the Sutherlands. She couldn't count on such good fortune again.

In any case, she was smart enough not to do anything else rash. She'd made headway with her da. She had finally forced him to pay attention to her. More than that, he was forced to bargain with her. His anger and irritation were far better than him refusing to deal with her and locking her away, out of sight. She'd keep working on him, keep her guard up against Alber, and let the chaos in her mind and in her life play out until she saw a clear path. One that made sense for her, for the clan, for the Sutherland twins, and even Seamus, as well. That was a lot to take on her shoulders, but her da had placed much of it there, with more to come if or when she did become the MacKay laird. The rest, she accepted. She could make sense of all of this. She would.

CHAPTER 11

With tension tightening his shoulders, Stellan watched Seamus upbraid Mariota. He was tempted to intervene. Across the width of the keep's gate, they were still close enough that he could hear what was said when they raised their voices, but much of their conversation they held to low tones and strained expressions. Stellan's sympathy for Mariota was based on her danger from Alber and her father's inaction. Seamus adding to that mix seemed unfair, but the longer Stellan watched, the more convinced he became that Mariota was holding her own with her friend. Not just holding her own. Something seemed to crystallize within her. Her shoulders went back and she straightened as if she'd come to a decision. For her sake, he hoped it was a good one. The fact that they were out here watching her hawk hunt coneys demonstrated in a small way her determination to carve out her own future. Stellan's respect for her grew even more for that.

No lass should be treated the way her father had treated her. But things seem to be changing between them. If the man was sincere, he'd include her in meetings and judgements, giving her the training an heir should have in how to run a clan and mediate disputes. That would tell Stellan that the MacKay finally listened to his daughter and was taking her seriously. Respecting her determination to set things right, for herself and for the future of the clan, would be a significant step in the right direction on his part. Stellan hoped he lived long enough to see it happen.

He pulled his gaze away from the argument, now more of a discussion, taking place across the gate's wide opening. He was out here to keep watch, but the only thing he had been watching was Mariota. Despite the presence of other guards with them, Seamus had been focused on her, and so had he. That was foolish.

He glanced up and grimaced as his heartbeat suddenly accelerated. Alber leaned casually on a merlon, watching Mariota from the wall walk. Damn it, how long had he been up there? Any time Stellan saw Alber anywhere near her, in the great hall, the bailey, or anywhere in passing, the man watched her like a wolf scenting prey, still and focused, with deadly intent. Despite his deceptively relaxed stance, this was no exception. His eyes were narrowed and his jaw clenched, like a wolf ready to jump on its prey. Alber noticed Stellan staring at him and returned the stare with open hostility, then dragged a finger across his throat in a parody of using a blade.

Stellan took a chance and turned his back. Alber wouldn't dare strike while Seamus and others could see him, no matter how much he wanted to.

It was no secret that he, as Anders, had been chosen to lead the Sutherlands here, not just to keep Mariota safe, but for a possible betrothal. If Alber thought she was about to be wed to a warrior who could defend her better than her father ever had, he might move up his timeline and take advantage of any opportunity to attack her sooner.

Seeing how blatantly Alber displayed his malice, Stellan swore no matter if he never wed the lass, he would not leave her to be assaulted by that man again. Even the serving lasses seemed to give him a wide berth as they passed by his seat at the table. Alber clearly was not to be trusted around lasses, not just Mariota, but what effect was he having on the rest of the clan?

Stellan had already seen factions forming among the MacKays. Some smiled at him, trying to make a good impression on the man who might marry their next laird. Some glared, like Alber, as if he were the enemy, to be vanquished. Did their attitudes reflect open disrespect for their laird? They certainly felt free to glower at an important guest. This clan seemed to be at a dangerous crossroads in leadership.

Stellan was sure there was more going on here than just one angry man threatening a lass. He'd never had such feral glares directed his way, never so many hopeful, pleading glances, either. Something was wrong here. Surely some of that had reached the MacKay's ears. His inaction remained a mystery Stellan wanted solved.

He needed a word with her father and soon. Given their past conversations, how to protect her without insulting the laird would be tricky. Too bad he wasn't Anders. His twin's diplomatic skills were greater than his. But Alber's open hostility toward Mariota made another confrontation with the MacKay inevitable.

⁂

MARIOTA NOTICED Anders glaring up at the wall walk. She suspected Alber had appeared, but she would not look up and give him the satisfaction of having her attention on him. If he had been doing more than watching, if he'd been threatening her or Valkyrie, Anders would have moved her somewhere safer than standing below the keep's wall. But he seemed content to continue the staring contest he was engaged in, so she moved a few steps farther away and trusted that he or Seamus would let her know if anything changed. She liked the idea of giving Alber her back. It would insult him, infuriate him, and might provoke him to action that her guards could react to, that the other MacKay guards on the wall would see, and that would convince her father to banish him.

Nay, that would mean if she left the keep, which she would do, he would still be free to threaten her— and with vengeance in mind, she knew he wouldn't go far. She didn't like where that thought led, but she'd had it before, and that the reality of the alternative— seeing him dead —might be the only way she'd ever have peace in her own home.

She glanced around at Anders. He had turned his attention from the wall walk back to her. Alber must have gone away from his post. Anders moved into the open gate, watched the bailey for a few minutes, before turning to her.

"Alber?"

"Aye. He went into the keep."

"Good."

Seamus approached. "I saw ye staring at him. He'll take that as provocation, ye ken."

"Good," Anders told him, echoing her word of a moment before, then he grinned at her.

Seamus nodded and left them, making a circuit around them, checking with the other guards.

Mariota expected he would let them know he'd seen Alber go in the keep, but that didn't mean he'd stay there.

She watched her friend for a moment, grinned back at Anders, approving his feral implication. If Alber challenged him, it would not go well. She also liked that she was starting to see cracks in Anders' reserve. The twins were incredibly alike, but the Anders at home in Dunrobin she recalled was much more lighthearted than he'd been since they left there. Since then, he'd been much more like his twin who'd first brought her to Sutherland. Could it be that because he was in another clan's stronghold, he was subdued by the potential danger? MacKay and Sutherland were not exactly enemies, but not fully allies, either. Unless she married him. She studied his face as his grin faded. The more solemn his expression, the more he reminded her of Stellan. Was that why she'd felt the heat of attraction with him lately? Because he'd been acting more like Stellan than himself?

Valkyrie's call pulled her attention from him to her raptor, approaching now with her prey clutched in her talons. Mariota held up a fist, signaling to her to drop the coney. It landed at her feet, and Mariota opened her hand, allowing Valkyrie to wheel away to continue her hunt.

"She's enjoying this," Anders said, bemused, his gaze shifting from the dead coney to Valkyrie and back again.

"'Tis what she's trained for. She can feed herself, but she also provides meat for the pot, which Cook appreciates."

"What else can she do?" He frowned and shifted his gaze to the side, clearly thinking.

"Besides protect me from Alber?"

"She got away with it once. He'll be ready for her the next time."

"If there is a next time. If I continue to make headway with my father, I expect to convince him to take action so Valkyrie never has to confront Alber. And never has to fear him."

"Nor should ye need to. Seamus is right. Ye have friends here, not just him."

"Why have they no' spoken up to my da?"

"Perhaps they have."

That stopped her for a moment. Perhaps they had. And if they had, what was between Alber and her da that kept him from acting in her best interest? Seamus had offered to speak to the older warriors about the time when Alber joined the clan, to see if any recalled the circumstances. He was headed their way, so she waved him closer.

"Have ye had a chance to talk to anyone about how Alber came to be here?"

He shook his head. "Nay. We've only been back the day. And I have a feeling 'tis best done carefully."

She nodded, as did Anders. "Aye. Something doesn't seem right between them, but Da may no' want whatever it is dug up."

"Would it go easier coming from a Sutherland? As a stranger to the clan? Wondering why Alber seems to get away with so much?"

Seamus shrugged. "It might, at that. If one of yer men could bring it up in a group, yer man might hear naught but speculation, but there might be a kernel of truth in what he learns."

"Very well," Anders agreed thoughtfully. "'Twill be only one of mine, to keep word from getting out that questions are being asked. But he may never get the chance, ye ken."

Mariota nodded. "I hope he does. We may uncover the truth of this yet."

"Ye may still get it from yer da, if ye ask again," Anders said. "'Twould be best coming from him."

He was right. "If Da would answer, and if I could trust that he told me the truth, aye, it would. I will try."

Seamus glanced skyward. "Here comes Valkyrie again."

Mariota smiled at her hawk and raised a fist. Another coney landed at her feet. She waved off her raptor.

"I'll let her get a few more for the pot before we go in. Cook will be pleased. And thank ye both for today. 'Tis good to be outside."

Both men nodded and stepped away from her. She watched Anders move to his position on the other side of the gate. Save for Anders' grin, she really could not tell him apart from Stellan. They looked, sounded, moved, and thought much the same. Only their temperaments differed slightly. Why shouldn't she consider him for her husband instead of his brother? He was not tied to Sutherland as its heir, and he would make a good partner for her at MacKay— strong, thoughtful, cheerful, even wise. They seemed to have developed an attraction for each other that could grow, perhaps even into love. She would not be settling. She would be making a wise decision. Anders would be the best choice for her and for her clan. So why couldn't she be happy about that?

❧

AT SUPPER THAT NIGHT, Mariota suddenly stiffened like a hare confronting a wolf. Alber watched her, careless of who saw him giving her a sickening grin. Seamus was on the wall walk, back on night watch. She was not sure who was sitting beside her, Anders or Stellan. And her personal wolf was too near, licking his chops. Nothing seemed right. Little about her situation made sense to her. And having to tolerate Alber's attention, even at a distance, made her regret letting her father force her into returning to MacKay.

She still had no idea what punishment her da exacted on him. He seemed not to have suffered at all. Why wasn't he in the MacKay dungeon? She looked to her da, hoping to bring Alber to his notice, but his attention was elsewhere. And in front of the clan was no place to confront him. "Da," she leaned toward him and said, "I wish to speak with ye in yer solar after the meal."

He studied her for a moment.

Mariota held herself still and kept her expression calm. She didn't want to give him a reason to turn her down.

"Very well," he finally said, agreeing.

Mariota nodded and turned away from him, suddenly wishing she hadn't requested the interview. She could only enrage her father, no matter how she asked the question at the front of her mind. Was Alber punished? And if not, why not? What did he mean to her da?

But she consoled herself that she'd made progress with him by being bold, confident, assertive. These questions were at the heart of her problems at MacKay. Her da owed her an answer.

137

In his solar, her father became as furious as she expected when she posed the first question.

"Ye should be more interested in yer future husband than Alber," he told her with narrowed eyes and a furrowed brow.

"If Alber has his way, I willna need one," she asserted. "I'll be his. Or I'll be dead."

"I am keeping Alber away from ye—"

"Aye? Who was that, glaring at me at supper? Even when he canna reach me, he can threaten—"

"Which does ye nay harm. I'll speak to him again."

"Why has he no' been punished before now? Ye ken what he's done. He should be in the dungeon or banished from MacKay for his attacks on yer heir." Anyone else would be dead.

"Ye dinna ken what ye speak of."

Mariota clenched her fists, not caring if he saw her do it. He still wouldn't reveal what hold Alber had over him. "I ken fine, Da. Ye thought ye'd have a son to follow ye, but ye were left with me. If ye dinna support me, if ye canna ensure I am properly trained to manage MacKay, all of it, then the laird who follows ye may well lose all ye have worked for. Is that what ye want? Or are ye thinking of naming another as yer heir? One of yer men?"

His sudden stillness spoke volumes.

"Nay Alber," she pleaded. "He'll ruin MacKay in his first month."

"Nay, I would never consider him."

"Too bad he doesna ken that. He might leave me alone. Then who? And why will ye no' tell me what I've asked of ye?"

"Ye dinna need to ken."

That came as another punch to her gut. He would never do anything about Alber. "If ye mean to leave MacKay to me, ye owe yer clan to prepare me as ye would yer son so that I can lead and my husband can support me— and MacKay. I'm yer daughter, nay a son, but I am one of the best archers ye have, and a hawk mistress who can aid in the hunt. I have tried to learn what a laird must ken, but I havena had much help from ye. So I'm telling ye now. Ye must train me. Or tell me what else ye plan so that I can live my life elsewhere as I see fit."

He stared off into space for a moment. "'Twill be yer husband's problem to protect ye in the future, and to act as laird where ye arena capable. He must be someone who can be the clan's war leader since ye canna."

Her heart cracked in her chest at this confirmation that her father didn't care about her, only about replacing her, or making a strong alliance with someone who could lead in her stead. He expected her husband to become laird in all but name. She fought back tears, and before he threw her out of the solar, she told him, "Factor this into yer planning, my laird. Since ye refuse to act, long before ye are gone and I become some semblance of laird, before he can hurt me again, I will see Alber dead."

"Ye?" Her father's laughter followed her out of the solar.

Aye, me, she thought, too angry for tears. There were many ways she could end Alber's harassment. And if she failed, her future husband could avenge her. But first, she had to spend time with Anders Sutherland, seduce him into wanting her, supporting her, doing what must be done if it turned out her da was right and she could not. Her da might refuse to believe it, but she knew she was in a fight for her life.

$\mathcal{S}$tellan arrived at the laird's solar in time to hear Mariota threaten her attacker, then she burst out of the room, followed by her da's laughter, and ran right into Stellan's arms.

He pulled her aside. "That sounded intense. Are ye well?"

She shook her head. "Nay, I dinna think so."

"Is there anywhere we can go to talk? To be private?"

She glanced out toward the great hall, nodded and without a word, led him away from it, down the corridor to a storage area.

After he closed the door, he turned to her. "What happened when ye talked to yer da? From the little I heard, it didna go well."

She broke down in tears. He reached for her but she shook her head and stepped back. "I'm angry, Anders. Furious, nay sad," she said around gulps of air and fresh bouts of tears.

Stellan pulled her against him into his arms and took a breath when her arms went around his waist, her hands on his back, clutching his *leine*. She fit against him so well, he wasn't sure he could force himself to release her. Her body aligned with his, breasts to his chest, hips to his hardness, thighs touching, her head on his shoulder. He didn't know how he could give her up, not to Anders, or any other man.

"I dinna ken where the betrothal is going," he said, "but I will protect ye as best I can for as long as I and my men are here. I dinna want to leave ye to face yer problems without my help." He hoped reminding her she wasn't alone would make her feel better. But her answer surprised him.

"Take me with ye back to Sutherland," she said. "I still dinna ken why, but I have nay future here. My da— if ye marry me, ye will rule MacKay in all but name. Or he will name one of his men to follow him instead of me. He has made it clear he has no confidence that a mere lass can be a good laird."

Stellan didn't see how he could take her away, now that she was back home. "Both our fathers would go daft— or go to war," he reminded her.

"Mine doesna care," she asserted. "And Alber thinks to rule the clan. He will ruin me to force Da to let him wed me if he gets the chance." She shuddered. "I canna even tolerate the sound of his name, much less his presence. Nor his taunts, or his fists," she added.

Stellan vowed silently to kill the man if he came near her again, despite knowing full well he'd cause trouble for himself and Sutherland. "Ye dinna deserve any of those. Ye deserve loving arms around ye, warm lips to worship ye and strong hands to protect ye."

"Yers?"

He didn't think. He dipped his head and brushed his lips across hers. Soft, so soft, and delicious, with a trace of cider and tears, sweet and salt.

Instead of pulling back, she wrapped her hands around his neck and lifted onto her toes, putting her mouth close to his for one heart-stopping moment, then she kissed him back. Her lips parted on a sigh and he took that as an invitation, though he knew he was daft to do it. He sucked her lower lip gently, slid his tongue into her mouth and tasted, stroking hers, making her sigh again. His body reacted with heat and need stronger than he'd ever known.

Her chest lifted, pressing her breasts against his chest as she stepped fully into his embrace, molding her body tightly to his. "Dinna stop. I want more. I need more."

His body reacted instantly, hardening. He pulled her with him until he could turn her back against the wall. He slid his hands down to cup her arse and lifted her, all the while tasting her mouth, her throat, her shoulder where her chemise had slipped aside. He pulled it farther askew with his teeth and nipped the muscle he uncovered, making her cry out softly. Her warm breath scorched his neck, loosening his control to dangerous levels.

Mariota wrapped her legs around his waist and clung to him, arching against him and driving him mad. The real Anders had enjoyed many lasses in the time since Stellan last did so. He was full of pent-up need, and had no doubt his desire for this woman was going to be his undoing.

❧

MARIOTA KNEW she was risking everything. But what she felt in Anders' arms had nothing to do with seducing him into doing her bidding and everything to do with heat and longing that flared between them. She'd never felt like this before, except near Stellan. They had never kissed, never touched like this, but the heat, the need, filled her and weakened her as they had only done with Stellan. Now, Anders had lit the fire within her, not his brother, and she didn't understand how that had happened, or what to do with it except to see where it led.

She wanted to climb him like the trees she'd loved to climb as a lass and cling to him forever, sheltered in his arms like the branches of her favorite tree had sheltered her. She had thought she was attracted only to Stellan. Now it turned out that Anders had something fierce that called to something primal within her. *If this was Anders.* The thought kept echoing in her mind. *If. If. If.* Why didn't she know?

She only knew she wanted more, things she didn't know how to name, and in this moment, was willing to risk him overpowering her. Sensation ruled her rather than thought. The Sutherland twins held the key to opening the wellspring of new feelings driving her to heights she'd never experienced. Surprised at herself, she vowed to enjoy this, wherever it led, especially if it led to her escaping MacKay again. Forever this time.

But something held her back. *Which twin was this?*

STELLAN FELT himself losing control exactly as he had once feared. Exactly what he had hoped to avoid. But the more he kissed her and the more she kissed him back, the more her legs tightened around his waist and her sighs and moans teased him, the more he wanted. But he couldn't. She thought he was his brother.

That stung.

Before they went much farther, he loosed his hold and let her slide down his body until her feet were firmly on the floor. He'd never felt such sweet torture, such overwhelming need, but he fought to control his body and stepped back from her. "Ye are playing with fire, lass. Getting burned will set ye on a path ye may not want to follow."

"That sounds like something Stellan would say, nay Anders." She studied him for a moment. "Which twin are ye?"

Her question shocked him into immobility. How had he raised her suspicions? And how to fix this? He dared not let his dismay show on his face, so he forced a hint of annoyance into his voice. "Ye ken who I am. *Anders.*" He hated lying to her but he had to. Anders' warning about ruining the lass and being forced to marry her rang in his ears. He could see it now. The wedding, with him still posing as his brother, the marriage record with his brother's name, but the wedding night with him.

The honorable thing to do would be to confess all before that happened, and stand proxy for his brother, breaking the oath they'd sworn as young lads. Anders would be forever tied to MacKay, close by, but not in the way they had planned. And of course, no wedding night would happen until the real Anders arrived to consummate the union Stellan had forced him into. The very wedding night Stellan's traitorous body wanted more than anything.

This pull between them was too fraught with disaster to continue. Should he tell her the truth she asked for? Could he? Nay, the repercussions would be felt all the way to Dunrobin, hell, to Sterling and Islay, too. The Sutherland heir at MacKay under false pretenses. Impersonating his twin. No one would believe he was here simply to protect the lass in his arms, and to learn more about her. He'd be seen as a spy, the worst sort of liar. Any hope of an alliance between the two clans would be lost. Sutherland's reputation would be tarnished.

How had he let himself be talked into this? In truth, he hadn't needed much convincing. And what could he do now that they'd kissed? Now that he wanted her even more than before their lips had touched. Their bodies. Clothes had been no impediment to the fire raging in his blood. He'd sensed every curve. Every bit of pressure she exerted with her thighs around his waist had made him crave what lay between them. Her breath had made him drunk with need for her.

He'd made a mistake. Possibly the biggest one in his life. If he could not have this woman, he would not be able to breathe.

He should leave MacKay, but he couldn't leave her at Alber's mercy. Nor could he take her with him back to Sutherland. He was trapped between impossible alternatives. The only honorable solution was to get word to Anders to meet him, switch places with him, and let the real Anders continue what they had begun to its inevitable conclusion. Betrothal. Marriage.

Was he willing to do that? To give the woman in his arms to his brother? Never to let her know the fire she felt with him was started by Stellan, not Anders? To grow old watching his brother make a family with the woman he wanted for himself? Or would she know the moment Anders approached her? Was the magic only with him, and seeing Anders after this would tell her exactly what he and his twin had done— switched places in a dangerous game that could only hurt them all.

He stepped back from her and pulled his hands from her lush body. "We canna continue this, Mariota. Too much depends on yer marriage. On ye being wed the right way, nay because ye are ruined and ye must. That would make me nay better than Alber."

She watched him for a moment, eyes wide and liquid. He feared her tears would start to fall at any second and he hated the idea that he had caused them. He never wanted to hurt her.

Instead, she surged forward, knocking him back, and his arms went around her of their own volition.

"I dinna care. If I have to choose between ye and someone like Alber, I want more from ye," she said and met his mouth again, sucking his lower lip and tracing her tongue over it as he had done to her.

His body roared to life just as the door opened behind her.

CHAPTER 13

As Stellan registered the noise at the door, he pulled away from Mariota. They were not touching when it opened, but the damage may have been done. They should not have been alone like this. And most certainly they should not have been found, both breathing hard and flushed with sensual need. Need that could never be met.

Mariota whirled around, stiffened, then relaxed. "Fionnuala."

The woman looked like an older kitchen lass to Stellan, but Mariota must have been a favorite of hers because she put her finger over her lips and stepped out of the room, closing the door behind her. Stellan went to it and opened it again, then tilted his head in an "out" gesture to Mariota. She gave him an apologetic smile and left the room. He waited a moment, giving his pounding heart a chance to slow, then followed.

"I be sorry, lass," the woman said. "I…" She gulped and continued, "I didna mean to interrupt."

"Ye didna," Stellan told her, determined to protect Mariota. "We had things to discuss and needed a quiet place for it."

"Sure and ye did," the woman answered, her gaze on the floor, then left them in the corridor without explaining what errand had brought her to the storage chamber.

"That canna happen again," he told Mariota once they were alone. Though his body was telling him he wanted it to— right now. And the pulse beating in Mariota's throat signaled the same. She wasn't the only one playing with fire.

"It can if I wish for it to."

"Nay, it canna, and ye ken fine why." He ran a hand through his hair and down the back of his neck, praying for the whirlpool to calm that was swirling blood from other parts of his body into his groin. "Now tell me what yer da said. Ye confronted him, aye?" It was the best way he could think of to lower the temperature between them. Recalling the confrontation with her father would surely distract her from the blood singing in her veins. He hoped it would do the same for him.

"There's naught more to say than I told ye earlier. I ken what ye are trying to do. But ye canna deny what is between us."

"I must, Mariota. 'Tisna my place— or my wish —to risk ye that way."

"Nay yer wish? What was that then?" She asked and pointed at the door they'd hidden behind. "For it seemed like ye wished it well enough while we were there."

"I… things got out of hand, lass."

She frowned at his words, her brow wrinkled and her lips pressed tightly together. "Did they, *Stellan?*" she said. "Or did the lie finally become truth?" Anger blazed in her eyes. Or was it contempt? "Do the men with ye ken who ye really are? Are they meant to protect ye rather than me?"

Mariota's words stabbed Stellan in the chest, right through his heart. This is what lies wrought, he thought as his blood turned cold, and he deserved it. But he didn't have to like it.

"Ye ken?" His heart beat hard against the wall of his chest. She desired him, *Stellan,* enough to know the difference between him and his twin.

"I have for a wee while. I couldna be sure until—" She waved at the door behind them. "Ye and yer twin may look exactly alike, but ye are no' the same at all, no' in the way it matters to me."

She touched his chest with her fingertips, making his breath catch and his heart threaten to beat right out of his chest. How could such a simple touch destroy his restraint?

"Ye are nay the same here," she said, her gaze on her fingertips. Then she looked up at him with eyes showing moss rings around deep, dark wells. "Ye dinna have the same smile or laugh, and ye dinna have the same heart. Anders' eyes have never burned into me the way yers do. The way yers are right now. He has never made me crave his touch the way ye make me crave yers. How could I no' see the difference? It took me a while to believe what I sensed. I was willing to go along with whatever ye two were planning, deceiving my da so ye could come along in Anders' place, but why did ye have to try to deceive me, too? I always felt something with ye, and naught with yer twin."

The pressure of her touch forced him to fight his urge to reach for her. He wanted nothing more than to pull her into his arms, close a door behind them, bar it this time, and make love to her as his body demanded. As hers, from her beating pulse to the scent of her arousal told him she would welcome. But he couldn't. He was too relieved that what he'd sensed from Anders had also been true. Friendship, but no attraction with Mariota.

She wanted him. And God knew he wanted her.

"I'm sorry, Mariota. I am. I had to lie. 'Twas the only way to be with ye. To see if these feelings between us were real. I still mean to keep ye safe, nay to be the one to dishonor ye. To ruin ye."

She took a step back, and now the tears did spill from her eyes. "Nay, ye'll let Anders have that honor. That's why ye came as yer twin, aye? Yer da agreed to the betrothal— in his name?"

He shook his head. What could he say? Anders' reputation was well known, even by Mariota after the time she spent at

Sutherland, and he had to keep up the charade, for all their sakes. "Naught is final. Ye ken I willna allow that to happen."

She crossed her arms and glared at him. "How do ye think to prevent it, when ye are as tied to Sutherland as I am to MacKay?" She shook her head, her sudden sadness making her shoulders drop. "Yer brother will be a poor substitute for ye," she said. "And he will ken it. God, how I pity him. What ye have done will break all three of our hearts." She shook her head, turned, and stalked away.

Stellan stood in the hallway and watched her go, unable to move to find a way forward or backward. He'd made a mess of this. A mess that could quickly become a disaster if he didn't keep his distance from her. But he'd gotten the answer he came for. He wanted Mariota. She wanted him, not his twin.

But she would soon be betrothed to Anders, and for Stellan, no other lass would do. He spun and beat on the oaken door, oblivious to the damage he did to his fists. The pain in his heart and the fury over what he and Anders had done to Mariota over-rode every other sensation.

MARIOTA, blood still singing, made her way to her chamber and locked the door behind her. She leaned against it, needing the stout oak at her back to support her, pressing her palms into the grain of the wood, fighting to feel something other than the desperate longing within her, the pulse of her blood in her nipples and her core, and the melted butter warmth that filled her lower belly.

Stellan had come to MacKay to be with her for what time they could spend together. Not enough. Not close to time enough.

She was bound for a powerful alliance with Anders, a man she liked but did not love. Or she could have a vastly different future than she'd ever imagined with Stellan, the brother she'd left in the hallway downstairs, the brother who lit her body on fire and made her ache for his touch, his kiss, and more. The brother who'd had that effect on her from the moment he first touched her waist to help her down from her horse while she protected Valkyrie. Anders would be a friend. Stellan, her lover, the man she wanted with her every night, filling the deep ache within her, and waking her every morning with kisses and caresses that proved his need for her. His love.

If she was forced to wed with his twin, she and Stellan would have to live in the torment of not being able to be with each other. Anders would share in their misery. He would know she could never love him the way she loved Stellan. Never desire him the way she desired his twin. It was so unfair. It made her wish Stellan had not come. If she had never truly known what his touch, his kiss, would do to her, she might have been able to live her life with his brother, content, if not deliriously happy.

Did Stellan love her? Could he?

Stellan would be as conflicted as she now was. He'd all but told her how torn being with her made him. His oath to his clan was even tighter than hers. He was a male heir, the expected heir. She? She had been responsible for her twin brother's death— or so her father believed. She was not the heir her father expected or wanted. She was the one he blamed for the loss of his son. No wonder he hated her so. No wonder he didn't protect her from Alber.

Then why had he bothered to take an army to Sutherland to fetch her back? Why did he even want her to stay here if he didn't want her to be laird? What would he have done if she hadn't run away from her clan?

She pushed away from the door and paced to the window. From it, she could see the mews and the stable, both symbols to her of freedom. How different would she feel if she looked out on the ocean or the smithy or… she shook her head.

Stellan Sutherland had her head spinning, her emotions in a tangle and her body still thrumming with unmet needs. He owed her a way to fix this. And she would get it from him if it was the last thing she did in this life.

⁂

FRUSTRATED by his situation with Mariota, and with Mariota's rejection by her father, Stellan went to speak to him again, something he'd meant to do before now. It might not be his wisest move to confront the man when his own blood still roared in his veins, but some things called for passion. Calm reason seemed not to have worked. So he'd do this now and do what he could to steer the MacKay to a better outcome for his daughter. As he stalked down the hall, he pondered how to protect her without insulting the laird. He wished again Anders was here. None of this would have happened. He would never know how much he wanted and needed Mariota. His twin would be the kind of leader who could improve the lives of the people at MacKay. And for this confrontation, Anders' diplomatic skills would likely prove much more successful in making the laird see sense.

And he knew every bit of that was pure bollocks.

MacKay welcomed him into the solar. If the man knew what Stellan and Mariota had been doing only a few minutes before, Stellan was certain his welcome would have been different. Frostier. More dangerous. Then again, he was about to beard this lion in his den. That could be the most dangerous thing he'd done since he arrived.

"What can I do for ye, Anders?" The MacKay gestured Stellan to a seat and leaned back in his own, hands loosely clasped over his belly.

"I'm here to appeal to ye again about Alber. He remains a threat to yer daughter."

MacKay snorted. "She's an emotional lass. He's a rough man. A warrior. But he willna actually harm her."

Was her father being deliberately obtuse? "He already has. I dinna ken why ye discount the danger he presents." Stellan held up a hand to forestall MacKay. "He threatened her and he put his hands on her. Have ye forgotten I told ye the last time he got her alone, he tried to smother her? Mayhap she didna admit to ye that he has also attempted to ruin her. Ye ken he nearly killed the hunting hawk, Valkyrie."

"After he was attacked."

"Nay. Before." And why was MacKay focused on what he'd said about Valkyrie and not about the threats to Mariota? "Ye must accept the threat is real and banish Alber."

MacKay straightened up in his chair, stood, and planted his fists on the desktop. "'Tis my decision to make."

Damn, he had taken offense, just as Stellan had feared. "Of course it is," Stellan told him. "I wouldna suggest otherwise. But I dinna think ye have been told the full extent of Alber's harassment of yer daughter. Yer heir. I urge ye to take it seriously." Did MacKay not realize how Alber's actions could be perceived? As an insult and challenge to his laird, so public and ongoing that Stellan judged the clan must consider their laird weak, since he let it go on. Stellan had sense enough not to compound the challenge MacKay faced by telling him what he was thinking. But the man should have figured that out on his own and done something about it. For his sake and his daughter's. And his clan's.

MacKay resumed his seat. "'Tis nay so simple as that."

"With a betrothal pending, nay, 'tisna. If Alber thinks she will soon wed a warrior able to defend her better than anyone yet has, what do you think he's likely to do?" Stellan took a breath. He'd almost said her husband would be able to defend her better than her father ever had, but had caught himself just in time. "For some reason, he covets her birthright. He wants to be laird, any way he can."

MacKay frowned, giving Stellan hope than his words were penetrating the thick shield the man kept around his thoughts and feelings. What would it take to get through to him?

"Mariota had nay reason to lie while at Sutherland about what happened to her," Stellan said, pushing his argument. "And nay reason to lie to her father and laird."

MacKay's nod spurred Stellan on. "Ye should be working together. As my brother and the Sutherland do." As *he* and his father did, he almost said, but saved himself from the gaffe.

"In what way?" MacKay seemed genuinely interested.

"Stellan confers with the laird daily, attends all meetings, judgements, and the like. He plans for the clan with our da. Crops, buildings, new crafts, fairs. Da has given over some tasks to him, such as visiting outlying crofts and seeing to their well-being."

"Only the heir, and nay ye, the spare?"

"I do as well when I can. He uses me in other ways, as well."

"Interesting. But I canna see a lass riding to outlying crofts…"

"Why no', with sufficient guard? She wants to learn from ye. For the good of MacKay, she must. She may no' be able to swing a longsword to go to war for the clan, but she is reputed to be a skilled archer, and can defend MacKay's walls. And train other lasses to do the same. She could name a war leader to command MacKay warriors in the event they are needed. I have seen how well she has trained Valkyrie. She has values beyond the alliance ye contemplate that perhaps ye havena taken advantage of."

Someone knocked on the door, forestalling any reply MacKay might have made. He glanced up and called out, "Come."

Stellan stood, knowing he'd lost MacKay's attention. "I'll leave ye to think on what I've said," he told him and left as a man he didn't know entered. Stellan thought MacKay heard him. Perhaps he would change his thinking about the value of his daughter and heir, and do more to protect her.

CHAPTER 14

Two days later, Stellan was wondering if he would ever get a chance to be alone with Mariota again. She was angry with him, and he didn't blame her. He was angry with himself. He'd made her want him— someone she couldn't have. If the pain she felt was anything like the pain he carried in his heart — and lower —she might never speak to him again.

He was no better off. Though his men stood watch over her, he'd passed up the chance to go hunting, instead hanging around the keep hoping to run into her, or at least to see her from a distance like a lovesick lad. Disgusted with himself, he'd retreated to the stable to care for his horse. He straightened from checking its hooves and put a hand on its mane. Looking at the animal, he saw a way out. He really should leave. Send for Anders, meet him in the woods and swap places. Put an end to this torture and do his best to forget what Mariota meant to him.

He couldn't. He owed Mariota more than to disappear suddenly. She would know the real Anders had arrived. Leaving was a cowardly move. He wasn't a coward, and she deserved better. So did his twin. So did he. He just didn't know yet how to clean up the mess he'd made.

He patted the horse's neck and left the stall. He was crossing the bailey when the laird's hunting party came back.

The rusty stench of blood filled the air. The laird, injured and insensible, rode double with one of his men, held upright by an arm around his chest. Blood drenched his clothes and the man supporting him. Another man leapt from his horse and ran past Stellan into the keep, shouting for the healer as several others pulled their laird down and carried him toward the keep's now open door.

Stellan went to the man who'd supported the laird on his horse. "What happened?"

"The boar got him, but he got the boar, too."

Only then did Stellan notice a boar, dripping red from several wounds, draped over the back of another horse. Once the laird was injured, they hadn't had time to field dress it.

"Damned bad luck it twitched when he bent over what he thought was the dead beast and got a tusk in his side for his troubles," the man added.

"Is yer healer good?"

"Aye. Good enough? We'll see."

"Where was Alber?" Stellan knew he'd gone with the hunters, but worry that he might come back and cause trouble was another reason Stellan had stayed in the keep.

The man eyed him, then tilted his head toward the other horses abandoned in the bailey by the men carrying their laird to the healer. "With one of the men. He didna do this."

Where was Alber now? Stellan looked around the bailey and spotted him entering the stable, leading two of the hunting party's horses inside.

Where was Mariota? In her chamber? She must be told. She might need to be with her da to get his orders when he awoke. If he did.

Stellan charged inside and up the stairs to her chamber. The door was closed, and probably locked since he'd seen his men down in the great hall. They would have seen the MacKay brought in and heard what was going on. He pounded on her door, then knocked even louder when he got no answer.

"Coming." He heard her voice softly through the thick wood. "Who is it?"

"Ste…Anders," he said. He needed to be more careful. If he'd said Stellan, and someone overheard, he'd have a lot of explaining to do.

He was still frowning when Mariota opened the door and looked up at him, a question in her moss-colored gaze.

"Is something wrong?"

"They just brought in yer da, injured by the boar he killed. He's been taken to the healer."

Her eyes widened and she gasped, turned and ran for her boots. "Help me," she pleaded, jamming a foot into one. Stellan set aside his relief that she would accept his help, knelt and got her other boot on and laced, then pulled her to her feet. She was shaking and breathing too fast.

"Calm yerself, lass. 'Tis likely the healer is still working on him. He'll need ye to be steady enough to listen if he has anything to tell ye or any orders for ye. And ye need to be calm for yer people."

She nodded and headed out the door, leaving Stellan to close it behind them. He followed her rapid footsteps to the herbal and paused in the doorway, not certain whether he should go in. The men who'd carried in their laird had gone. The healer was alone with her patient. She finished stitching up the laird's side as Mariota approached and blanched. Stellan moved behind her and led her to a seat.

"I'll be done in a wee," the healer said while slathering a foul-smelling poultice on the wound. "Yer da is made of strong stuff. The tusk didna penetrate too deep, so despite all the blood ye see, he should be fine in a fortnight, I'd say. He'll need rest and someone to handle his responsibilities for a few days. That would be ye, lass, aye?"

Mariota nodded. "Has he said anything?"

The healer shook her head. "Nay, ye can see he lost a lot of blood. I got a draught in him for the pain so he should sleep a while yet. While I clean up, sit with him in case he does wake. Ye, too, lad," she said to Stellan. "He may wake thinking the boar is still moving, and try to avoid it. Ye need to keep him still until he realizes where he is."

"I will," Stellan promised, his gaze on Mariota. Tears glimmered in her eyes. After all her father had done to, and not done for her, she still cared about him. Perhaps even loved him. It hurt to see someone you cared about injured and suffering. Even if you didn't like them much. Mariota had little reason to like her father, but he was still her father, so Stellan sympathized with what she was going through.

The healer left to see to herself, leaving the two of them to sit vigil over the MacKay laird. Mariota alternated between sitting by her father and pacing around the chamber, walking off her anxiety. Each time she passed near Stellan, he wanted to reach for her hand, to offer what comfort he could, but she avoided his touch and kept going. As time passed, a few from the hunting party looked in for a moment, but let them be when they found nothing had changed.

"Cook has the boar," one reported. "I'd wager the MacKay will enjoy eating that bastard more than most."

Mariota, again sitting by her father, choked out a laugh. "Aye, nay doubt he will."

The man gave her a grin, nodded to Stellan and to his sleeping laird, and left them.

"Boar broth is very good for a wounded man," Stellan said, trying to reassure her. "Or so the Sutherland healer often says. Though perhaps she means it much as yer man just said, as a way to get revenge on the beast."

"Which would make the meat even better when he's ready for it," Mariota agreed, giving Stellan a sad smile. "'Twill be a day or two, I'd guess, before he'll want that."

"Mayhap, but the healer said the wound wasna bad."

The MacKay twitched.

Stellan stood and went to stand by him in case he did as the healer feared and thrashed about.

"Canna tell them," MacKay muttered.

Mariota stood, eyebrows creased under a frown. "Canna tell what?"

"Promised her."

"Promised who, Da? Promised what?"

He mumbled some more, then subsided.

Stellan traded a frown with Mariota. "What did that mean?"

"I dinna ken."

"The lad is called Alber," MacKay suddenly said. "After his da."

Mariota paled and her eyes went wide as she studied her father, then looked again at Stellan. "I dinna like this."

He didn't either. It wasn't much of a leap to think that the MacKay had promised a woman to raise her son. Who was the father, and why was he important enough to the laird to take in a lad who was not his? Stellan could see another possibility, that he had a child with his friend's wife. That would explain why Mariota hadn't been told, and why he had let Alber run wild as he had. Did Alber know?

Nay, that didn't feel right. "We shouldna jump to conclusions, lass." Though he had, and he knew she had, too.

"Da has much to answer for if this means what I fear it does."

"I dinna think it does. There's a simpler explanation."

She clenched her jaw and shook her head. "Ye are right. That doesna make sense. He's no' been pleased to have a daughter as his heir. Alber is older than I by at least two years. Why would Da no' claim him? He could have been named heir already."

"Because he isna yer brother," Stellan told her, sure of the feeling in his gut. MacKay would have acknowledged a son, and he called Alber someone else's son. "There's something else going on."

"But what?" Mariota's frustration was evident in her tone and her clenched fists. "What could Da have promised to a woman about Alber?"

"None of those things may be connected, lass," Stellan told her. "He's injured and dreaming, talking in his sleep. They may be as random as—"

"As a lass fleeing her home running into the only honorable group of hunters in the Highlands?"

After the lies he'd told her, she could still say that? Her words warmed his heart and he smiled. "I'm glad ye think so."

"So we wait. And when he does wake up, it will be time for him to tell his heir the truth."

Stellan's chest twinged. The MacKay wasn't the only one keeping secrets, and though Mariota now knew his, Stellan dreaded her father's reaction when he found out.

❧

MARIOTA KNEW one thing for certain. While her da was recovering from his injury, she had to act in his stead as laird. "I dinna want to leave him in case he says something else, but I need to get a look at his desk, at what he's been working on, so I can carry the load for him until he's better," she told Stellan.

"I think that can wait a wee," he told her, taking her hand and urging her to a seat. "At least until the healer returns, ye should stay with him. I'll stay, too, if ye wish."

She smiled at him and nodded. "Of course I do. While we wait, perhaps ye will tell me more about what Sutherland shares with his heir so I have a better sense of what to look for."

"Yer da hasna trained ye as he should have to take over when he's gone. I'm happy to help as much as I can."

"He seems to think he'll live forever," Mariota said. She looked over at his sleeping form and frowned. "That, or he's been training someone else while letting me— and the clan —believe I am his heir."

"Do ye have any reason to think he has done that?"

She pressed her lips together, then shook her head. "Nay, no' really. Just a sense that I will never be laird. He has hinted that he is considering others. I overheard him talking to one of his council about naming a *tanist*, someone who could step in for me. I suppose he thinks I'd be a figurehead, nay more."

"Ye have a sense? Do ye believe in such feelings?"

"Do ye?"

"I dinna ken. All I ken is that my twin and I know things about each other that others dinna sense or feel the way we do. 'Twas stronger when we were lads, and one reason Da fostered us apart. We think he wanted us to lose the ability. We almost did. 'Tis different than kenning the future, but 'tis…"

"Strange and wonderful? I envy ye being so close to yer twin. I —I never got that chance."

"What do ye mean?"

Should she tell him? Explain why her da treated her with such disdain? It might not explain all, but it might help him understand, and perhaps she'd feel better by sharing the pain of the tragedy that changed so many lives.

"I had a twin brother," she admitted and glanced at Stellan to see his reaction.

He looked surprised, but gestured for her to continue.

"He was eldest by some minutes, I was told. No matter who was eldest, he would have been the heir, and all my father's concerns about no' having a lad to follow him would never have happened. But I was the more adventurous twin, even at a very young age. I'd always been fascinated by birds. Their colors, their songs, their flights, the way their wings caught the sunlight, the sound of their bairns in the nest. 'Tis why I was able to climb to a hawk nest and secure eggs for the mews. Why I have Valkyrie. Over the years, I grew strong from running and climbing trees to reach the height of a hawk's nest." She shrugged. "We were seven when I climbed up a tree and my brother, who'd been teased by some older lads and called a bairn, decided to follow me."

Stellan pressed his lips together, then asked, "He fell?"

"Aye. I've been told most of this. I dinna remember it clearly. His head hit a rock. I remember screaming at all the blood, not knowing what else to do. My twin was dead as soon as he hit the ground." She hugged her arms around her middle. "I could see below me, people running and my da scooping his son up and running back to the keep with his body, crying out the entire way. After seeing my twin fall, I was terrified to climb out of the tree. But I think once I stopped screaming and started crying silently, everyone forgot I was there. I had to be brave and get myself down. I knew what had happened was bad, but that was all I could comprehend at that age."

"I'm sorry, lass. I canna imagine losing my twin. How that must have felt."

"Dinna be. Mother did her best to protect me, but she was as devastated as Da was. And a year later, she was dead of the next bairn she tried to give him— another son." She took a breath. "I... I canna recall what she looked like. Only that I've been told I resemble her more than my da. So did my twin."

"So ye remind him—"

"Of her, aye. And of what he lost. Of how unsuitable I am to take my twin's place. I think 'tis why he does little to protect me from Alber. I'm certain he blames me for what happened."

"'Twas nay yer fault. Ye were a wean, like yer brother."

"And now I'm grown, and he isna. And my da is older and needs an heir who can be the MacKay in truth. I've done everything I could to be the son he wanted, but naught I do is ever good enough. I'll never be good enough as laird, either. He's made certain of that."

"Age doesna always bring wisdom, lass, or forgiveness. But there's still time." Stellan frowned at her sleeping father.

"Nay enough, I think. And I often think this isna the life I want. Nay the life I should have. There are men in the clan who would make much better lairds, men who can fight if the trouble between Domnhall and Mar continues. They will see me as weak and MacKay as ripe for the taking, along with Ross. If only Da would make that decision and free me from MacKay to marry elsewhere. But he's stubborn, and he's got it in his head my only value is to marry for an alliance with another clan. To bring a strong husband here to be the laird in deed if no' in name."

"Would ye be happy with that? To be a figurehead?"

"It would depend on the man, would it no'?"

Stellan shook his head. "No matter the man, I dinna believe ye would."

The healer returned, and since her da had remained deeply asleep and silent, Mariota opted to leave him in her care and go to his solar. Stellan asked Mariota to stay with her long enough for him to check in with his men and assign two to escort her and to stay with her while she worked. She was grateful for his care, but worried how he'd think of her now that he knew she'd killed her twin. Nay, he wouldn't think that way. It had been a tragic accident. Despite how her father continued to punish her for it, she hoped Stellan would not.

EVERY TIME STELLAN learned more about Mariota's history, his heart broke for her a little more. He knew better than to fall for the fallacy that she needed rescuing. She was doing her best to rescue herself, while still hopeful that she could bring her father around to treating her as a father ought. As a laird ought.

But if she wanted him to, Stellan would be proud to help her in any way he could. He would, though that fact surprised him.

He wanted to help her succeed, even though he didn't want her to remain at MacKay. The irony was not lost on him.

Given the lack of training she'd gotten from her father, he suspected that helping her make sense of whatever was on his desk in the solar would be of the greatest immediate use of his skills.

He rounded up Camus and Gregor and sent them to escort her to the solar and to stand guard outside the door. Then he headed up to his chamber to get the one thing he suspected he would need while pouring over someone else's cramped hand-writing and columns of numbers— his spectacles. It annoyed him that he sometimes needed them, when Anders never did. Thank-fully, both of them had excellent distance vision. But Anders had not spent as many hours as he had with their father going over Sutherland's ledgers. And Mariota had never seen either one of them reading anything, so she would not have suspected Anders for using them. Not that it mattered any more.

He carried the folded-up spectacles concealed in one hand. He didn't want anyone to know the Sutherland heir used them. It was a weakness that vexed him, but at the same time, it was one he shared with his father who was one of the most powerful lairds in Scotland, and in his day, one of the most feared on the battlefield. Stellan was glad the wee bits of glass helped keep things clear for both of them.

He nodded to his men in passing and entered the MacKay's solar. Mariota wore a frown of concentration— or was that confusion? She didn't notice him come in.

"Mariota," he said softly, hoping not to startle her.

She looked up and her expression smoothed into one of relief. "Ach, ye're here," she said and leaned back. "Ye said ye worked with yer da on Sutherland's ledgers. Do ye think ye could help me make sense of Da's?"

"If it will help ye, I'd be pleased to try."

She stood and carried the one she'd been bent over to the

table in the middle of the chamber. "I ken a wee about planting schedules and such, but this doesna make sense to me."

She gestured for him to take a seat.

One glance at the page told Stellan his spectacles would be needed. He unfolded them, wiped them clean on his sleeve and put them on the bridge of his nose.

"What on earth...?"

"They're called spectacles. They help me read small hand-writing and numbers."

"How?"

"They make things look larger and sharper."

"Does Anders use them, too?"

"Nay. I need them because I've spent more years reading and helping Da with his ledgers."

"Of course," she commented and studied his face. "Will they fall off?"

"Aye. Sometimes. When I look down, I hold them in place."

"That must get tiring."

"'Tis tolerable."

She grinned. "Somehow, they make ye seem— I canna believe I'm going to say this —but they make ye seem even more attrac-tive. Wiser. As if ye keep secrets ye willna share."

Stellan fought not to react. His very presence was a secret he couldn't share with most, though she now knew. Instead of replying, he gave her an Anders grin and bent to study the ledger page puzzling her.

Two hours later, they'd made sense of most of the notations in it. "Dear God, Da has been sending raiders into MacLeod," Mariota exclaimed near the end. "And does this indicate one into Sutherland?" She pointed to several marks. "The count of cattle and sheep increased suddenly after each of these."

"I found nay evidence of recent raids on our crofts. Why MacLeod?"

"I dinna ken, but that must stop or we'll have more trouble on our border. Whether the incursion into Sutherland was real or only rumored, I appreciate yer da's forbearance. I wonder if Da does."

Stellan approved of her intentions. That revelation was only one among several that no other clan should be privy to, but Mariota had needed help and Stellan reminded himself that he could keep secrets, especially those that didn't affect Sutherland. Still, her father would be furious if he ever found out she'd shown him this ledger. "Ye willna tell yer da I saw this. He willna like it."

"Nay, I canna. He'd be furious. We've altered naught, and now I understand his thinking, I can take care of most clan business until he's better. I ken enough now to ask him to explain the rest — like those raids."

"Good, lass." He folded his spectacles.

"I couldna have done it without ye. Thank ye, Stellan. I… I'm sorry I got so angry earlier. I—"

He pressed his lips together and nodded, regret tearing at the edges of his satisfaction for helping her. "Ye had reason, lass. I regret what Anders and I did. What I did. The lies. For the trouble it will cause. But never for the chance to be with ye." That mattered to him. He was more and more certain that he wanted it to matter to her just as much.

To distract himself he asked, "Do ye want to go check on yer da?"

"The healer wouldha sent someone if anything changed." She closed the ledger and pushed it away, lifted her arms and stretched.

The movement lifted her breasts and tightened the fabric across them, making Stellan's mouth water. He was glad she'd leaned her head back and closed her eyes, or she would have seen him staring at her. And seen the hunger in his gaze. When she dropped her arms and opened her eyes, he looked away. He'd told her an encounter like they'd had in the storeroom could not happen again. But his gaze would have made a lie of that, and the way she tempted him, if she touched him again in response, might have made stopping himself impossible.

He stood and stepped away. "I'll see ye at supper?"

A frown flitted across her features, faster than a falcon could dive on its prey, then she nodded. "Aye, supper."

He left her before anything else could happen between them.

CHAPTER 15

$\mathcal{W}$atching Stellan's abrupt departure, Mariota's heart sank. She'd hoped for some time alone with him to— well— she wasn't sure what she wanted to do. Pick up where they'd left off in the supply closet? A frisson of remembered yearning tingled along her nerves from her belly to her fingertips and back. She wanted his arms around her, his hands stroking her, his lips teasing her, but none of that might ever happen again. The thought made her regret turn to frustration with herself for letting Stellan walk out. She stood and flattened her hands on the tabletop. She should have stopped him when he stood, grabbed his hand and pulled him down to kiss her. If their time together was limited, shouldn't they enjoy it before they lost each other?

He'd done his best to build a wall between them, to keep their feelings for each other from running wild, a conflagration neither of them could control.

But she didn't know why.

Yes, she did. Her father would be apoplectic if he knew what they'd done already, much less where her thoughts were straying now. She didn't want to find out what he would do if he knew what was simmering between her and the Sutherland heir.

She sank into a chair, her knees suddenly weak with both worry and relief.

Stellan. Not Anders. The pull between them had been with Stellan all along.

That should make her feel better, but it complicated things, too. Before she'd met Stellan, she'd wondered if she would ever be accepted as the MacKay laird. With Stellan in the keep, she was becoming more and more convinced that this was not the life she wanted. Her father's refusal to explain Alber's presence and his neglect of her training had taken a toll. But no matter how miserable it made her, until he was better, she would do what she must for the sake of the clan. Still, she couldn't keep her traitorous heart from imagining life with Stellan at Sutherland rather than here, with Anders.

She probably shouldn't depend on Stellan's help with any more of her da's ledgers. Her da would be furious that she'd shared as much of them with Stellan as she had. Not that he'd seen anything she thought he could use to harm MacKay in the future. Still, her da would call it one more reason she was ill-suited to be laird. Was there a MacKay she could lean on? One of her da's advisors? Would Seamus know enough to be able to help her?

And what would Alber be doing while the laird spent time healing?

"Mariota." Seamus called her name from the solar's doorway. "Though they ken me, these fine lads willna allow me to enter without yer leave."

"Aye, come in," she said, grateful that his arrival distracted her from her thoughts.

"I have some news ye will want to hear," he told her, pulling a chair out from the opposite side of the table and seating himself with a sigh. "I have more to add from some of the old warriors about Alber's early days at MacKay. They are all in agreement that yer da brought him when he was about eleven years old."

"Why dinna I remember more about him?"

"Because ye were younger, I guess. He was homesick as a lad. He didna fit in. Didna try to fit in. Kept to himself and sulked because he didna get the attention from yer da that ye did. Played at being the heir. He thought himself better than the rest of us for having been chosen to come here by the laird, and only obeyed yer da."

"Because Da saved him? No one told him why?"

"Perhaps. I didna find out anything about that."

Mariota thought back to what she'd overheard her father mutter in his sleep. "Is there any chance he could be my da's bastard son?"

"I dinna believe so, but whether he is or nay, perhaps he thought he was, and it shaped him, made him boastful. Even convinced him he would replace ye in yer da's affections and become his heir. "

Mariota snorted at that. She tried to summon some sympathy for the young Alber Seamus' tale made her picture. But she couldn't. "He was old enough when it all happened, he should remember his parents. And he has had plenty of time and support in MacKay to get over any childish notions he might have imagined."

Seamus shrugged. "I would say he never did."

Mariota nodded. "I would, as well."

❧

TWO DAYS LATER, the MacKay had recovered enough to resume desk work in his solar. After spending time with him going over what she'd done while he was resting, Mariota judged him well enough to confront him. She wanted to hear his explanation for what he said while injured and under the healer's sleeping

171

potion. She told Stellan where she was going and let him escort her to the solar, but refused him entry. She needed to have this out with her father in private. No Stellan, no James, no Seamus. No one but the two of them.

Initially, he reacted much as she expected, with his usual denials and demands to keep out of anything to do with Alber. But perhaps he was weaker than she'd judged, because before long, he gave in.

He leaned his elbows on the table where they sat. "Ye want to ken why Alber is still at MacKay? Because I made a promise to his poor mother. His father was a friend. I cared about his family." At her frown, he added, "Nay, no' like that. I loved yer mother." He sighed and sat back. "Alber is nay my son. If he were, I wouldha claimed him years ago."

Her belly tightened. Of course he would have claimed a *male* heir. She pressed her lips together and let him talk.

"His village was burned on a day I was supposed to be there but didna go. His father and most of the men in the village were killed trying to put out the fire. At the time, I thought their deaths were my fault because I was often seen there, and believed someone had tried to kill me— to eliminate the MacKay heir. We never found out who did it. It could have been accidental, but as fast as it spread?" he said and shrugged. "Nay. I've carried guilt over those deaths ever since. His mother couldna care for her young son, and begged me to take him with me. To care for him and see that he grew up to be a man. I couldna refuse her and leave the lad to his fate in a ruined village."

It was a sad story, but it didn't explain why he allowed the grown-up Alber to threaten her. "Da, some in the clan think he believes that he is yer bastard, and that belief is behind his arrogance, and his resentment of me. Partly, at least."

"Why partly?"

"Because years ago, he tried to accost me. I did what Cook taught me and disabled him."

MacKay winced, then gestured for her to continue.

"He's never forgiven or forgotten that I bested him. Worse, that I have had to do so twice more lately. The first time with Valkyrie's help."

Her father shook his head. "'Tis worse than I kenned."

That made her hackles rise. "Ye did ken. Or ye wouldha had ye listened to what I told ye again and again." She pushed back from the table and stood. "I canna believe ye continue to honor a promise made to protect a young lad until well past the age when ye shouldha forced that lad to grow up. Or forced him back to where he came from. 'Tis yer fault Alber is the way he is."

"Hold yer tongue, daughter. Ye may no' speak to me that way."

"Nay? Someone must. Ye have ignored the danger to me and excused the source of that danger again and again. Who else will he harm before ye see who he really is? Must I lie before ye, ruined and forced to wed with him so he can take over our clan—or even dead once there's a son he can act as regent for —before ye believe me?"

"He will do naught. I will see to it."

She'd heard that before. "Ye owe me yer oath. What will ye do about him?"

His silence lasted long enough that Mariota didn't know if he was thinking or fighting to control the fury she had aroused in him. He looked away from her and drummed his fingers on the table top. Then his mouth pressed into a thin line. "I dinna ken, but I will deal with him," he promised.

"Send him away," she insisted. "He deserves to be banished or worse. I tell ye again, he tried to ruin me. He tried to crush my skull, then flattened his palm on my face to smother me. He nearly killed a valuable hunting hawk. The other lasses avoid him. He's hazarded more than ye will ever want to hear."

He closed his eyes as if trying to unsee the images she painted with her words. "I will consider it, lass." Then he met her gaze and frowned. "Ye have yer friends here. Keep them close by for now. The Sutherlands, too, I suppose. Though I think they've overstayed their welcome. They should leave soon. Their presence says MacKay guards are no' enough to protect ye."

Mariota's heart clenched at the thought of Stellan leaving her behind. "They havena been. And later? Ye are right that the Sutherlands canna remain forever. Neither can Alber, Da. If ye canna deal with him, I will have to. He will force me to."

WHILE MARIOTA MET with her father, Stellan called his men together in his chamber.

"We dinna have much time. Mariota is with her da, and I dinna expect that discussion to last long. Ye need to ken our time here is no' unlimited. We may leave soon, either by being asked to depart, or by summons from Sutherland. Either way, be ready to go."

Their reaction was exactly what he expected. They didn't want to leave until they knew Mariota would be safe from Alber, and that things at MacKay were stable.

"Ye make me proud, lads, that ye take her safety so seriously. I do, too."

"Ye care about more than her safety, Stellan," Erik said.

"Ye kenned?" Stellan's mouth fell open, eliciting a laugh from the others. He shrugged, then grinned. "I shouldha guessed. Ye've been careful no' to call me by either name. Thank ye."

"We're with ye, no matter when or why we stay or go," Camus told him. "Ye ken that."

"I do, and I'm grateful. Naught is decided, but I hope Mariota will go with us."

They broke out in cheers that fell silent as Stellan waved them off.

"We kenned there was something between ye," Elias said, and

rolled his eyes, then turned his wide-eyed gaze on Gregor, making the others laugh.

Stellan did, too. He couldn't help it. He had chosen these men purposefully, some of the best warriors at Sutherland, but some of its best men, too. "Ye must no' breathe a word," he cautioned. "No' even to discuss anything we say here now among yerselves lest ye be overheard. Dinna tell a soul, I dinna care how deep in yer cups ye are. Just prepare for any eventuality. Alber is still a threat. Stay sharp."

At that moment, he heard the scrape of a boot on the plank flooring outside the door. Signaling for quiet, he stood, rushed to the door and flung it open.

No one was there. Had he imagined the sound? He looked down the hall toward the stairs in time to see Alber's shoulders and head disappear down them. Nay!

Was he off to tell the MacKay? Or to hole up and think how to use what he heard against the Sutherlands? Stellan considered chasing him, even took a step out into the hall toward the stairs, but he knew it was too late. Alber could have gone in several directions from the great hall. Stellan closed the door and turned back to his men. "I am discovered," he told them. "Alber was out there."

The men jumped to their feet, ready to give chase, but Stellan gestured for them to sit back down. "He may have heard naught, but we canna depend on that. We can be certain he will use anything he knows against us. Against me. We may be leaving sooner than expected."

"We have to do something. He's the source of trouble here, and now he thinks to take on Sutherland? We canna allow that."

"*Dinna fash,*" Stellan said firmly. "We willna allow him to. His days are numbered. He just doesna ken it yet."

He let them talk for another moment, then held up a hand. "Elias and Erik, head down and hang out near the solar. Mariota should leave there soon. I dinna want Alber anywhere near her.

Gregor, check the stables. If he's gone there, he's going to leave the keep. That makes him too hard to track. Find out. Camus, stay by Mariota's door. If Alber comes back up, let him think she's in there. Wait a wee after he leaves, then come down to the great hall and settle down as if ye are off duty. That will confuse him."

"What are ye going to do?"

The question was on all their faces. Stellan grinned. "Wander about. Give him a chance to find me rather than her. When she leaves the solar, as long as Alber is nowhere nearby, take her to the healer. I'd like him to think she's locked up tight in her chamber, just waiting for him to try something. But I dinna want her anywhere near that."

"Why no'? The lass has beaten him before."

Stellan nodded at Erik's question. "She has. How many times do ye think he'll fall for her tricks?"

Erik pursed his lips. His expression was his answer.

"Aye, never again. He's angry and out for vengeance, but that doesna make him stupid."

"I'd like to make him dead," Camus muttered.

"Get in line," Stellan told him, then grinned. "Ye each ken what to do. Out with ye."

After the men left, Stellan made certain he was fully but discretely armed, with extra blades tucked in his boots, the small of his back, even up a sleeve, secured by a tie sewn inside the shirt. Let Alber try something. He was ready.

CHAPTER 16

Though Stellan sometimes got a vague sense of feelings that he might have picked up from Anders, he didn't expect to hear from him. But later that evening, after wandering the keep but never finding Alber, a ghillie brought a note from his twin, signed "*Stellan.*" He grinned at that before he read the missive. The rest of it was not as amusing.

News about Mar being on the move had reached Sutherland. Domnhall still held Dingwall, but for how long? It lay south of Sutherland territory, but close enough to require watchfulness on Sutherland's part, especially as Mar was determined to boot Domnhall back to Islay and out of the disputed Ross territory on mainland Scotland.

Their da was watchful but not expecting Mar to bring trouble north to Sutherland. Rather, he'd stay on Domnhall's tail and continue the disagreement over Ross territory. Anders helpfully informed him that Sutherland had sent a missive to MacKay with what they knew, offering to share information and ally, with the MacKay's consent, for mutual protection, with or without a betrothal between their clans.

Stellan could understand their concerns, but was glad he did not have to be the one to inform the MacKay. As the second son away from home, he would not normally have been privy to Sutherland's thinking and didn't want to have to explain why he had been informed.

But the last bit of news from Anders disturbed Stellan the most. In keeping with his concerns, Sutherland wanted "Anders" to return home, and intended to send him on a scouting mission to see what he could discover about Mar's intentions. If there had been no further threat to the MacKay heir, he was instructed to leave her in the care of her father and her trusted MacKay guards.

Stellan fought the urge to crumple the missive into a ball in his fist. Should he refuse his laird's order and send word to Sutherland that the situation here was still precarious? Anders would convince their father why he was reluctant to leave Mariota. Without Sutherland guards' presence to keep her father honest in his efforts to protect her, Stellan couldn't predict what would happen. The news about Mar added a sense of urgency to Stellan's concern over Mariota's safety. She was still in danger within her keep, but if MacKay was forced to get involved in Mar's incursion, taking many of his best men with him, he could leave his daughter in an even more precarious position.

Was he even recovered well enough to ride and fight? That would be a question for the healer to answer.

Stellan ran a hand through is hair. Should he and his twin switch back? He'd have to return home so that Da would see the two of them together, then he could send the real Anders out on the scouting mission. That would keep Anders busy and away from MacKay. Stellan trusted his twin. But he knew him well. If the real Anders came to MacKay, he would spend a lot of time around Mariota, perhaps fall for her himself, even though she professed to love only Stellan. And with Anders at MacKay, the betrothal their father had proposed could proceed— against Mariota's wishes. And his own. That, Stellan could not allow.

WHEN THE MACKAY summoned him to his solar the next day, Stellan was still wrestling with what to do about the Sutherland's summons and whether it made sense to switch places with his twin. That would pull Alber's fangs and make anything he'd overheard less useful, though not useless. He could still cause trouble for Mariota and by extension, for Sutherland. Stellan walked into the solar and stopped inside the doorway. The laird sat behind his desk, but across from him, Mariota sat, glaring at the woman standing off to the side. Fionnuala.

Stellan knew instantly that all his concerns about his brother's missive and perhaps even what Alber thought he knew were about to become inconsequential. "Laird MacKay, ye sent for me?" He nodded to Mariota, then turned his attention back to her father, doing his best to remain calm.

"This woman brought me an interesting tale," MacKay said, but his frown made it clear he wasn't amused by her storytelling. "Perhaps ye would like to repeat what ye told me, Fionnuala."

She opened her mouth, then closed it again.

Stellan could see her tremble, and gave himself a moment to feel sorry for her, but she'd brought this on herself. If she was about to say what he expected, she could have kept it to herself. She could have protected Mariota. She should have.

In a quavering voice, she related what she saw when he and Mariota came out of the storage closet. "I held my tongue for days, but finally told my mate and she spread the tale from there. I'd guess by now the whole clan kens."

MacKay glanced at his daughter, gestured from Fionnuala toward the door, and said, "Ye may leave."

"Thank ye, laird," the woman said and got out as fast as she could.

Stellan was surprised to see how calmly Mariota seemed to be taking this revelation. Then again, he shouldn't be. She'd sworn to be strong around her father. But the effort must be costing her.

"Mariota, is her story true?"

"Aye." Mariota spat the word, the only indication of the anger simmering in her. "She came into the storage chamber where we were having a private conversation. We told her so, but she obviously imagined aught else."

"Did he ruin ye?"

"Nay, of course no'." She frowned at her father. "He cares for me."

"More than he should before ye are formally betrothed, it seems," MacKay said in agreement. He turned to Stellan and narrowed his eyes.

Here it comes. Stellan kept his breathing slow and even, waiting for whatever punishment MacKay would choose to mete out.

"Ye have two choices. Marry my daughter or leave. For Mariota's sake, I give ye until the day after tomorrow to decide. Daughter, ye have that much time to prepare yerself for yer wedding, or nay. 'Tis up to him and whatever influence ye may have over him."

When Stellan opened his mouth to object, MacKay waved him to silence. "Make yer peace with what ye did or leave MacKay. And be glad ye are who ye are. Any other lad would be on his way to the kirk right now. I extend Sutherland the courtesy of allowing ye to choose in the hopes that if ye remain, ye will be the husband my daughter needs, and the strength of the clan when I am gone that she canna be. Now get out." He turned his glare on his daughter. "Both of ye."

⋅≫⋅

STELLAN HELD the door for Mariota. She left the solar with her head high and her back straight. He had to admire her courage, though his heart broke for her yet again. Her father had not given her the choice of what to do. He'd given it to the Sutherland right in front of her. Once again, Mariota's wishes, and her value, were ignored by her father.

"I'm sorry, Mariota," Stellan told her back as she paced away.

She kept walking, traversing the great hall and yanking open the keep's heavy oaken door, dodging horses in the bailey until she passed outside the keep's gates and marched around the wall away from any guards on the wall walk. There she whirled and pinned him in place with one finger. "Dinna dare tell me ye regret what we did. I willna accept that."

"I willna tell ye that. I dinna regret a moment of it and given the chance—" he paused and swallowed, not daring to go on or Mariota would be in his arms, their mouths fused together and he wouldn't know how to stop. "But there is aught else I must tell ye."

She frowned, then looked up at the wall walk. Stellan glanced up at the same time to ensure no one was up there to hear what they said to each other.

"Well?"

If he wasn't still intent on wooing her, Stellan might have made light of their situation and asked her which of the options her father gave him she preferred. But first he had to take care of his immediate problem.

"I've been called home. I must leave tomorrow at the latest. I dinna wish to. I would stay here with ye if I could. I'm the twin who wants to wed ye. Never doubt that. But I canna. And for the same reason, ye canna. And if I tell yer father who I truly am—"

"He'll have ye lashed and send ye on yer way. Is that what ye think?"

"Or force us to wed and damn the consequences. I dinna want to steal yer birthright from ye, lass. No' if that is the future ye truly desire. I wouldna want anyone to do that to me, either, so I will understand if ye decide—"

"If I decide? I have nay say in this. The laird gave the choice to ye."

"I willna make a decision like that without ye. It affects ye as much— or more —than it does me. I willna treat ye as yer da often does." He hesitated. "There's more. Alber was outside the door and may have overheard my men and I discussing when and how to leave. Whether to take ye with us or nay. And it became apparent they've kenned all along which twin I am. If Alber heard any of that, he will use it to make even more trouble."

She crossed her arms and began to pace, taking short, sharp steps, but only three or four, in one direction, twisting about and returning before twisting about and repeating her steps again. "I could kill ye for what ye have done," she said, though her voice lacked conviction. "Am I to assume the real Anders is at Sutherland impersonating ye?"

"He is."

"He has the easier role to play. Ye were never very good at capturing his humor or the way he flirts with every lass in sight. I dismissed it as the result of being here, in another clan, unsure of yer welcome, yer position here. I couldna have been more wrong."

Stellan wanted to give that the laugh it deserved, but knew if he did, she would never forgive him.

"I have lied to ye—" And how many times would he have to apologize for those lies? Would she even give him the chance? He'd drop to his knees before her if he thought it would soften the anger toward him that he could see in her flashing eyes.

"I ken it. I even understand it. I dinna have to like it." She crossed her arms, making Stellan lament that they weren't wrapped around him. "I must consider what to do."

"Can I help ye?"

"I think ye have done quite enough," she said, turned, and without looking at him, stomped back to the gate and inside the bailey.

Stellan wasn't so upset as to leave her to Alber's tender mercies if she ran into him there, so he hurried after her in time to see her open the door to the keep and enter.

His men were in the great hall. They would stay with her and stand guard outside her chamber door, if that was where she went. Unless— was she going back to her father? To refuse any offer of marriage Stellan might make? Or to ask for his banishment? Stellan hurried inside, didn't see her, so went next to the solar door. It was open and the laird was working at his desk. Stellan moved on, preferring not to be seen. His men were missing, so that told him where she'd gone. To her chamber to think. Or to sulk or to vent her fury in private.

He'd ruined his chances with her. He might as well saddle his horse and ride for home right now. But hope held him in place. She hadn't said no. Would she ever say yes?

CHAPTER 17

Mariota couldn't believe how the fates had conspired to befuddle and confuse her, but how well they'd resolved her dilemma—or most of it—in the end. She'd been torn, fearing she felt for Anders what she'd felt for Stellan, but it was Stellan all along who weakened her knees, whose kiss drove her to madness, whose touch made her desperate for more. Not his twin. *Stellan*, the man she'd been attracted to since he put a hand on her boot and gazed up at her when she rode, half-asleep, into his camp. Stellan, who'd helped her down from her horse, his broad hands spanning her waist and heating her blood while at the same time, melting her heart with the care he showed both her and Valkyrie. Stellan, who risked the ire of both their fathers to be with her, to protect her from Alber, by impersonating his twin. She shook her head. She should have recalled sooner the stories she heard at Sutherland about how when the twins were younger, they often switched places and identities with each other.

But now she had a decision to make. She didn't have to waste more time wishing for a different life. She could grab it with both hands, or she would have to remain here and wait for the real

Anders to arrive to be betrothed to her. She pounded her fist into her other palm. The wrong twin.

Or she could spend the time grooming her father for the decision she'd been torn about making, but which now seemed simple and necessary. She knew she would be out of her depth as laird. The time she'd filled in for him while he recovered from his injury showed her that. Once her father was gone, it would be even worse. He hadn't been much help to her, but he was here and she could pry answers from him, at least some of the time. Later, when she truly became laird? Nay. She would try to do her best, but the clan would be safer with another person as laird, especially if the trouble between Domnhall and the Earl of Mar continued and spread north. She'd known before she overheard her father talking to his councilor, James, that if the council wanted him to name a *tanist*, support for her as a wartime laird was weak.

But who would she recommend to replace her? If she was in a position to do so, who would she name to carry the burden of MacKay? The only person she trusted completely was Seamus. Though MacKay blood ran in his veins, he was not a close cousin to her father or her. But he was a well-respected warrior, chief of the night guards, and well liked. Her gut told her abdicating in his favor would be a good decision. Perhaps the best she would ever make as laird.

Knowing she'd been falling for Stellan all along made the idea of relinquishing her heritage in Seamus' favor more attractive to her. She could marry the man she wanted, the man who made her blood sing, and help him at Sutherland when he became laird there.

Perhaps she was being selfish. Anders was fully capable of helping her if she married him and remained here, but their situation was not the same. What she felt for him did not approach the way she needed Stellan, and it never would. Anders felt to her like her brother, not a man she would lie with and bear his children. Nothing more than the love they shared for Stellan would ever exist between them.

§

STELLAN KNEW he had to leave. He couldn't delay much longer or MacKay would have them before the priest, still thinking he was Anders. Or Alber would expose him. Even if that complication didn't exist, Sutherland had called him home. If Stellan didn't return with due haste, his father would send men here to rival the army that MacKay had taken to Sutherland's walls to retrieve Mariota.

But he couldn't leave without her. He wanted to take her with him. Needed to take her with him. Would she agree? He had no doubt she wanted to. But would her sense of duty demand that she remain to support her father and someday replace him?

He found Mariota working in the clan's summer garden, pulling weeds and from the look of it, working off some anger or frustration. One of his men stood nearby, staying out of her way but on guard. Stellan waved him off, then said, "Mariota, is Cook going to be unhappy with ye?"

Mariota looked up from the rich soil between her fingers, then back down at the pile of limp greens laid out in the dirt, already drying out in the sun. "Aye, I think she might. I wasna paying attention to what I was doing."

"What if we put them back where ye found them?"

"We can try, I suppose." She looked dubious, but shrugged and picked up a green shoot, made a hole in the loose soil and patted it in.

Stellan knelt by her and did the same. Before long, they had repaired the damage Mariota had done, assuming the insulted plants managed to survive. From the looks of some of them, he wasn't optimistic.

"I think ye may still be on yer cook's bad side," he said with a smile, "but I can save ye. Come home with me."

The hope on Mariota's face tugged at Stellan's heart, so badly did he want to give it to her.

"I would like nothing better," she told him. "But how?"

"We could appeal to Seamus for help. Failing that, we'll find a postern gate or climb the keep's walls and get ye out. Valkyrie, too— let her fly and that problem will be solved."

"That risks clan war, and Sutherland throwing us into his dungeon, or worse, my da tossing us into his," Mariota argued.

"We can do it. We must. I canna leave ye unprotected. Even more, I canna leave ye behind." He would have cupped her cheek but he would leave dirt there. He didn't care. He reached for her, but she shook her head and brushed dirt from her hands as she stood.

"It willna work, and I fear my da would have ye killed for trying to steal me. 'Twas bad enough when I left on my own. I dinna want to put ye in that position."

"MacKay willna kill the Sutherland heir."

"He doesna ken he holds the Sutherland heir. He thinks ye are the spare, and Anders is worth less to him, save as a way to bargain with yer da, or to force me to comply with his wishes."

While Stellan digested that, Mariota put a hand on his arm. "I dinna wish to sneak away from my da. That will only cause more trouble. I'm going to tell him he needs to name another heir, and that I've decided to leave MacKay with ye."

Stellan felt a smile bloom on his lips that grew from the depths of his soul. "I would like nothing better, but will he allow it?"

"I willna give him a choice."

"He's the laird. Yer father."

"And he kens he has failed to prepare me to take over from him. He must accept my decision and name someone more qualified."

"Lass, I respect yer decision and yer determination to see it through, but yer da may be more of a problem than ye ken. I willna let ye face him alone. I will come with ye."

"Nay, Stellan. This is a conversation best had in private with him."

MARIOTA'S pulse beat fast in her ears, whether from the decision she'd made, from the support Stellan proudly gave her, or from anticipation of the confrontation she would soon have with her father. But when she reached the solar, the door was closed— nay, it had not shut completely, and she could hear the discussion going on inside.

"Word has come that Mar is on the move," her father was saying, though she didn't yet know to whom. "If Mar succeeds in claiming Ross, he will drive Domnhall back to the Isles to stay. Domnhall's aspirations of territorial expansion will be checked."

"But if it comes to fighting," another man said, "MacKay will be in a weak position with its laird recovering and his heir a lass."

"We have many strong and skilled warriors. Survivors of Harlaw most recently, and other battles," her father said.

"If the worst happens, laird," another man said, "MacKay will not be safe with yer daughter as laird unless she marries soon. Our coastline is potentially too tempting for Domnhall to use to outflank Mar. They'll force Sutherland, who stayed out of Harlaw, to pick a side."

The conversation ceased for a long moment that Mariota supposed was due to her father considering his councilors' words.

"I fear ye are right," he said after the long pause, "but MacKay is done with Sutherland unless Anders accepts my daughter and marries her the day after tomorrow. If no', there are other clans, other potential alliances to be made with her marriage. I am out of patience with Sutherland's presence and interference in MacKay affairs. I have banished Alber, so they no longer have a reason to remain. If one of theirs wishes to affect MacKay, let him do so as the laird's husband and the clan's war leader. If no', in two days, I will send missives to other clans proposing alliances. My daughter will do her duty to MacKay."

Mariota wanted to charge into the solar and deny her father his plans, but common sense held her back. Confronting her father in front of his councilors would gain her nothing and only cause him to dig in his heels. This was worse than she could have imagined. She expected him to argue with her about replacing her, but that he would be relieved to no longer have the burden of a weak heir weighing on him. Instead, now, he seemed even more determined to make her laird, so long as the plan James had proposed that she wed someone strong could be enacted. Well, she didn't want that, not if it meant losing Stellan. She would speak to him after the men left, and after she had a chance to calm the fury that filled her. And her surprise at his revelation. Alber was gone? A tide of relief rolled through her, but didn't last long. He was still out there, somewhere.

And how dare her father continue to plot without her. And to plot against her, now that he was thinking of wedding her to someone else. She didn't care who else. Stellan was the only man she wanted. The only man she would have. Her father could make his alliance some other way, because she was leaving.

Despite her sensible decision not to charge into the solar in a rage, the urge to confront him still burned within her. Should she interrupt the council and suggest Seamus to them then and there, or come back another time and speak privately with her father?

Suddenly the tone shifted in the room. She heard chairs scraping and men getting to their feet. James' voice rang out. "Laird? What is it? Laird! Someone get the healer!"

CHAPTER 18

One of the council ran out of the solar. Mariota ran in, took in the situation with a glance and knelt by her father's side on the floor behind his desk. His hand lay clenched like a claw over his heart.

"Da! What happened. What can I do?"

He looked up at her with apology in his eyes, then terror.

Mariota clutched his hand with one of hers and with the other, stroked his face. "'Twill be all right, Da. Just relax. The healer is coming." What was happening? Why did he suddenly look ashen and sweaty? "Da?"

His eyes closed and he shuddered. Beneath her hand, she felt his heart stutter.

"Nay, Da! What are ye doing? Ye canna leave."

She thought he heard her. He took a breath, lifting her hand along with his. Only then did she notice how cold his had become.

He seized, arching onto the back of his head and his heels like a bowstring pulled back too hard, and collapsed.

The councilors all stood in an arc at the side of the desk in silence for a moment, then one began praying and in a moment, others joined in.

The healer arrived in a rush, knelt on her father's other side, and made her assessment without hesitation. "Laird Mariota, I am so sorry. Yer father is dead." She glanced up at the councilors. "The auld laird is dead." She looked back to Mariota, sympathy in her gaze. "I will call for the priest, my Laird."

Mariota had the presence of mind to realize the healer was calling her Laird in front of the council intentionally. She felt a swell of gratitude fill her chest, but the council members looked less than pleased. Two were still praying and she heard them calling for intervention for the MacKay clan, but James and others grimaced at the scene she, her father's body, and the healer set.

"What happened to him?"

"He's been ill for a long time. Worse lately, since the boar gored him. He kenned this could happen, but he didna want ye to *fash*."

Heartbroken at the suddenness of her father's passing, scared and, yes, angry that he'd left her to succeed him with little preparation, she met the healer's gaze and nodded. "Thank ye, Healer. 'Tis time." She looked to the councilors. "Send for the priest."

THE NEXT DAY, after the council finished discussing preparations for her father's burial and attendant ceremony appropriate for a laird of his stature, Mariota understood what it felt like to hold one's temper in both hands. She clutched hers tightly in her fists on her lap to keep from lashing out at the men sitting across from her father's, now her, desk. MacKay's council. Her father's, not hers. Of the five, she would choose to keep perhaps two of them, and fill the other places with Seamus and Cook and someone else she hadn't decided on yet. It would be unexpected to make up a council with such a mix of ages, skills, and genders. But she saw no value in having all of her councilors with the same experience and the same viewpoint about everything of import to the clan. It was time for a change. She was the change, and she would do more. "We will lay my da to rest in the morning. He wouldna appreciate what ye propose, nor would he have approved it, as ye ken fine. I will send missives to our allies advising them of the bereavement MacKay has suffered and the change in leadership, and thank them for continuing to honor their alliance with us. "

"But we dinna do aught like that," one man continued to mutter.

"My point exactly," Mariota repeated. "Thank ye for seeing the difference I intend to make for MacKay. More diplomacy. Fewer bloodied swords, no' until all other venues have been attempted. We canna continue to lose our young men at the rate we did at Harlaw, just to name the latest example. Da kenned this, but he was wedded to the auld ways. I am no'."

"That is what *fashes* us, lass."

"Laird MacKay, ye mean?" Mariota said, sweetening her tone to a level that even that daft man would hear the iron in it. She was no longer a lass. She was a laird. And she was discovering that she hated it as much as she'd expected she would. Or even more.

"'Tis past time for the Sutherlands to leave MacKay. How much have they learned about us that they can use against us in the future?"

"Dinna pick a fight with them," she said with a smile, "and 'twillna be a problem."

"Lass," another said, his voice strident, "ye dinna take the danger seriously."

She sighed and tried again. "*Laird* MacKay." She was getting nowhere with these old wolves, and she blamed her da for leaving her out of his meetings with them. She should have followed her instincts and burst in every time he sat with them. Staked her claim in front of all of them. But she hadn't, and now, they didn't take her seriously. "If ye were to speak to members of the clan other than yer closest friends, ye would find that MacKays welcome the Sutherlands who have been here. Protecting me. What makes ye think those same men would go back to Sutherland and conspire against us when they have ensured that I am able to assume the position I was meant to take."

"Rather than yer wee brother?"

She wasn't sure who muttered it. The voice had been low enough that at first she wasn't sure she'd heard the words correctly. When she played it back in her mind, her control snapped. She wanted to surge to her feet, but realized she would have more impact if she kept her seat and her voice level. "That is enough. All of ye, get out. I will select a new council. Dinna hold yer breath waiting to hear yer name called."

They looked at each other for a moment, the shock of her pronouncement registering quickly in one or two, much more slowly in the rest. One by one, they stood and filed out. James left last, a small smile lifting the corner of his lips as he met her gaze. Did he approve of her decision or was he laughing at her? She was certain he knew about her father's illness. It explained why he'd pushed for a *tanist* or a strong husband for her. Well, if she had any say in the matter, he'd get his way on the latter. She narrowed her eyes at his back as he walked out the door, then shrugged. His opinion no longer mattered.

Only then did Mariota rise and go to the door. Rather than slam it shut, she beckoned to the Sutherland guard standing outside. "Erik, can ye please have someone fetch Ste...Anders, and Seamus as well."

"Of course, Laird MacKay," he said and smiled before stepping toward the great hall and signaling to another Sutherland.

Well, that certainly proved that he had heard much of her first council meeting. But his smile and his tone of voice reassured her. She had detected no smirk, not even lighthearted teasing in his smile, his tone, or his words. Why did it take a Sutherland to give her her due as Laird MacKay?

The sense of approval he gave her was a lovely gift and seemed unconstrained. If she were the Laird of Sutherland, she'd be able to count on at least him.

The stray thought stopped her and distracted her from watching him relay her request to his clansman. Where had it come from? She was not the laird of Sutherland.

She could be married to Stellan, and be Lady of the clan. His partner, his helper, in a place where she would have much more freedom to be herself, to train hawks and falcons. To train the lasses in archery to guard the walls of Dunrobin in a way she'd never been allowed to do at MacKay.

And even as MacKay laird, she might not be able to break through the attitude that something had always been done a certain way. Some things she could affect, but lasses as warriors would be a huge change at MacKay. Seamus may have done her no favors in teaching her to shoot. Each thing he learned, he taught her as soon as they could arrange it, telling her that it helped him to learn and remember the lessons, the technique, the purpose.

Longing rose in her again, sharp and bittersweet. Could she have that kind of freedom in her future? Should she? Alber had disappeared and, she prayed, was no longer close by, though he could still be a threat in the future. Were there others? Others who were opposed to a lass as laird? To her specifically for her role in her brother's death, the one they considered the rightful heir?

Was she giving up too easily? She'd barely assumed the title and responsibility. But she was not the only person at MacKay who could be laird. There were better choices. Men, aye, but good men. Men like Seamus, hungry to learn and to teach, to protect and to help others enjoy life. Men who could fight and kill when the need arose. As she had done. She was not so different from them, except in one major way. Not her gender, but her desire for the position, the title, the responsibility and the acclaim that went with it. She lacked that crucial factor. She could do the job, but she would never think of it as hers and hers alone.

She heard voices outside and a moment later, Seamus entered, followed by Stellan. "Laird," Seamus said.

While they settled, she tried to recall whether Seamus could have any idea who Stellan really was. He was no fool. He might have figured it out, too. "Take a seat. I need yer wisdom."

The men exchanged a glance and sat down. "What do ye need, Mariota?"

"Call yer man on guard inside, too," she told Stellan. "Erik overheard much of the last meeting. He may have impressions I missed."

Stellan went to the door and fetched his guard, then closed the door behind them.

Mariota gestured them to a seat and explained what had happened in the council meeting, and her thinking since then, all except her thoughts about Sutherland and her possible future there.

Stellan's man added only that as the councilors left, they went from silent and introspective to egging each other to anger. "It doesna bode well, my laird. They will cause trouble for ye and whomever ye choose for yer new council."

"Overt trouble can be handled," Stellan observed. "Danger lies in the ones who remain silent and strike suddenly from an unexpected direction. People ye ken and trust— and shouldna."

"Seamus? Yer thoughts?"

"Ye will win them over, Mari, in time. Ye are capable, more than any other lass in the clan. More than they will expect."

"Thanks to ye, no' to my da. And thanks to what ye and Cook

taught me, else Alber might have done what he wished with me. Instead I was able to fight him off. Still, I dinna believe I have time," Mariota admitted. "Nor do I have the will to do this job as it should be done. I intend to abdicate in yer favor, Seamus. I will leave MacKay, and all of the problems associated with me being laird will go with me. Ye will have a fresh start. Ye are a man the clan admires and respects. Ye will do well here."

"Mari, nay."

"I recommend ye choose yer own council. Dinna make the mistake of adopting Da's. They are moribund and will be nay help to ye."

"Ye truly mean to do this?" Stellan's brows winged and a hopeful smile lifted the corners of his lips.

"I do. Do ye still want me to go to Sutherland with ye, Stellan?" Despite the import of his answer, she couldn't help glancing at Seamus to see how he reacted to her revelation.

He grinned. So he had suspected.

"Ye ken I do. But Mariota, what ye will be giving up—"

"Naught that I want. Everything I wish for is with ye." It took strength to turn away from the joy reflected in Stellan's eyes, but she looked to Seamus and stood. "Ye may as well begin now. I have some packing to do. We will make the announcement to the clan at supper and leave in the morning."

"Have ye considered, Mari, that I mightna want the job either?" He asked as he and Stellan got to their feet, too.

"Nay, I havena, because ye are perfect for it and will be a much better laird than my da was. Than I could ever be."

She walked around the desk and went first to Seamus, kissing him on the cheek. "My friend, I entrust MacKay to ye. I ken ye can handle it better than anyone." Then she turned to Stellan and took his hand. "Let's get ready to go. I'm eager to start a new life with ye."

MARIOTA FELT like holding her breath the entire way back to Sutherland, fearful that something would happen to force her to return to MacKay, or that she would wake up and realize this was a dream and she was locked in her chamber by her father, with Alber pacing outside her door. Only Stellan's calm presence at her side helped her accept that this change in her life was real. His men surrounded them, along with an honor guard of MacKay's best warriors chosen by Seamus to accompany her to her new home. Over his objections, she had refused his presence, reminding him that he had much to do to cement his place as MacKay's laird.

Stellan reached over and took one of her hands from the reins she clutched. "*Fashing* again, love? We've no' far to go, and we'll be home."

She summoned a smile for him and released a sigh. "I'll be glad to see Dunrobin. I keep expecting something to happen—"

"Naught will, lass. We're well protected and have been on Sutherland land since we camped last night. Besides, ye should worry for me. Once Da finds out what Anders and I did, he's likely to skelp the both of us. But dinna fear. He'll welcome ye."

"I hope so. Ye canna ken how much I hope all of Sutherland will welcome me. And support our marriage."

Stellan's face lit with one of his rare, heartfelt smiles. His eyes twinkled with mirth, making her laugh.

"What is it?"

"Ye ken who will support it the most? Anders. The lasses will now have to put all their hopes on him, and believe me, he'll take advantage of that."

"That sounds terrible."

"Nay, 'tisna. They've chased both of us for years. Anders is well-capable of enjoying them— and of fending off any lass he doesna want or trust. What the lasses may no' yet realize is that Da wants Anders to wed outside of Sutherland, too, and bring home a bride and an alliance to benefit us."

"I think I hear hearts breaking already."

"Aye, if ye dinna, ye soon will. Look— there's Dunrobin."

Mariota looked where he pointed. Indeed, the tops of the highest towers were just becoming visible above the intervening trees. "Almost home," she said on a breath.

"Almost home," Stellan repeated and squeezed her hand. "Better?"

"Aye. Thank ye for distracting me from my worries."

"I'll always care for ye, lass."

"I ken ye will. And I will take care of ye the same. And someday, our bairns, as well."

This time, Stellan gave her a smile that held heat rather than humor. "The sooner we wed, the better, I think."

"I think so, too."

An arrow flew out of the woods and buried itself in the pommel where Valkyrie perched, pinning several of her claws to the wood.

Stellan pushed Mariota down over her and threw his body across hers. "Find that shooter!"

Mariota did her best to control Valkyrie's thrashing while several MacKays took off into the woods. Her hood had come loose and Mariota knew the hawk, in her struggles, could rip out her throat without meaning to. "Let me up, Stellan!"

"Nay, stay down."

"I need to secure Valkyrie, and free her claws. She's got her hood loose enough to come off."

"Damn." Stellan sat up and pulled Mariota back against him, then reached around her and grabbed the arrow, working to get it loose and free her hawk.

Mariota secured Valkyrie's hood, then went to work helping Stellan. As soon as they managed to work the arrow loose enough for Stellan to pull it out of the pommel, Mariota told him, "I'm going to let her fly. She's safer above the trees than here."

While she worked at the ties of Valkyrie's jesses, Stellan asked, "Will she fly for Dunrobin's mews?"

"I hope so," Mariota told him as she got Valkyrie free and pulled off her hood. "She lost a claw," she said as the hawk wasted no time launching herself skyward. "Fly on!" Mariota shouted at her, then swept her hands, streaked with blood, forward. The blood had to be Valkyrie's. Her fingers were uncut, and she hadn't noticed any blood on Stellan's. She looked up in time to see another arrow track Valkyrie, but it missed. "Fly, lass!" Even bleeding, she should reach Ian at Dunrobin.

"Damn it, he's still out there," Stellan said. "Stay down and let the men wall ye off," he said and leapt for his horse.

"'Tis Alber," Mariota shouted as he rode toward the source of the arrows. "It has to be. He's a terrible shot." She didn't know if Stellan heard her. Two of his men and four MacKays closed in around her too quickly for her to see whether he acknowledged her or not. His remaining two Sutherlands took off after him as soon as they saw she was surrounded.

"Ride, lass," Stellan's man Elias told her. "We're for Dunrobin as fast as we can."

The men kicked their horses into a gallop, forcing hers to keep pace, and raced for Dunrobin's gates. No more arrows came their way, confirming Mariota's sense that the shooter was Alber. He tried to kill the hawk that damaged his face and neck, she was sure of it. If instead, he hit her, she was sure he'd consider it a bonus.

The castle proved to be farther away than it appeared, as was often the case in the mountains. But her guards refused to let up their urgent pace and rode hard. The men beside her kept sweeping her with their gazes, making sure she was up for this rough pounding. She gave them a nod and bent lower over her horse's neck. She would stay with them, no matter how fast they rode, for as long as her horse could keep up.

They maintained the pace far longer than Mariota expected

but slowed to rest the horses by a fast-moving burn. By now, she was certain they were in no danger from Alber— or whomever shot at Valkyrie. She had to admit the possibility that she'd been wrong. In any case, she hoped her hawk had made it to the mews. Her first concern now was Stellan.

She twisted in her saddle to look behind them.

"He'll be along," Camus told her.

"With Alber's head dripping gore on his sword, I hope," she muttered. That man had been a thorn in her side, and a danger to her and to Valkyrie for entirely too long. Her da had finally sent him away. A bad decision, that.

And today, she was certain, Valkyrie had paid the price of a claw. She hoped that was all her hawk had suffered, and that the Sutherland hawk master, Ian, would recognize her and realize she needed care.

She looked skyward but saw no sign of a circling hawk. Valkyrie had to have obeyed and gone on ahead. She couldn't bear to think of the alternative, that an arrow had found her and she lay dead in the woods behind them. Tears burned the back of her eyes. She blinked them away. She would not borrow trouble. Not that. Never that. Alber could not win.

"How far have we left to go?"

"Over that next hill, across a glen and through the gates," Elias told her.

So the answer to her concern was closer forward than behind. She kicked her mount into motion. Stellan had men with him, his arms, and his prowess. Valkyrie had her, and perhaps Ian. Dunrobin was close. She'd never thought to reenter it without Stellan at her side, but she would do what she must. She always had.

CHAPTER 19

Stellan hated leaving Mariota behind, but she was well shielded by the men surrounding her. He'd heard her call out that the shooter was likely Alber. He thought so, too. He didn't think hitting Valkyrie— or near to her —was a coincidence, or an accident. Alber hated that hawk as much or even more than he hated Mariota.

With Gregor and Erik at his side, Stellan slowed as they approached where he judged the arrows had originated. As he expected, the shooter was gone.

"As soon as his first shot missed, he saw us coming after him," Stellan muttered. "He took a chance with the second one."

"Aye. The coward would run as far and as fast as he could," Erik said, agreeing.

"Unless he wants us to think that," Stellan told them, then signaled for them to go right and left while he continued forward. It was a risk. He knew enough about Alber to think he'd hang around to see what more trouble he could cause before he moved on. Or had he followed the group with Mariota at its center?

That gave Stellan pause. Was the shooter still here? Was it truly Alber or someone else?

Mariota might have been the target, and might still be in danger if the shooter trailed her, or rode parallel to her, hoping for a clear shot.

He had to trust the men around her. And her instincts. They'd reach Dunrobin soon at a gallop. The best he could do from here was to confirm the shooter, discern his movements, and if possible, capture him.

Erik whistled from the left, so Stellan turned in his direction.

"Here's where he waited for us," Erik told him once he arrived and pointed out the open view of the path they'd ridden on. Gregor showed up a few minutes later, as Stellan and Erik were studying the ground and the trees where Erik found signs of disturbance, and a broken arrow. The fletching matched the one Stellan had pulled from Mariota's pommel.

"Did he climb?" Stellan studied the branches above them, and those of the nearby trees. A man could move from tree to tree in this part of the forest, the branches were so thick and interwoven.

"If he did, he jumped down here," Gregor said and pointed to deeper heel marks in the forest loam beneath the tree. "He's heavy enough to have made those."

"Assuming 'tis Alber."

"Where would he go from here?"

"'Tis what *fashes* me," Stellan said, still studying the surrounding trees. "He might think Mariota would charge at whomever shot Valkyrie, so he'd move far enough away, but no' so far as to be unable to see her coming. But he realized too late that our men were holding her back and keeping her safe. Seeing that, he would expect the whole group to go with her, so he'd move in the direction of his horse, and ride away. Free to keep threatening her."

"Which way, do ye think?" Gregor, too, was studying the branches above them.

"See any broken twigs? Torn or crushed lichen or moss? Anything?" Stellan moved quietly forward. His men flanked him at angles. "There," Gregor said, pointing up. He marched forward, then studied the ground beyond where he stopped. "The horse was here, but the branches start too high to jump safely from here. That's why he went back where we saw the boot prints. Aye, he's gone. The horse tracks go that way."

Stellan nodded. Toward Dunrobin. "Ye two follow his tracks. Find him. Capture him if ye can. But kill him if he gives ye nay choice. I'll no have ye harmed. Or Mariota having to bear any more of this."

"Where will ye be?"

"I need to follow Mariota and her guards. She is on her way to Dunrobin, and so is Alber, by one path or another. I have to find her before he does. Ye find him."

&.

THE NEED TO catch up to Mariota and make sure she was safe burned in Stellan and drove him to run his mount faster and farther than he should have. It was showing lather by the time he reached a fast-flowing burn to rest and water his horse. He chafed at the delay, but pushing his horse until it dropped would not get him to Mariota— or get him home —any faster. Likely he'd miss her altogether, something he could not tolerate. She was in danger, and he was not with her, not able to protect her. That was not something he would tolerate for a moment longer than he had to.

He walked his mount to cool it, then let it drink before walking it a few minutes more. Satisfied that it was ready to continue, he mounted.

The first arrow caught him in the upper arm, the second in

his shoulder. Shocked to have been unaware of someone nearby more than by the pain of his injuries, Stellan wheeled his mount to face the shooter.

Alber walked out of the tree line upstream. "Ye're no' much of a threat now, are ye? Ye've stood between me and that lass too many times, but nay more."

Fury tightened Stellan's gut. Apparently Alber had missed earlier shots on purpose, to panic Mariota and her hawk. He could shoot well enough to injure Stellan without killing him. He gritted his teeth, reached up with his good hand and snapped off the arrow shafts. "I can fight ye with one hand."

From the feral glint in Alber's eyes, that was exactly what the man wanted. To fight, and to kill. To pay Stellan back for protecting the woman he wanted to harm. "Ye didna have the courage to fight me without trying to weaken me. 'Twas yer first mistake."

If Stellan survived this battle, someone would dig out the arrow heads for him and patch him up. If he didn't survive, Anders would be pissed that he had to become laird. And Mariota— Stellan couldn't think of her now or he'd break down. He couldn't leave her. She loved him, not Anders.

Alber charged.

Stellan stayed mounted, guiding his horse with his knees and shifting weight to meet Alber's attack. He swung his sword, scoring a wound on Alber's shoulder similar to the ones inflicted on him.

"Now we're even," Stellan taunted. "Are ye sure ye want to continue this?" He was grateful that his growing battle lust was dulling the pain in his left arm and shoulder. He could fight. But the harder his heart beat, the faster he would bleed.

"Ye're no' going to last long," Alber said and sneered. "Ye must be feeling weak by now. I can take ye." He swung for Stellan's head.

Stellan blocked his strike, his sword and good arm vibrating

with the power of it. "Dinna be so sure. I have much to live for."
And much to love for. *Mariota.*

Alber laughed and swung again, but missed. "Mariota
MacKay? Ye think ye're going to be the first? Ye are only the
latest in a long line. Did ye ken that?"

"But never ye," Stellan taunted. "Have yer bollocks recovered
yet?"

"She'll find out when I finish with ye."

With a growl, Stellan knocked him from his horse.

Alber bled more freely after his fall, his shoulder wound
gaping, crusted with dirt. If he lived, it was sure to fester.

Arrowheads blocked Stellan's wounds from bleeding heavily,
though he could feel some blood seeping around them and dripping down his arm— enough, he supposed, for Alber to assume
he was in worse shape than he actually was. But the more he used
that arm, the more the arrowheads would cut the muscle they
lodged in. He let it remain by his side.

Alber stood as Stellan swung off his horse and slapped its
rump to get it moving out of the way of what was to come. The
duel continued on the ground, Stellan circling and thrusting,
looking for weaknesses in his opponent, just as Alber did, and
both trying to wound the good arm the other fought with.

Stellan couldn't help trying his link to Anders. Would it still
work? Was he close enough? Would Anders hear him and know
that he was thinking about him? They might have grown past the
ability they shared as young lads. Their connection had not
always been reliable even then. Now? Still, he had to try. He was
in a fight for his life. Alone. Wounded. *Take care of Mariota if I
dinna make it back*, he fought to project as he blocked another of
Alber's thrusts. *Dinna let this man near her. If I fail, kill him.*

The fight seemed to go on forever. Stellan was panting, but
Alber was both panting and pale from the multitude of cuts
Stellan had inflicted on his bad arm, his torso and one leg. None
were deep enough to finish him, worse luck, but they bled, so

until they both exhausted every reserve or failed to block an attack, the fight would continue.

Stellan had taken a few cuts, the most severe a slice along his ribs under his good arm. He fought not to let it slow him down. Even with only one arm, he was faster and more precise in his thrusts than Alber. Still, blood loss was becoming a factor, shaking Stellan's confidence and making him start to fear he wouldn't win.

Alber might have had good reason to brag about Red Harlaw, despite what Mariota believed. The man wouldn't give up. Stellan could see in Alber's eyes that despite his wounds and exhaustion, he was enjoying this. Was his adversary toying with him? The thought threatened to steal the strength from Stellan's legs. Or was Stellan's own exhaustion making him see things that weren't there?

Like Anders, who Sutherland noticed as a mirror-image stutter of movement in the corner of his eye.

Alber lurched forward and stumbled over a half-buried rock as he swung at shoulder height.

That rock saved Stellan from his distraction. He blocked Alber's swing with a dangerous chop that forced both swords down till the point of Alber's penetrated the ground. Stellan lifted his and ran Alber through.

Alber's shocked cry ended on a gurgle.

Stellan jerked his blade up.

Alber slid backward off Stellan's blade and fell to the ground.

Stellan kept his gaze on him long enough to be certain he would not get up again. He wasn't certain anything else he saw was real. With a disbelieving glance at Anders and some Sutherland men approaching him, Stellan collapsed.

CHAPTER 20

Mariota leapt from her horse once she and her escort crossed under Dunrobin's gate. "Ian!" She called for the hawk master as she ran for the mews, certain the stable lads would care for her horse. She needed to find Valkyrie. The hawk master came to the open door of the mews just as she reached it. "Is Valkyrie within?" Her heart was thundering so loudly, she was certain the man could hear it.

He gave her a nod and gestured for her to enter as he stepped out of the way. "She's here, lass, and she's well," he told her, while wiping his hands on a cloth. On it, streaks of blood mixed with water varied from red to pink. "She lost a claw somewhere, but other than that, she's unhurt. What happened?"

Mariota ran to Valkyrie's perch. The hawk sat there calmly, watching her mistress approach. "Ach, my poor wee *eyas*. I'm so sorry ye were harmed." She studied the wrapping Ian had put on her foot. "Will she be well?"

"Aye. She will. Ye needna *fash*, lass." He gave her a smile. "Ye sent her, then?"

"We were attacked." She told him about the arrow that did the damage he'd repaired. "Stellan and two of his men stayed behind to search for the shooter."

"Stellan? I just saw him an hour ago."

Mariota wanted to kick herself. She should not have said anything. "I mean Anders."

He shook his head. "Nay, ye didna. So the lads are up to their old tricks." He chuckled for a moment, then frowned. "The laird willna be happy."

"I willna tell him. Will ye?"

"Nay, but the lads will. And they'll bear whatever punishment he deems suitable. They may be too clever for their own good, but they're honorable lads."

Mariota thought back over all Stellan had done for her since she'd stumbled into his camp. Honorable, indeed. Anders, too, in his own, more playful way. But it was Stellan she cared about. Stellan she loved.

Where was he?

"Ye look as though ye had best go inside," Ian told her. "Get some food and have a rest. The lads will be along soon."

"I'm sure ye have the right of it," Mariota told him with a smile. "How can I ever thank ye for taking such good care of Valkyrie?"

"Naught needed, lass. Yer hawk and I are old friends, now, are we no', lassie?" He said, turning to her hawk. "I'll see her fed and will fetch the healer if she shows signs of being in pain. Go get some rest, lass."

Mariota nodded, and on impulse, reached forward and gave him a kiss on the cheek. "Thank ye," she said again and headed out into the bailey. The lads were still dealing with the horses, so Mariota grabbed her pack from hers and thanked the stable lad for his care of her mount, then went inside. Ian had given her good advice. She tossed her pack onto the nearest bench and sat beside it, waiting patiently until a serving lass brought her something to eat and asked, "Would ye like ale or cider?"

"Cider, please, and some bread to go with Cook's wonderful stew, if ye please," Mariota told her.

"Are ye well, milady? Is there anything else ye need?"

Mariota realized she must look worse than she knew. "Just tired, thank ye. I'll be fine after I eat."

"I'll hurry back to ye, then," the lass said and rushed away.

People at Sutherland were so nice to her, it brought tears to her eyes. She blinked them away. She must be more tired, more shaken by Alber's attack, than she'd realized. The scent of the stew, when it arrived, made her mouth water. She reached first for the cup of cider and downed it, then tore of a chunk of bread and dunked it in the stew. She'd taken only a bite or two when her benefactor returned with a pitcher and replenished her cider. "I thought ye might need more than one cup," the lass told her.

"Ye are wise beyond yer years," Mariota said with a tired smile. "I'm Mariota. What's yer name?"

"I'm Anna," the lass told her.

"Pleased to meet ye," Mariota told her, stopping with stew-soaked bread in her fingers long enough to speak.

"I'll leave ye to eat in peace. Tell me if ye need aught."

"Thank ye, Anna," Mariota said, once again grateful for the treatment she received here, so different from how she was regarded at home. Nay, *at MacKay*. This was now her home. That made her smile again, and she dug into her meal.

She finished and started to wonder how long she'd been sitting here. Was Stellan back? Surely she would have seen him enter the great hall, probably to report to his da in the laird's solar. And he would have seen her and come to her. But the hall bustled with people coming and going, none of whom were Stellan or Anders. Where were the twins?

Anders sometimes had an uncanny sense of what his brother was doing. She could use his reassurance right now. But first, she'd take her things upstairs, come back and ask if anyone had seen either of them.

In her chamber, her bed— and Ian's advice to rest —called to her, but she left her pack and went back downstairs. Anna, the first person she approached, knew nothing, nor did the healer when she ventured back to the herbal.

"Check with the lads in the stable. They ken everything," the healer advised.

Mariota had to laugh. "Of course. Stellan would leave his horse there when he arrived. If he was back, they'd know, and might know where he'd gone. She could follow her instincts to the laird's solar, but she feared interrupting their da at work, and worse, winding up explaining why one of his sons was missing—assuming she could keep from him which son it was. Nay, she'd rather not betray Stellan and Anders' duplicity. Ian said they'd confess to their da, so she must keep silent.

She was in the stable when thunderous hoofbeats shook the ground and made her run for the entrance. So many horses galloped through the keep's gates, she couldn't count them all for the dust they kicked up. But one caught her eye and stopped her heart. Anders, holding his bloody twin slumped before him, rode at the fore. Or was it Stellan holding Anders? And why were they together when Anders had been left behind in Dunrobin?

She knew better than to rush out into the bailey in the middle of the melee, so she gripped the stable's doorframe and waited until all the riders had their beasts under control, then ran to the twins. "Stellan?"

"Hurt, but he'll be right once the healer sees to him," Anders told her, confirming her worst fear.

"Dear God, what happened?"

"Alber ambushed him, and they fought," Anders told her as he beckoned several men over to help him get his brother down. They carried him inside.

Mariota watched them go, her feet sliding side-to-side in her anxiety to follow them. But Anders was still talking.

"He— I kenned something was wrong and rode out with some

men. We found him just as he killed Alber." Anders dismounted and handed his reins to a lad. "Ye needna fear him ever again."

"Stellan killed him?" Unconsciously, her hand covered her mouth. "I must go to him."

"Let the healer see to him, lass."

Mariota ignored him and ran for the herbal. Anders called her name, but she kept going. In a moment, she felt him following on her heels.

Several people filled the herbal, watching the healer work on Stellan's wounds. One arrowhead was already out of his arm and the wound packed with healing herbs. The healer frowned as she cut around the one in his shoulder. Mariota held her breath until she pried it out, examined it for broken edges, probed the wound and removed one small bit before letting it bleed freely for a moment to ensure it was free of debris, then packed that wound as well.

That Stellan's father was already there and watching the healer cut his son surprised her. One of the men who carried Stellan in must have fetched him, and now several waited against one wall in case they were needed again. Mariota and Anders crowded along the wall next to them, across from the laird.

"His other wounds are no' deep," the healer announced a while later as she finished cleaning the last one. She turned to the laird. "I'll pack and wrap them and watch to make certain they dinna fester. When he wakes up, he'll be given cider and ale to drink. He lost a lot of blood, so liquids will help him recover faster than aught else."

"How long?" Sutherland's face and voice held concern.

"I canna say, laird. I'll watch over him."

"I'll help," Mariota said, the words out before the thought formed in her mind. She couldn't bear the thought of Stellan waking up alone, in pain. She would help the healer so that he had someone with him all day and all night.

"So there," the healer said, smiled at Mariota, and turned back to the laird. "He'll be well cared for."

"I dinna think 'tis appropriate for a lass—"

"Of course it is," the healer argued. "Who do ye think helps me with most of ye brave lads when ye come in dripping blood?"

Stellan groaned and turned his head from side to side. Anders hurried to him and placed a hand on his uninjured shoulder. "Fight's over, brother. Ye won."

Stellan calmed, then croaked out, "Mari…"

"I'm here, Stellan. I'm safe. So are ye."

The healer approached with a cup. "I want ye to drink all of this, lad," she said and nodded for Anders to lift his head, then held the cup to his lips. Stellan managed to swallow most of it, sighed and passed out again.

Mariota made a sound of protest, terrified he wouldn't recover, but the healer held up a hand.

"Have faith, lass. I put something to help him sleep in that draught."

Anders put a hand on her shoulder. "Remember how ye said our healer is formidable? Trust her."

Mariota nodded, mostly because she knew that's what Anders expected, and she didn't want to hurt the healer's feelings. But she worried for Stellan. He looked so wan, so less than himself, lying there. Despite knowing his father would see, she put a hand on his cheek. "Sleep well," she told him, then looked to the healer. "What do ye need me to do?"

"At the moment? Go rest. Ye look as knackered as he does," she said and nodded toward her patient. Come to me after ye have slept a few hours and we'll talk."

Anders took her arm and escorted her to her chamber. "Dinna *fash*, Mariota. Now that he's home, I'm confident he'll be better soon. Ye should be, too."

Tears she'd fought to contain since she'd seen Anders ride in with Stellan in his arms finally wet her eyes and trickled down her face. "I'll try," she told him as he pulled her into his embrace. So like Stellan's, and yet… not.

"Ye need sleep. Go rest. I'll keep an eye on him until ye come back down."

"Thank ye, Anders." She stepped out of his embrace and into her chamber. She closed her door and stretched out on her bed, heedless of the state of her traveling clothes or anything else, save that she'd thanked more people since she arrived at Sutherland than she had at MacKay in months. She'd be grateful to be able to thank the healer for saving Stellan, for bringing him through his recovery and back to her. And she'd do everything she could to help him. With him, her life was going to be so much better. She loved him, and he loved her. If Alber had stolen that from her, she'd curse his name and wish she could kill him all over again. She didn't miss MacKay or the loss of the lairdship. Those things were in her past. Stellan was her future. Sutherland was her future. And as soon as Stellan was healed, she had so much to tell him. So much to thank him for. He must get better soon.

STELLAN CAME AWAKE to pain everywhere, but the worst seemed to be in his arm and shoulder. Then he remembered. Alber's arrows caught him there. He opened his eyes, not certain where he was or what he'd see. Alber standing over him about to thrust his great sword through Stellan's chest?

Nay, something much more reassuring. Anders, leaning over him, smiling.

"'Tis about time ye came back to us," Anders told him. He reached aside, then offered a cup. "I'll lift yer head so ye can swallow this. Ye'll feel better once ye do."

"No more sleep," Stellan protested. "Mariota."

"She's in her chamber, resting. Ye are stuck with me for now. Ye've been here four days and the lass has barely left yer side. The healer is going to steal Mariota from ye and train her as her replacement unless ye get better soon."

"If she wishes to, aye, but Mariota is mine."

"Aye, she's made that clear to anyone who will stand still long enough to listen. Ye gave her a scare, brother. All of us, too. For most of the first day, we werena certain ye would make it. But ye are strong. And Mariota and I wouldna let ye go."

"Good."

"Yer lass was making herself sick worrying over ye. She loves ye, brother. Never doubt it."

"I ken it."

"Then heal and marry the lass. She doesna love me. Never has, betrothal agreement be damned. I'm no fit substitute for ye."

"And don't ye forget it," Stellan told him, summoning a smile.

"Oh, and by the way," Anders said, "we're both in trouble with Da."

Stellan tried to laugh, but it hurt too much. He'd know from the moment they concocted this crazy scheme, switching places with each other, that in the end, they'd have to confess to their father and he'd probably flay their hides. Instead, Stellan asked, "How did ye show up in time? I remember seeing ye right after I killed Alber. Or I think I did. Were ye there?"

"I was. I felt ye were in trouble long before Mariota got to Dunrobin. I rode out with some guards. Our connection led me to ye."

"Ye felt I was in trouble?"

"Aye. That may be the longest reach of our connection so far."

"I thought it was gone. Grown out of it. But I was desperate. Thought I was about to die. Needed ye to ken. To look after Mariota."

"And be laird in yer stead. Ye ken I never intended to do that by myself. Ye swore an oath with me."

"Kenned ye'd be angry."

Anders snorted. "Ye were right about that. What made ye charge off by yerself?"

"Chasing Mariota and the men. Two of mine following Alber. Too slow, I guess."

"Aye. They were shocked when they arrived home to hear what had happened. Likely ye'll see them before long. They're eager to apologize. To see that ye are getting better."

"Me, too." He fought to clear his throat.

"Thirsty?"

"Aye."

Anders picked up another cup, lifted his head and held him so he could drink. When he finished, Anders told him, "That one has some sleeping potion in it." At Stellan's frown, he said, "Dinna blame me. The healer wants ye to rest, so sleep well, brother."

Stellan barely heard the last word before the dark crowded in. He took a breath and let it cover him.

❧

MARIOTA'S favorite pastime had become watching Stellan's chest rise and fall with his breathing as he slept. Over the last few days, each breath had gotten deeper and lasted longer, a sure sign, the healer told her, that he was healing and very soon would be well enough to use those breaths to start complaining.

Mariota hoped so. She couldn't recall hearing Stellan actually complain about anything, unless it was her father's treatment of her. Or his failure to deal with Alber. Stellan deserved to complain about that, certainly. If she could speak to her da, she'd not speak, she'd yell and scream and point fingers until he understood what his inaction had led to. The man she loved lying here, breathing.

At least Stellan *was* breathing. The fight with Alber could have gone so much worse. His arrows had wounded Stellan, but they could have killed him. It seemed Alber was a much better shot than she'd given him credit for. He'd missed Valkyrie twice— if she didn't count her missing claw —and he'd missed her, too, all on purpose, she now suspected. Stellan lived because Alber wanted to fight him, not because Alber's killing shots didn't land where he intended.

Suddenly, Stellan groaned and opened his eyes.

"Stellan, how do ye feel?" She reached for the cup of cider the healer had left for him, first in a line of them. She was to ensure he drank every one by the time the healer came back from her rest.

"Better," he said and rolled to his side on his good arm. "More sleeping draught?"

"Nay, just cider in this cup. Ale in the next. I'm to send for some warm broth and start ye on yer way back to eating."

"So no sleeping draught."

She started to hand him the cup, thought better of it and set it aside. "Do ye want to sit up?"

He thought for a moment, pushed up on his good arm and swung his legs off the bed. The sheet moved with him, keeping him covered, and he straightened to sitting. And wobbled.

Mariota put her arms around him to steady him. Despite his enforced inactivity, his muscles bulged under her hands and his skin was taut and warm. Not hot, thank God. He felt big and solid in her arms. A man she could count on to protect her when she needed it, and care for her when she needed that, too.

He rested his head on her shoulder, bringing tears to her eyes. "I thought I was going to lose ye," she told him as she rubbed his back, careful of the wrappings around his torso holding the healer's salves against his wounds. "Anders said ye were too mean to die. I prayed he was right."

"He was. He is," Stellan said against her neck, then lifted his head. "Cider?"

She reached for the cup and put it in the hand he held out, her gaze flicking to his broad chest and etched muscles of his abdomen. He was so much more imposing upright than he had been, lying unconscious, while she watched over him.

She wanted to trace every curve and ripple of muscle she could see. To brush her fingers over his nipples and see if they reacted to her touch as hers did when he had kissed and held her. To pull the sheet askew and admire every inch of his body. Instead, she wrapped her arms around her middle and turned away from the temptation he presented.

"What were ye thinking, fighting Alber alone?" She asked while he drank.

He emptied the cup and handed it back to her. "He ambushed me. I didna have a choice."

"Where were yer men? They should have been with ye."

"Hunting him. My orders. Too bad he found me, instead."

Mariota nodded, at a loss for what to say to that.

"But he's gone now," Stellan continued and took the next cup she offered. "At least I think I remember finishing him." He drank.

"Ye did. Anders was there in time to see the end of the fight. Damn my father for no' dealing with him as he should have long ago."

Stellan set the empty aside and cupped her face. "If he had, we never would have met, or not until ye were wed to my brother."

She shuddered. "I dinna want to imagine that. I like Anders as a brother, but ye are the man I love. Ye must hurry and get well so we can marry." She paused, not knowing whether she should tell him of the missive she'd recently received, but Stellan needed to know. "Else, Seamus may send for me."

"Back to MacKay? Nay!"

"Word has come that Mar has taken Dingwall, claiming Ross. Yer da kens. Seamus worries Domnhall will come at Mar via MacKay." Should she have stayed? For a moment, she allowed herself to feel torn. But nay. She belonged here now. "Seamus can handle whatever happens. I will never leave ye."

CHAPTER 21

Stellan walked slowly down the stairs to the great hall. It had felt good to spend his first night in his own bed since returning wounded from MacKay. Anders waited at the bottom of the stairs, ready to assist him if he needed it. He was determined to prove he could handle himself. Most of his injures, the shallow ones Alber had inflicted with his sword, were well healed, a new set of pink scars decorating his torso, arm and leg. The arrow wounds were slower to close, but the healer judged them well on the way and dismissed him from her care, save for daily visits to allow her to watch for infection setting in.

Also at the bottom of the stairs, hands clenched over her heart, eyes wide, Mariota stood waiting for him. Each day, she became more beautiful to him. More precious. Not just for her care of him during the last sennight, but for the love she bestowed so fully and openly to him. The wisest decision he had ever made was to switch places with Anders and escort Mariota back to MacKay. There, he'd learned he loved her and did not want to live without her, and she felt the same for him.

"Finally ready to break yer fast, are ye?" Anders chided. "'Tis time for the midday meal and ye arrive all slugabed."

"Dinna listen to him," Mariota advised with a laugh as he reached the floor and she came into his arms. "'Tis only a little past sunup."

"Either way, I'm hungry," Stellan told her and turned her within his arms. He walked her to an empty table, Anders following behind.

In moments, food and drink arrived. Anders must have signaled from behind his back, Stellan mused. "Thank ye, brother. I am truly famished."

"No doubt, having spent a sennight subsisting on cider, ale and broth."

"And bread and stew and honey cake," Mariota added. "Ye'll get no sympathy for that last."

They passed the meal in pleasant conversation, interrupted by well wishes from everyone walking by until Stellan could eat no more. "'Tis time," he told his twin.

"Da is waiting in his solar."

"Let's go see how angry he is," Stellan said and stood.

"I'm the cause of this. I'll stand with ye," Mariota offered.

Stellan shook his head. "Nay, lass. This has to be between our da and us. 'Twas my decision to make the switch. Ye were no' involved."

"I was! If no' for me, ye wouldna have done any of what ye did. Ye wouldna have made the trip, nor risked yer life."

"I did what I wanted— what I needed to do to keep ye safe. I will answer to the Sutherland for that."

He knew he'd won when her shoulders dropped and she turned her gaze on Anders. "Ye, too, then?"

"Aye, of course. We'll be fine. Da will yell at us, and may put us on duty cleaning out the stables, but we willna be harmed."

"He'd best no' or the might of MacKay will fall upon him."

Anders laughed and held up a hand, then cut off the laugh when he saw the determination in her eyes.

"She's impressive, is she no'?" Stellan asked, grinned and stood. "Let's get this over with before Mariota sends for Seamus."

He leaned down and kissed her soundly on the mouth. "Stay here. Likely ye'll be able to hear most of what is said," he told her.

"Hmmmph," she replied and crossed her arms. "If I hear steel sliding, I'm coming in."

Anders laughed again. Stellan gave her a grin and joined his brother walking toward the solar.

"Are ye truly ready for this?" Anders asked, concern on his face now that Mariota could only see their backs.

"Aye. Let's get this over with. The sooner we do, the sooner I can be married."

Their father stood when they entered. "I'm glad to see ye on yer feet, son," he said by way of greeting, and gave Anders a nod. "Ye may remain standing while ye tell me what the hell ye were thinking."

His tone remained mild, but Stellan wasn't fooled. Their laird was displeased. He explained how the attraction he felt for Mariota would not let him simply give her to Anders and how they arrived at the decision to impersonate each other.

"I thought ye had grown past such nonsense," their father told them. "I thought ye had grown enough, and learned enough by now no' to indulge in such risky behavior. Ye do ken how wrong this could have gone. How wrong it did go," he added with a glance at Stellan's shoulder. "And ye compound it by riding home alone though ye kenned there was trouble in the area. Not to mention bringing the MacKay heir back to Sutherland. What do ye think her clan will do about that?"

Stellan exchanged a glance with Anders. "About that— she's nay longer the heir. She was the laird, but she's nay the laird, either. Nay longer. She's free to wed with me."

Sutherland spluttered. "What the hell did ye do to clan MacKay while ye were there?"

Stellan laughed, groaned with pain, then told him the story, sparing only a few details such as his time in the storeroom with Mariota, but including what happened to her father and how she decided to abdicate in favor of Seamus MacKay.

Sutherland was silent for a few moments after Stellan finished speaking, then he surprised him, taking a breath and saying, "Well done, lad." Then he, too, laughed. "Yer lass already told me much of that. They're stronger and have a good man in charge. Ye will have a good wife to help ye here, as well." He glanced at Anders, who nodded his support. "Ye may wed when ye can laugh without groaning in pain," he added to Stellan. Now go, rest and finish healing."

Stellan took that as a challenge and began light sparring sessions as well as eating more and spending time in bed under the healer's watchful eye. But it took days more, days he spent with Mariota, with Valkyrie, who did lose a talon, but no more than that, much to his relief— for her sake and Mariota's.

He left the practice field one afternoon to find Mariota teaching archery to his cousin Nan and to Anders' friend Brìghde, along with several younger lasses. Once they finished, she came to him and admitted she'd begun on her own, but had sought and received permission from his father.

"Ye talked to my da about this, too?"

"Of course. He and Anders have been very good to me while ye recovered."

"What else did ye talk about?"

"Many things. Much about MacKay, as I'm sure he told ye. 'Tis natural that he would be curious. About Da and Alber, Da and me, Seamus and why I chose him to succeed me, MacKay and Domnhall, and ye at MacKay."

"So he learned all ye ken about MacKay's capabilities, did he?"

"I kenned what he was doing. He learned what he needed to ken."

The idea of his father interrogating Mariota irritated Stellan. Anders laughed when he complained to him about it.

"Ye have it all wrong, brother. Mariota didna tell Da anything she didna wish to. And in the process, he became as smitten with her as ye and everyone else. Never fear, yer betrothed guarded her clan as she needed to, but ensured two things: that Sutherland would be an ally to her friend Seamus as laird of his clan, and that she'd be welcome in yers."

"She didna need to do that. She already was."

"Aye, but she's a wiser lass than Da kenned. He was impressed."

"Good."

"Especially since he's none too pleased with us at the moment."

"Aye, well, he'll get over that."

"He will, but Mariota just smoothed the way."

MARIOTA HAD NEVER BEEN SO happy. Stellan was so much better that his father had decreed that their wedding could go forward. She was in love and no longer in danger, and she had made friends here who would help her prepare for her new life.

Despite hours tending Stellan before he healed well enough to leave the healer's care, despite spending as much time with him since as his training and duties as heir allowed, she had explored every nook and cranny of Dunrobin, learned a great deal from hawk master Ian while flying Valkyrie, met most if not all of the people, and found a few favorite places within the keep. One of which was the weaver's, where the woman was close to finishing the four-seasons tapestry Mariota had seen at an earlier stage before her da had taken her back to MacKay.

"I could spend hours staring at it," she told the weaver during her latest visit. "Ye have a wonderful talent and skill. I look forward to seeing everything else ye create."

"Ye are too kind, milady," the weaver told her, blushing at the praise while her gaze lingered on the work she was finishing with the final touches of embroidered flowers in the spring and summer quadrants.

Mariota noted several new additions since she'd last seen it, including tiny leaping fish in the firth depicted along the eastern edge. "Nay, ye are justifiably proud of yer handiwork. I look forward to displaying it." She took her leave then. She'd agreed to meet Nan, who promised to help her find something suitable to wear to her wedding. Mariota didn't believe there was time to make anything new, but perhaps they could alter something. Nan and Brìghde had both offered to find dresses that might fit her.

They were waiting for her in the great hall when she entered the keep. "There ye are. Ye must have been visiting Valkyrie again," Brìghde said, greeting her.

"Nay, the weaver. She is finishing that most amazing tapestry we saw when I first came here. I canna wait for everyone to see it. But look at what ye have brought! How many dresses to ye think one lass needs to be married?"

"Only one, but the right one. And I ken the rest of yer belongings just arrived from MacKay, but I doubt ye have a gown to wed in since ye never mentioned having anything suitable."

"'Tis because I never wanted to marry. I never imagined I would, no' truly," she said as she mounted the stairs. "I ken that sounds daft for a lass who was the laird's heir, but I fought my da on every betrothal he suggested."

"Ye were waiting for the right betrothal. The right man," Nan told her as Mariota opened the door to her chamber.

She stopped and gaped at what confronted her. The trunk she'd had all her life to hold her clothes sat at the foot of her bed. But on the bed lay other things she didn't recognize. "What is all this?"

"There's a missive on top," Nan pointed out.

Mariota picked it up and read. "Gifts from MacKay to celebrate my wedding," she read. "Linens and other things made by the crafters in the clan. And Seamus sends along things that belonged to my mother, dresses and jewels, he says, that he found in the laird's chamber when he moved in. Da never told me he'd kept anything of hers." She started digging through the piles until she located a velvet bag.

"We should let ye explore this in peace," Brìghde said. "Ye may now have a suitable dress. But if nay, Nan has made something for ye."

Mariota blinked back tears and turned to her friends. "Nan?"

"No' made exactly. Altered and embroidered." She moved aside two other dresses on her arm and held up an ivory silk kirtle embroidered down the front and around the hem with leaves and flowers.

"The seasons! How did ye find time to copy the weaver's work?"

"Nan is an artist with a needle," Brìghde told her, making Nan blush.

"Do ye like it?"

"'Tis beautiful!" Mariota wiped away tears. "I canna believe ye did this for me."

"I recalled how much ye liked the tapestry. It seemed the proper theme for yer wedding. The weaver was good company while we worked, each on our own projects."

Mariota hugged Nan, careful not to crush the kirtle over her arm. Then she turned to Brìghde and did the same. "I dinna ken how to thank ye. Either of ye."

"We must ensure ye can wear it. Do ye want to try it on now, or look through the things Seamus sent ye."

"Try it on, of course."

"It laces, so if 'tis long enough, it will fit, I think," Nan said, slipping it over Mariota's head after she removed her day dress and stood in her chemise. "Aye, it nearly brushes the floor." She fussed for a few minutes with laces at the back and sides, then stood away and let Brìghde hold up a polished metal mirror.

"'Tis beautiful on ye," Brìghde told her.

Mariota found herself speechless. "I've never worn a dress so fine. So beautiful. Thank ye, Nan, for yer thoughtfulness. Brìghde, too. I dinna ken what to say."

"Yer face says it all," Nan told her. "I'm so pleased ye like it."

"I love it. Stellan will, too."

Nan chuckled. "Another reason for the lacing. He willna have to rip it from ye to remove it."

"What! He wouldna dare."

"If he does, I'll repair it," Nan promised with a wink. She loosened the ties so Mariota could remove the dress, took Brìghde's arm, and they left her to explore the rest of her treasure.

Mariota sat in her shift on top of her trunk, contemplating the fabrics and handiwork piled on her bed. She reached over and plucked the jewel bag from the midst, opened it, and let the contents spill onto her lap. She couldn't believe her da had kept the keepsakes she saw and never said a word to her about any of it. There were not many pieces, but the ones she saw were exquisite. Three rings, three gold necklaces, one set with gems, even a chatelaine's chain belt of hammered silver, rings for keys empty and waiting for her new station. Seamus could have kept all of this and never told her of the treasure her da had hid from her. But her friend had always been honest with her, even in this.

For one heart-stopping moment, she missed Seamus and MacKay, but then she heard Stellan's voice through her open window from down in the bailey. He was laughing at something one of the other men said. She slipped the rings on, one by one, then took them off again, her gaze on Nan's gorgeous needlework. MacKay was her past. Stellan Sutherland was her future.

STELLAN STOOD on the kirk steps awaiting his bride and squared his shoulders. Aware of all the eyes on him, he fought not to wince as the arrow wound pulled. It was taking longer to heal than the one in his arm, but he'd kept that fact from everyone except the healer, who could see the difference when she examined him. Right now, he didn't care about the remaining pain. His focus was on Mariota, gliding toward him on Seamus MacKay's arm, seeming to float on the air, looking like an angel in a white dress embroidered with colorful flowers and leaves. His summer angel. Someone had arranged her hair and placed a garland of summer wildflowers and roses on her head. She looked young and fresh. The smile she gave him made his heart leap with more joy than he'd ever felt in his life.

She was about to become his. He had to be the luckiest man alive. He wanted to dance, to sing, to hold her in his arms and never let her go. And he knew he needed to get his exuberance under control or the entire clan would think he'd been into the ale.

Truth be told, he, Anders, their father, and younger brother Cameron who'd come from Clan Rose for the wedding with his bride and laird Mary Elizabeth Rose, had shared a toast, but only one. This exhilaration filling him was all for Mariota, and for the life they would share, the family they would make, the clan they would shepherd into the future. He couldn't wait to begin it all with her.

When she reached him, Seamus leaned over and kissed her cheek, then gave her hand to Stellan. That kept Stellan from punching Seamus for kissing his bride. But Mariota arched a brow at him, as if reading his mind and warning him to behave. Stellan grinned and leaned in to kiss her fully on the mouth. There, Seamus couldn't do that.

Seamus gave him a knowing grin and stepped away. Over his shoulder, Stellan saw Anders roll his eyes. Did everyone know what he'd been thinking?

He didn't care.

"I didna ken Seamus would come and stand in for yer da," he

whispered to her as he turned her to face the priest. "'Twas good of him."

"'Twas his obligation," she reminded him. "As the MacKay laird, to attend the wedding of the former heir and laird, to be wed to an ally's heir. 'Tis all very important to our clans, and to our part of Scotland."

"Aye, of course 'tis," he said, reflecting the gravity with which she regarded the ceremony.

"Besides," she added, giving him a cheeky grin, "he was my best friend. Of course I wanted him here."

Stellan chuckled at that. "I understand, lass. Ye did well."

The priest cleared his throat, signaling that he required their attention. The ceremony was blessedly brief. After Stellan slipped his mother's ruby ring on her finger, they went inside the kirk for a short wedding mass. Through it all, Stellan fought to control the elation that filled him, thinking it would not be fair to Anders. Stellan feared their link, which had recently connected them from a great distance, might now at such close quarters overwhelm his twin. And it seemed unfair to force such strong emotion on his brother.

At last, the priest finished, and it was time to sign the register, to record their marriage for all posterity. Stellan signed, then handed the quill to Mariota, careful not to drip ink on her lovely dress. She gave him a smile, and her whispered, "Thank ye," spoke to that as much as his courtesy.

It was done. Stellan took the hand his wife offered him, overcome with relief and joy that she was his. He wanted to shout, to run, to kiss his bride and never stop.

But the Sutherland laird, arm in arm with the MacKay laird, stepped forward to announce the new husband and wife, then led the way into the great hall for the wedding feast.

"There is a sight I never thought to see," Mariota told Stellan as they crossed the bailey. She nodded at his father and Seamus. "They look like old friends."

"Old drinking buddies at the very least," Stellan said in agreement.

"They'll achieve that this night, I have nay doubt," Mariota said as he handed her up the steps into the keep and walked her to the high table. "I hope ye'll agree with me to get through this celebration as quickly as we may," she said while he seated her. "We have much to accomplish in private."

Stellan's pulse kicked up at her intimation. He quickly took his seat beside her. "Is now too soon?"

Mariota laughed at that. "I fear 'tis so. We must eat and perhaps dance before we can slip away."

Later, while Mariota danced a women's dance with the other lasses, Anders dropped into the seat beside him.

"How are ye?" Stellan was truly concerned how his feelings were affecting his brother.

Anders gave him a penetrating look. "I have sensed enough from ye to understand how true love feels. No' lust, no' just an enjoyable tumble with a different lass every night. Ye have taught me that I've been missing the most important thing in life. *Love.* I will carry that knowledge with me until I find a bride of my own. Ye have shown me that only one lass can make me feel what ye feel for Mariota."

"Anders, I had nay idea." Stellan didn't know whether what he felt was shock at his brother's admission or joy that he now would seek out and find the very thing that lit Stellan's life from the inside out— a love like he had with Mariota.

Anders sat back and raised his cup. "Enough of that. I promise to get drunk or go hunting and get far away. Or both. All of those." He gestured into the middle of the great hall. "How do ye like that? Cameron brought Mary with him. See? She's dancing with the other lasses. We have three lairds attending yer wedding. That might be some kind of record."

"I think ye are well on yer way to fulfilling yer promise to get drunk, brother. Have a care ye dinna drink too much."

"I'm nay so far gone as I will be. Never fear, several lads are going with me to ensure I dinna fall from my horse and break anything. Congratulations, brother. Ye have a fine wife. Ye are a lucky man."

"I hope soon ye will be as lucky," Stellan told him.

Anders shrugged and stood. "A quest for another day, brother. Have a successful night. I'm on my way— elsewhere."

Stellan watched him go, weaving a bit but still in control of his movements. As long as Anders had men with him, he would be well, but it still worried Stellan that he felt he had to take these measures. After a moment's thought, he realized Anders was doing it as much for his sake as for his own. For Stellan's privacy. And Mariota's. In that moment, he could not have loved his brother more. Their twin connection had brought them closer together than most siblings could ever imagine being, but there were limits. Anders recognized that and was taking measures to give Stellan the space he needed.

"Fare well, brother," he said softly as Anders left the great hall. "I'll speak to ye tomorrow."

Mariota returned to him breathless from the dance and grinning. She put a hand on the back of his chair and leaned in close to his ear. "'Tis time? I saw Anders speaking to ye."

"Aye, lass, 'tis time."

"Good." She stepped back to let him stand, then took his hand.

CHAPTER 22

Stellan was never clear if he walked her across the great hall or she walked him. Either way, they were greeted with applause, laughter, and catcalls. Mariota took it all in stride but wasted no time mounting the stairs. Stellan stayed right with her, not sure how much she had to drink and whether she could injure herself on the steps. But neither of them did.

Their chamber was lit with a multitude of beeswax candles. The scent of honey filled the air, along with the scent of roses. Bunches of them had been placed on every table, and when Stellan stepped forward and glanced into the bedchamber, he saw rose petals scattered on the bed.

"Courtesy of Nan and Brìghde, I'll wager," Mariota said as he closed the door behind them— and locked it.

"'Tis lovely," Stellan told her, "but nay so lovely as my wife."

Mariota blushed and dropped her gaze, then raised it again. "Ah, look!" The weaver's four-season tapestry had been hung on the wall across from the hearth where it would be safe from soot and flames. "I've admired that so. She finished it just in time!"

"What do ye mean?"

"She said she was making it for the clan's new lady. I guess that is me. Or will be, someday."

"Sooner than ye think," Stellan warned her. "Da will recruit ye to serve as hostess and chatelaine. Ye'll be well practiced by the time ye must do both for me."

She nodded, suddenly serious. "Long years from now, I hope. Yer da is strong and hale. And a good laird."

"He is all of that, but I dinna wish to talk about him. This is our time. I wish to make love to my bride. To make ye mine in truth."

"As do I. Shall I help ye?" She reached for the Sutherland pin holding his sash on his shoulder.

"Aye, please do. My shoulder still pains me a bit," he said and rolled it, grimacing.

She knew exactly what he was doing. "This is nay the night for sympathy, my love. I ken ye will be strong and yet tender and will ignore any twinges yer injuries may still give ye."

He pulled her to him before she could unbuckle his belt and kissed her soundly. "I will, love," he said and began undressing her. "And ye ken how eager I am to see all of ye."

"As I am to see ye," she replied and opened his belt, let it fall to the floor and watched the yards of his kilt's woolen fabric join it in a plaid puddle.

He stood before her in his *leine*, determined that his brave bride would join him. He reached for her kirtle but she held up a hand.

"If ye tear this, ye will have three women after yer blood, and I will be one of them. Brìghde and yer cousin Nan, who made this, will be the other two. I suggest ye take yer time and loosen the laces, husband, before ye make a fatal mistake." She grinned.

"Ye three planned this to frustrate me," he accused, then sank to his knees and worked on each set of laces, loosening them enough to let the kirtle slip from her shoulders and down her body.

She stepped out of it, picked it up and laid it reverently over a chair.

In moving around the room, the candlelight and firelight of the hearth glowed through her fine lawn chemise, giving him sweet glimpses of her form through the semi-sheer fabric. He stood, unable to resist holding her any longer. "Come here, Mariota."

She came into his arms and pressed against him. "'Tis time, aye?" She turned her head and looked toward the window that overlooked the gates to Dunrobin's walls.

"Ye worry for Anders?"

"I ken ye do. He should be far enough away by now."

Surprised, he said, "So ye ken about that."

"I've heard tales."

"He is. And well sotted, too. But that is no' what I meant. Ye are no' ready. I want ye to remember this night with joy— and delight. Nay with pain."

"Then delight me, husband. I'm eager to be yers."

THE FIRST THING Mariota had noted when she entered Stellan's chambers was not the candlelight or the roses. The four-season tapestry hanging in the chamber she would now share with Stellan delighted her. It had been hung in the public room, where others might visit and see it. A doorway led to the inner bedchamber. Stellan's space was larger than the laird's chamber at MacKay, and so fine, she wondered how much nicer the laird's chambers at Sutherland could be.

She'd find out in due time. For now, she was alone with Stellan. Her husband. And she could not wait for the rest of the evening to begin.

She was nervous, but hid it in playfulness, teasing him out of his clothes, then threatening his life if he ruined her wedding finery. He met her challenge and before she knew it, they were both naked and lying on Stellan's bed. It was much larger than the one in her chamber. Her former chamber. Of course, it had to be large enough for two.

He kissed her, did it again, moving from her lips to her eyelids, her cheeks, down her throat and farther still. She forgot everything she'd been distracting herself with, forgot her nerves, forgot even where she was. There was only Stellan. His mouth, his hands. His scent. The rough texture of his body against hers, his whiskers teasing over her sensitive skin.

Every touch made her blood swirl and dance in her veins, every kiss made her warmer, needier, hungry for sensations she couldn't name. Stellan answered her every cry with a kiss or caress until she was writhing with unnamed need.

"'Tis time, husband," she gasped as he began kissing the insides of her thighs. "I canna take much more."

"Ye can, love, and ye will," he murmured, then put all his attention on her center.

Something within her shattered, scattering light and heat and a liquid surge of satisfaction throughout her body. She dared not open her eyes. The sky was already too full of stars falling behind her eyelids, and the cries and whimpers she heard were her own. When the storm passed, she lay quiet, just breathing.

"Now," Stellan told her, "'tis time."

He moved over her and supporting his weight above her, entered her slowly. At first she didn't realize what was happening. Then she smiled and lifted to meet him, welcoming him, wanting him to fill the aching emptiness within her. "I need ye, husband," she murmured. "All of ye."

He surged forward, and for the briefest time, a sharp sting surprised her, but it soon faded away, and there was Stellan. Filling her.

"Ye are mine, now, Mariota. Forever, my love. My wife."

"As ye are mine, Stellan, forever, my love. My husband."

He began moving, and before long, she met the storm again and vanquished it, then rested in Stellan's arms, secure in the knowledge that she would never be lonely again. Or afraid. This man loved her and took care of her. She would do the same for him as long as she lived. And for any children they were blessed with. And for their clan. Today— and tonight —she'd taken on more than just this man, but she did so gladly, with hope and happiness for their future.

"I love ye, Stellan," she told him. "With my whole being."

"As I love ye, Mariota," he whispered and caressed her cheek. "Ye mean more to me than anything in this world. I will love ye always, and never leave ye."

She put a hand on his chest, over his beating heart. "That is all I ask of ye."

EPILOGUE

DUNROBIN CASTLE, SCOTTISH HIGHLANDS, SPRING 1413

Mariota patted her rounding belly and smiled at Cook from her seat at the long worktable in the Sutherland kitchen. "I dinna ken how much of this is the heir and how much is yer excellent honey cakes." She'd just finished another piece, and while she knew she didn't need another, the bairn inside her seemed to have other ideas.

"Time will tell, lass," Cook told her with a grin and put another small square, dripping with golden honey, on her plate. "Ye are eating for two. *Dinna fash.*"

"I try no' to, but my feet have hidden from me for the last month. I canna see my slippers any longer." She laughed. "Stellan has to help me put them on," she added, eyeing the golden goodness waiting for her on the plate. "I'll be glad when this bairn comes and I can find the rest of me again."

"Like as no', yer husband will be glad to be able to find the rest of ye, too. And ye'll end up just like this again." She laughed and slapped the tabletop.

Mariota had to laugh with her. A few more weeks. She could do this for a few more weeks. The reward would be worth all that she'd been through, and the pain yet to come. She hoped the bairn was a lad. Stellan would be excited to have his heir, but she knew he'd be happy with a daughter, too. He would never treat her as her own father had treated her, even if it turned out their lassie bairn was fated to become the Sutherland laird after him.

"Ye are smiling more every day," Cook told her. "Ye seem happier than when ye arrived. Because of the bairn?"

"And Stellan. And all of ye. I'm a very lucky lass."

"A very smart lass, I'd say." Cook patted her hand and moved away to deal with the rest of her busy kitchen.

Mariota sighed and gave in to temptation. Just this last piece, and she'd go back to work. She wanted to organize the clan's library, which had fallen into disuse. She'd been overjoyed when she first saw it, a moment later, appalled as she realized how haphazardly books, documents, and maps were scattered about. Someone had cleaned as best they could, but really, everything would be so much more accessible and useful once she finished. Stellan heartily approved her efforts. Laird Sutherland was never much of a reader and had no opinion, Stellan told her, so she forged ahead. She was nearing the point when she would have to reach upper shelves, but Stellan had forbidden her from the library ladder, possibly forever. She would have him or Anders or one of the lads in the clan act as her arms and legs to bring things down to her so she could add them to the catalog she had created, then have them placed where they would belong in her system, and clean the upper shelves.

Archery was out of the question until the bairn came. She missed it, but she watched the lasses train, and more of them, old and young, joined all the time. Mariota knew they were eager to help defend their home, but she could also see they enjoyed spending time together learning a new skill. If only they knew how much that pleased her.

She loved her life at Sutherland. Loved Stellan more with each passing hour. Loved the people of the clan who had welcomed her from her first visit. Nan and Brìghde were still two of her closest friends. And the letters Seamus sent now and again told her he was doing well as MacKay's laird— as she'd known he would. The clan had a new leader and a new spirit of respect and cooperation that had sadly deteriorated during the last few years of her father's life. In passing the responsibility to Seamus, she had made the best decision for her clan.

She had just finished the last bite of the honey cake when Stellan found her. She looked up at him and had to laugh at his rueful expression, lips pursed, but laughter in his eyes. "Again? I pray Cook doesna run out of honey cake before the bairn comes."

She ignored his teasing. "Aye, ye found me."

"I looked for ye in the library. I shouldha kenned ye'd be here. I could smell fresh honey cakes from the great hall."

"Sit," Cook told him, approaching with another piece for him. "Dinna give this to yer wife. She'll birth a honey cake if she eats any more today."

"I'll be happy to help prevent that," Stellan said and dug in.

Mariota watched him enjoy the treat without a trace of envy. She'd had more than her share, and the bairn's share, too. They both were satisfied and ready for a nap.

"I see yer eyelids drooping," Stellan told her as he scooped up his last bite. "I'll take ye upstairs."

"I have too much work to do," she objected. "The library—"

"Will be there after ye have rested. Valkyrie, too, now the rain has moved off." He stood and held out a hand. "Come, wife."

Mariota gave him her hand and let him pull her to her feet. He moved the bench aside to make it easier for her to slip by it and away from the table. "Thank ye, Cook." She patted her belly. "We enjoyed it all."

"Any time, lass. Ye tell me what ye want, and I'll see it done."

"I see ye have Cook wrapped around yer little finger," Stellan told her a few moments later, as they crossed the great hall.

"I'm grateful for her care," Mariota said, "hers and everyone's here."

Stellan steadied her as they mounted the stairs, eased her to sitting on their bed, and knelt to remove her slippers. Instead of settling her back against the pillows, he stroked one of her feet, pressing and rubbing from her toes to her ankle, then moved to the other foot and back again until Mariota moaned from the pleasure of it. "Better?" He stood and helped her lean back into the pillows.

"Ye canna tell? 'Tis no' quite as good as... ye ken what... but aye, 'tis near as good."

He settled beside her on the edge of the bed. "Do ye want... what... before ye sleep?"

She gave him a grin for echoing her avoidance of a word for their lovemaking, then yawned. "Perhaps later," she told him and reached for his hand. "I love ye, Stellan Sutherland."

"I ken it. I love ye more than life, Mariota Sutherland. I still canna believe how lucky I am to be wedded to ye. Ye are everything I hoped for in a wife, a partner, and a lover. And soon, we will have our first bairn. I dinna ken how I could love ye more than I already do."

"As ye are life and joy to me, husband. Ye risked everything for me."

"And ye gave up everything for me. I'm glad I fought to win ye, fought to save yer life and mine from Alber, and fought to convince ye to upend yer life and yer clan's, and come live with me. Every struggle, every setback, every threat, and every drop of blood shed has been worthwhile."

She squeezed his hand. "But with ye, I have gained everything, too. I'm grateful to ye, Stellan. And grateful to whatever stroke of fate led me to ye in that forest."

"So am I, love. More than I can ever say." He bent and dropped a kiss on her cheek. "Now, rest well."

He left her in peace, but once he was gone, she realized the urge to sleep had left her. She heaved herself to sitting, slipped off the bed and padded to the window seat. Spring had come again after a long, cold winter. Midday sunlight glinted everywhere on wet leaves. Seeing the bright green of new leaves pushing out on the trees made her happy, as did the new shoots in the castle's garden. Cook had forbidden her from getting down on hands and knees to work the soil until after the bairn came and she was less prone to losing her balance, but she was eager to get her hands dirty planting and weeding and enjoying the warm sunshine.

She patted her belly and felt the bairn within it kick. "Soon, wee one, soon. I'll teach ye so many things. So will yer da, who is a wise man and a great warrior. Be ye lad or lass, ye will have much to do and much to learn. Ye dinna ken it now, but a grand adventure awaits ye."

DON'T MISS THE NEXT BOOK THE SERIES!

BOOK 6

Coming in March 2025, Anders Sutherland meets his match in
LAIRD OF SIGHS

Their clans say they're enemies, but their hearts disagree.

Now that his twin is blissfully married and starting a family,
Anders Sutherland longs for the same happiness. Lasses have
always favored him, but he refuses to settle for anything less than
a love match. Winning a bride worth keeping for life is a challenge he will enjoy—if he survives. When a storm at sea spits
Anders onto a hostile shore, he finds himself falling for the spir-
ited lass who nurses him back to health.

The handsome stranger who shows up at Ailsa Sinclair's clan
stronghold captivates her. Is he friend or foe? Her parents and
brother, the heir, are away, so the clan's safety depends on her
ruling. Then the stranger collapses at the gate, making the decision for her. As she cares for his injuries, she learns why all the

lasses sigh over him, and her spark of attraction to him grows into fevered longing.

But Ailsa soon discovers that no matter how he came to them, Highland hospitality be damned, she should never have allowed Anders inside her walls. Fearing betrayal, he has kept an important secret. He's the son of an enemy laird. Will she fight to save the man who stole the heart she has so carefully guarded for years, or will she let her family toss him in the dungeon—or worse, back into the sea?

ALSO BY WILLA BLAIR

Highland Talents Heritage

Highland Prodigy

Highland Memories

Highland Reckoning

Highland Dreamer

Highland Echo

His Highland Heart

His Highland Rose

His Highland Heart

His Highland Love

His Highland Bride

Laird of Lies

His Highland Heart Boxed Set

Highland Talents

Heart of Stone

Highland Healer

Highland Seer

Highland Troth

The Healer's Gift

When Highland Lightning Strikes

Other Novels

Waiting for the Laird

When You Find Love

Highland Beginnings

ABOUT THE AUTHOR

Willa Blair is an award-wining Amazon and Barnes & Noble #1 bestselling author of Scottish historical, light paranormal and contemporary romance, filled with men in kilts, psi talents, and plenty of spice. Her books have won numerous accolades, including the Marlene, the Merritt, National Readers' Choice Award Finalist, Booksellers' Best Award Finalist, National Excellence in Story Telling Historical Fiction Third Place Winner, Reader's Crown finalist, InD'Tale Magazine's RONE Award Honorable Mention, and NightOwl Reviews Top Picks. She loves scouting new settings for books, and thinks being an author is the best job she's ever had.

Willa loves hearing from readers!
Contact her:
www.willablair.com
authorwillablair@gmail.com

Sign up for my Newsletter
Find links to the rest of my books